DEAD RECKONING

McCord was growing impatient. He puffed his pipe angrily until the bowl grew hot to the touch. Malcolm kept shaking his head.

"Black Wolf knows the way," McCord said, "the quick way to the Columbia."

"You're taking him along?"

"Yes. And you're coming with me, Malcolm."

"For what reason? You got that Mandan. You don't need me."

"I need you so bad, I'm going to tell you why you're going to come with me to the Columbia. And after I've told you, you'll either come willingly or I'll have to kill you."

With that, McCord drew his flintlock pistol from his waistband and laid it on one leg, the barrel pointed at Flynn's heart.

Rivers West
Ask your bookseller for the books you have missed.

RIVERS
WEST

THE
COLUMBIA RIVER

Jory Sherman

BANTAM BOOKS
NEW YORK • TORONTO • LONDON • SYDNEY • AUCKLAND

THE COLUMBIA RIVER
A Bantam Book / January 1996

ISBN 0-553-29772-4

Published simultaneously in the United States and Canada

Bantam Books are published by Bantam Books, a division of Bantam
Doubleday Dell Publishing Group, Inc. Its trademark, consisting of the
words "Bantam Books" and the portrayal of a rooster, is Registered in
U.S. Patent and Trademark Office and in other countries. Marca
Registrada. Bantam Books, 1540 Broadway, New York, New York
10036.

PRINTED IN THE UNITED STATES OF AMERICA

OPM   0 9 8 7 6 5 4 3 2 1

For Tom Burke. Thanks for helping to smooth many a path along the way to a bunch of rivers.

A river seems a magic thing. A magic, moving, living part of the very earth itself—for it is from the soil, both from its depth and from its surface, that a river has its beginning.

LAURA GILPIN (1891–1979)
U.S. photographer

Foreword

John Jacob Astor. The name seemed possessed of a magic from the very beginning. This German-born American citizen who made New York his home and headquarters seemed destined for fame and riches not long after he set foot on American shores.

Astor had a vision that exceeded the expectations even of his ambitious peers. He exuded a spirit of adventure, an aptitude for enterprise that surpassed all others when the western lands were still a forbidding and forbidden place, when the French and English dominated the fur trade in the only area in the continent of North American legally open for trapping and commerce in animal peltries.

Astor began his meteoric career not long after his arrival in the United States, some say, in the year 1784. He started small, but soon expanded his influence and operations as he began to earn enough money to realize his vision. Fascinated by the wealth that was possible for an enterprising man, Astor traveled to Canada and bought furs. He learned to grade them and buy them for the best price. He opened his own markets in London, but he saw beyond them, envisioning the entire world as his trading ground.

He also dreamed of someday cornering the entire

fur trade of North America. Everywhere he looked he saw mismanagement and waste—even in the vast forests of Canada with its numerous lakes and rivers. He knew of the French, who had dominated the fur trade until 1670, when Hudson's Bay Company, under royal charter, established dominion in the territory of Rupert's Land, which later became known as Hudson's Bay.

The Canada Company came into existence in 1787 in direct competition with Hudson's Bay. It soon became known as the North-West Company, a bitter rival to Hudson's Bay. Shortly thereafter, as if to challenge the two largest competitors, a new company emerged to the south and called itself the Mackina Company. It was based on Michimilimackina Island.

Astor saw his opportunity as the arena enlarged. He established the American Fur Company in 1809, and set out to take advantage of the new lands explored by Lewis and Clark after the U.S. government bought the Louisiana territory from Napoleon. Astor bought out the Mackina Company in 1811, further expanding his American Fur operations. He called the new corporate body the South-West Company, thereby announcing to the world that he was in direct competition with the Nor'westers.

With this move, Astor now dominated the fur trade of the south and made plans to corner not only the entire territory east of the Rocky Mountains, but beyond. Like a general planning his attack, Astor's strategy encompassed the fur trade along the coast of the Pacific Ocean, a brand new field of battle, virgin lands teeming with beaver, marten, lynx, mink, deer, muskrat, and other animal riches from Canada to the sea, all along the Columbia River.

John Jacob Astor's dream began to grow and take shape. But there remained many challenges ahead.

For there were others who had the same dream.

THE

COLUMBIA RIVER

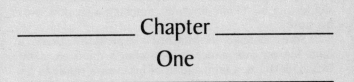

Chapter
One

The western sky a rage of blood. The river running
with the quiet carnage, crimson as the gutter in
an abattoir. Shadows puddling up under trees
along the shore; nightbats slicing the sky like dark scal-
pels. The two men in the canoe caught in the incarna-
dine blaze like racers from a forest fire, their faces
flushed and maddened with the glow of the sky as they
rounded the wide bend of the Missouri River in late
March of 1811, their birchbark craft knifing through the
waters, their paddles leaving little bloody whirlpools
that disappeared as the surging current ironed them flat
as glass.

Randall McCord sat at the stern, as always, watching the Frenchman at the prow with a snake's steady
gaze, cold hazel eyes that flickered with the bloodhue
of the sky but so still in their sockets.

The Frenchman grunted and turned around. The
waft of sweatmusk on the halted air, the rot of flesh
under buckskin leggings like the reek of a public bath-
house. Both men wearing long-sleeved shirts tight at

the sleeves, necks closed with deerhide buttons. Boot moccasins giving off the rank odor of a bear staining the air after wallowing in ripe carrion.

"Eh, we are close, McCord," René Jessaume said. The hired guide's face was flocked with hair, hatbrim shadowing his Gallic features, cracking a shadow over his nose.

Some change in McCord's expression stirred a faint klaxon dissonance in Jessaume's mind. A slight twitch, perhaps, a faint squint of his eyes, a ripple in his brow, a furrowed wrinkle across his forehead. Something seen for an instant and then the image distrusted, faded from memory like a candleflame died, leaving only a puff of smoke lingering in the darkness, a sharp oily aroma of burnt wax tainting the nostrils.

René Jessaume did not trust Randall McCord, the strapping six-foot Scotsman who had hired him as a guide, along with a half-dozen others. There was something about the man that made him suspicious. And that pork-eating Frenchman McCord had brought along, Paul Vermeil. Jessaume considered him no more than an Accadian cutthroat from the docks of New Orleans, a sneak thief stealing the Scotsman blind. His bastard French was difficult to understand; his English a lot worse. A bad pair, in René's book, and he had known many such men who had taken to the frontier since 1794, when he had first come to this country.

"That is the Knife River ahead," René said, resting his paddle on the gunwale of the bullboat. "Where we meet the Mandans, eh?"

"This is as far as we go," McCord replied, a faint burr and the lilt of the Scottish highlands to his speech.

This was the country of the Mandans, once a populous tribe living near the mouth of the Heart River. The Sioux and white men's diseases, especially the smallpox epidemic of 1782, had decimated their ranks over the years. Forced to move out of the way of the Sioux migrations, the tribe had settled on the Knife River in 1790, living there in close proximity with the Minatarees or Gros Ventres.

"Like fleas in a blanket," Jessaume always said.

René had been to their villages many times over the last nine years, but there was something different about this trip. He did not know where McCord's ultimate destination was. McCord was licensed to trade and trap for furs by the Hudson Bay Company, but he did not act like a company man. Perhaps he was just naturally taciturn and secretive. He spoke passable French, but seldom said more than a half-dozen words in either that language or his own.

"We stop here? We do not go to the Mandans?" Jessaume asked. He had been hired by McCord to guide him up the Knife to the village. Nothing there for Hudson Bay. Wherever those *cochons* went, though, there was trouble, sooner or later. Much blood. Much fighting. Treachery.

"No," the Scot said.

McCord looked back at the others coming behind in bullboats—ungainly craft made of cured, tough buffalo hide and waterproofed with tallow. He and René manned the lead canoe, working well together despite their mutual distrust, plying their oars in the deep Missouri River through the clouds of bloodthirsty mosquitoes that attacked them in famished droves.

René lifted an arm, signaled to the boatmen behind, then angled the canoe toward the bank. McCord used his paddle as a rudder, and the canoe swung gracefully to its new course. The red sky began to rust as the colors faded on the high, thin cirrus clouds and the temperature began to drop.

The canoe glided toward shore. Behind Jessaume and McCord the other craft followed, the men's faces darkening as the sun fell deeper beyond the rolling prairie hills to the other side of the mountains. McCord looked back to see that they were following, catching a glimpse of Paul Vermeil in the stern of the bullboat directly behind the lead canoe.

"Why you no go to the Mandan village?"

"That's my business, Jessaume."

"Sonofabitch."

They beached the canoe on a wide sandy bank. Jessaume climbed over the prow. McCord scrambled to the fore and climbed out as well. The two dragged the canoe up onto the bank and waited for the others.

"When they all come ashore, I want to settle up, Jessaume."

"Settle up?"

"This is as far as you go. I want you to take your men and head back downriver tonight."

"What you do with all these goods?"

"That too is my business."

René went to the bank, helped land the bullboats and canoes. The other Frenchmen spoke excitedly, wondering why they were stopping there, so close to the Mandan village. McCord stood off, beckoning for Vermeil to join him.

The Accadian trotted over, a puzzled look on his face.

"When I finish up here, Paul, I want you to help unload those bullboats. We'll keep the canoe for ourselves. Give the men all the food they want for the trip back."

"What you do, eh? These men, they want to make big party with the redskins."

"We don't need them anymore."

Vermeil fidgeted, slapped at mosquitoes, looked at the other men ashore.

McCord's eyes never left the swarthy Accadian, his expression masking the disgust he felt for this laggard, this surly sluggard who whined and complained the whole trip. But that hadn't stopped his thieving hands.

"Why you want to let them go?"

"Vermeil, just mind your own store."

"But what about all the goods we brought? Who will carry them to the Mandans?"

"We can manage."

With that, McCord stalked off, the quibbling Vermeil following in his wake.

The five men with Jessaume stood next to the boats, lighting pipes, flapping dark hands at the clouds of mosquitoes foraging their faces, ears, and necks.

"Just unload the boats," McCord said. "Set the goods well up on shore. Then, Jessaume, you and your men can take those bullboats and leave."

"What about our pay?" Jessaume asked.

"Paul, fetch me that strongbox from my canoe."

The men gathered around as the Scotsman counted out coins for each man. He made them sign a document as receipt that they had been paid. They muttered among themselves about having to stay on the river instead of going to the Mandan village. But McCord did not want them around any longer.

"Take all the food you need, Jessaume. We'll get by."

"I do not understand, McCord. You pay us to bring you to the Mandans, and then you send us away. If you are going beyond, you will not make it, only the two of you, eh? Bad business."

"That is my choice. I want you all to go back downriver. Now."

After much grumbling, the Frenchmen packed up the bullboats, separated the trade goods and gifts McCord had brought. They shoved off from the shore, and McCord watched until they vanished beyond the bend. Then he turned to a nervous Vermeil.

"Where are we?" the Frenchman asked in English.

"Nowhere."

"Are we going on upriver?"

"Perhaps."

"But Jessaume says—"

"Jessaume is not in charge. I am."

"Where do we camp, McCord?"

"Any place liable to stay dry during the night. Go ahead and set up a lean-to, shake out the blankets. I'll cover up the trade goods."

Vermeil bent to the task with remarkable alacrity for one who had proved so lazy on the long journey up the Missouri.

When the task was finished, McCord walked three or four hundred yards in the dusk, scouting various places. Vermeil, puzzled, followed, a confused and fearful acolyte.

"You lookin' for something, McCord?"

"I'm looking for a spot where there is no track of man or beast."

"It'll be too dark to see pretty quick."

McCord stopped, peered around for landmarks, grunted his approval. He scooped a handful of loam from the ground. The soil was loose. "Here's where we'll cache most of the goods," he said. "Let's get to work."

Vermeil cursed. "We maybe should be setting up the camp, no?"

McCord did not answer, but headed for the river. He sorted the goods he would pack himself, helped Vermeil carry the others to the place of the cache. Vermeil dug a deep hole and they buried what they had brought.

"Cover it up," McCord said.

It was full dark when they finished smoothing out the burial place. McCord seemed to see in the dark. He walked back to where the canoe lay black on the shore. He turned it over on its side, propping it up with sticks of driftwood.

"Light a cook fire," McCord ordered.

Vermeil gathered firewood, set to building the fire with hatchet and knife. Soon he had the flames curling into the night, and they could see the mosquitoes at the edges of light, and then the bats came like dark whirligigs on aerial maneuvers, whipping by so fast they made the flames dance in the wake of their wings.

"What you want to eat, McCord? We have the goat meat."

Antelope, shot that morning by McCord himself. "Put on some coffee, Vermeil," he said. "You eat what you want."

"Ah, no hunger, eh?"

McCord did not reply. Instead he drew one of a pair of pistols tucked inside his sash. Big-bore .60 caliber chunks of iron and wood with French locks as intricate as a man's ear.

McCord cocked the pistol. Vermeil, squatting by the fire, jumped, rattling the coffeepot's lid.

"No last meal for you, Vermeil. This is as far as you go."

Vermeil's face drained of blood. He stood up on shaking knees. "Why you do this, eh, McCord?"

"I can't trust you. No one must know where I'm going—or why."

"I will never tell."

"You may hand over the gold coins you stole from me, or I can retrieve them from your corpse."

Vermeil spluttered, fought for air. He drew his own pistol, but he was slow, awkward.

McCord squeezed the trigger. Orange flame and white smoke flew from the muzzle. The ball struck Vermeil in the chest, just to the left of his breastbone. His hands went slack and he dropped his pistol. Blood and bone splinters erupted from his back and he crumpled to the ground, mortally wounded. Tendrils of smoke curled from the barrel of McCord's pistol. He blew it away, stuck the weapon back in his belt.

Vermeil made noises in his throat, but his eyes glazed over with the final frost of death. He shuddered once and then breathed no more.

McCord searched the dead man's clothing, found the pouch of gold coins hidden underneath Vermeil's sash.

He dragged the corpse to the edge of the shore and pushed it into the river. He stood there watching the body spin slowly and then float downstream. By the time he turned away and walked back to the fire, Vermeil's body had rounded the bend and was no longer visible.

All traces of the sun disappeared from the sky and the darkness drew shadows close to the campfire as McCord squatted, cleaned his pistol, and reloaded it with powder and ball.

Chapter Two

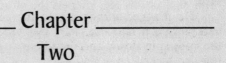

He did not know the name of the river. It birthed high in the Rocky Mountains somewhere to the north, in Canada, but here it flowed from a place where two small lakes stood sheltered among the sheer towering walls of mountains rising above verdant meadows like a massive granite fortress built by powerful and mysterious ancient gods.

Jared Flynn had seen grandeur before, but nothing like this. His pulse quickened and he could hear the thundering bloodbeat of his heart as he gazed across the still waters swarming with mayflies and yellow-winged butterflies. A trout broke the mirrored surface, leaping from the fractured lake in a scimitar-shaped arc, and Flynn felt he was witnessing the birth of creation. The stillness, the haunting poignant beauty that lay before him, left him speechless, but also awestruck that he had come this far, away from the memories and the horrors of home, through country that shattered his eyes with its beauty, only to see this place, like a god's garden, with summer's green mantle flowing over the

high meadow where the river slowed and widened into
a lake seemingly suspended in time and space.

Jared stood at the edge of the timber, the fierce-
ness in his eyes softened by the majesty of this place on
the very edge of the Rocky Mountains. He leaned his
rifle against his leg, slipped the straps from his shoulders and lowered the pack to the ground soundlessly.
His buckskin shirt swelled with the reverence of his
breathing, straining the thongs that laced the opening
at the throat.

An otter slid into the water near him and paddled
to the far shore, twin wakes streaming silently behind it,
rumpling the water, leaving a vee that widened until its
ripples lapped against the shore.

Gray Cat, the Mandan, stood next to Jared, like his
shadow. "Him big river," he said.

"Beautiful as a Galway mornin'." Jared spoke each
syllable distinctly, as if these were magic words.

The Mandan stepped away toward the spillway.

"Where you goin'?" Jared asked.

"Find cache. Many canoe. Hunt deer."

Jared watched the Mandan slip into the trees and
disappear. Gray Cat wore no pack, carried only a trade
gun, possibles pouch, two knives, a tomahawk. Jared's
other companion was David Pettibone, a man who had
lived with the Mandan and the Oglala. A most valuable
man.

"Jared, where you at?"

Flynn turned, looked back over his shoulder. Pettibone straggled through the trees, his buckskins, shape-
less and oversized, wrinkled beyond design or pattern,
his backpack riding high on his shoulders like some obscene hump, rifle pulling his right arm down six inches
beyond the other so that he walked at a starboard tilt.

Jared put a finger to his lips, waved Pettibone on.
"Come looky, Fur Face," he said. "Ain't it some sight?"

Pettibone grunted under the weight of his pack, his

face invisible under the tangle of wiry beard that sprouted from his round, plump face. Only his pudgy lips, his small feral eyes, and his sunburnt bulb of a nose gave his physiognomy a human appearance. He wore grease-stained buckskins that bulged around a middle that sagged over his five-inch, elkhide belt.

"Didja see where it falls yet? Just over yonder."

"I ain't seen the falls," Jared said. "But I can hear 'em plain." A roar such as a man seldom hears unless he be witness to some cataclysmic collision of planets in far deep space, or the thundering rumble of a gigantic landslide in the cold silence of winter, or is witness to the eruption of a South Seas volcano when it is said the gods are angry and speak to men from a throat spewing fire and smoke so dark it blackens the sun and lava thick as mortar, hotter than the furnaces of Hades.

"That be the Columbia," a panting Pettibone said as he slung his pack to the ground as if to kill it later with a pistol shot to its swollen belly. "Like I done tolt you."

"I believe it," Jared replied, still rapt from the jade-green trees that surrounded the meadow where the river leaped from the lake like some amazing Inca fountain built long ago for purposes man no longer imagined.

"Where'd that Gray Cat go off to?"

Jared pointed ahead to where the falls murmured like some kind of forest prayer. "He says he has canoes cached yonder."

"Then I reckon he has," Pettibone said. "He's been over these mountains often enough, he has. Like a damned pack rat. Knows the river well."

"So you keep sayin'," Jared said.

The journey to this place had been hard, harder than a man from the flatlands could imagine. They had sent the others back to Fort William with the winter's pelfries. To Pierre Lescaux, Jared had said: "Let the

North-West Company know that we have come through the mountains and the beaver are thick as fleas on a mongrel."

The others—Maurice Wakefield, Terrell McCormack, Red Wing, the Huron, and Paul Dubonnet—would follow the Missouri to St. Louis, then take the furs, all prime, to Fort William. His orders from the company were to push beyond to the mouth of the Columbia and make friends with the local Indian tribes. Pettibone knew the country, leading the men up the Missouri, then through the mountains to the Snake River, which emptied right into the Columbia, to this place where the river caught its breath and stood still and solemn under the vaulted blue cathedral of the sky.

To Jared, New York and Fort William seemed so long ago and far away. Prairie du Chien and St. Louis, just as far, like half-forgotten dreams, with his mind full of the wilderness and the wild country inside him now, so long inside him that the forts and towns were only blurred and faded etchings dimly seen on a distant wall. The years had only dulled the pain and scabbed over the guilt he felt over what had happened at home long ago, and now his father was dead, his mother and sister lost to him forever. He was still running to escape it, even to the ends of the earth, as if his sister Caitlin could escape, as if his mother, Bernice, could ever forget the horror, the blood, the mute graves on a Pennsylvania farm long since abandoned to rock and ruin.

"That river will take us where we're a-goin', I reckon," Pettibone said.

"But we're not there yet."

"No, son, but we got furs aplenty and our hair. Where we are is where we're at, sure enough." Pettibone looked back at the jagged rim of the Rockies scratching the sky like a dinosaur's ragged back. It had been a hell of a winter, and the others were well on their way back to Fort William with pelfries of beaver, marten, mink, and otter, worth many crowns back in Montreal.

Jared knew the riches of the mountains, for he had crossed through them and trapped the streams along the way. He had waded through ball-freezing water and hip-deep snows, sampling each place and heading westward, holing up through white storms and canoeing down swollen rivers where a spill could mean death in seconds. More than once Flynn had gotten so cold he could not think straight, and Pettibone had to build a fire to thaw him before the cold had snuffed out the tiny candle of life at his core.

"How far to the mouth?" Jared asked.

"I calculate sixty leagues, more er less."

"Less than two hundred miles."

"Yep," Pettibone said.

"Rapids?"

"Them too. But I ain't worried about no river."

"No?"

"You got to watch out for them Chinooks," Pettibone said.

"What's that?"

"Fish-eatin' Injuns."

"We got along with the Lakota just fine."

"Chinooks is different. And ain't all of 'em Chinooks neither."

"So, how do you tell?"

"Damned if I know. Some is friendly, some ain't."

"Ah, well-a-day," Jared said. "What about Gray Cat? He knows them, you say."

"Some he knows. Some he don't."

"Well, we'll just have to find out which is which—what, won't we?"

"Chinooks's been robbed so much they ain't likely to take to a white face."

"But you lived among 'em, did you not?"

"I did. Been a while."

"Why didn't you tell me all this before, Fur Face?"

Pettibone laughed. "Hell, I thought you'd turn back long before now."

"Why, you crafty sonofabitch? Did you think I would give up?"

The old trapper slipped his fox-fur cap off his head and scratched at the lice in his hair. He popped one between his fingers, flipping its cracked carcass toward the lake.

"I didn't rightly know," Pettibone said. "First snow can make a man think mighty hard about civilization and soft beds, a warm bath."

"Hell, Pettibone, I've seen winters before."

"Not in the Rockies you ain't."

"I figured high mountains would get high snows."

"Oh ye did, did ye?"

"We got to spring, did we not?" Sometimes Pettibone was a little too critical, Jared thought. As if he alone had beaten the wilderness, and all others who followed were trespassers.

"The onliest ones I ever seed take to the mountains were a-runnin' from somethin' back down on the flat."

"Huh?"

"Wife, kids, the law."

"What about you, Fur Face?"

Pettibone laughed wryly. "Me? I got tired of workin' a hardscrabble farm and payin' tax money to the county and blood money to the landlord."

Jared laughed. "Reason enough," he said, looking away into the emerald woods. Jared had his own reasons, but he wasn't about to confide in Pettibone. There was just nothing left for him back there in civilization, on the flat. It wasn't just civilization either that he hated. He hated what he had done, what he had had to do. He hoped he would not have to do anything like it again.

"Let's get going. Gray Cat probably thinks we took a nap."

"He's probably snoozin' hisself," Pettibone said.

"Before we go on, I want to leave a mark that I was here," Jared said. He walked to a thick pine and took out his knife. He carved his name into the bark: JARED FLYNN. Underneath, he wrote: *Apr 1811*.

"Good way to kill a tree," the old trapper said.

Pettibone and Flynn hefted their packs back onto their shoulders and hiked past the first falls. Here the river made a perpendicular cascade of some twenty feet. The water was very swift below it.

They walked a mile alongside the boiling rapids where the river made a swift descent. Then it drove between humped islands of black rock, dropping another eight feet between two rocks. Mist sparkled in the air above the falls, pulsing with sunlight and invisible air. Tiny rainbows shimmered in the depths of these miniature clouds, winking on and off with the vagrancy of the breeze.

Jared followed Gray Cat's tracks; small swaths of flattened grasses, a moccasin print in soft mud, a damp rock where the Mandan had stepped. Above the sound of the rushing waters, he listened for other sounds: the trill of a bird, the *scree* of a hawk, the *whap-whap* of wings, the crash of deer or elk through the forest.

He heard nothing, and instantly the silence pricked all of his senses as if some ghost wind had brushed against him, touching a frail finger against the back of his neck until the hackles rose in spiny bristles.

Jared stopped, stepped off the path. Pettibone halted too, a look of wonderment on his face. Jared put a finger to his lips.

"You hear somethin'?" Pettibone asked.

Flynn shook his head, cupped his left ear. He swung his rifle around until it braced against his abdomen.

"You don't hear nothin' and you're listenin'?"

Flynn nodded, stepped farther away from the river. He crouched and beckoned for Pettibone to follow.

"Damn foolishness," the old trapper muttered.

He followed Jared into the brush and along a course that kept the river in sight but also kept them off the trail that Gray Cat had followed. The younger man stepped slowly, stopping every so often to listen.

Pettibone had learned to respect the young man's instincts, his tracking ability, his keen sense of approaching danger. As he watched the young man stalk through the trees, using them for cover, he was impressed by such skills in one so young. Flynn seemed at home in the wilderness, and while he often looked at peace with the world, Pettibone knew that he was always on his guard. Yet Flynn had never talked about himself, and the company must have known of his skills to entrust one so young with such an important mission when there were others more able, more proven.

Men like Jared Flynn seemed to take to the wilderness as if they had been born there. Even the Indians, sometimes hostile to whites, treated such men differently, as if something in their eyes told the red men that some white men were kin to them, like brothers. Flynn had that rare quality. Pettibone had seen it work on the Mandans, the Crow, the Sioux, even the few Blackfeet they had encountered.

Wanderers. That's what men like Flynn were. They never put down roots, but seemed at home wherever they were. They carried a kind of song in their hearts, and you could see something shining in their eyes with each stretch of new country. And Pettibone had been watching Jared Flynn, all right. All the way from Fort William. Had seen how he looked at every curl and comb of river, every plant, every flower, every mark on the land made by man or beast. Pettibone had the eerie feeling that Flynn was making a gigantic map in his mind so he could always get back to where he had come from and would never be lost, not in this country or any other.

Flynn had never spoken about himself, nor did he ask many questions. It was as if he knew the names of everything that grew on the earth, and that he wove them into his mind until they were all one thing. The journey, the map, the names of things, and the tracks of men and animals were like a song he had memorized and could never forget because it was locked into his heart and had become part of his soul.

Indeed, Pettibone had heard Jared murmuring to himself, making up little rhymes about things. His eavesdropping made him feel self-conscious, as if he were prying into the man's diary, into his medicine pouch, and seeing objects he didn't understand.

Pettibone shook off the thoughts he had now. He had been down that trail before, lying awake at night, wondering what Flynn was thinking as he listened to him sing some melody to himself. It was as if Flynn was recording the day's events in some kind of memorable form.

Jared disappeared in the brush, and Pettibone felt a brief moment of unreasonable panic until Flynn reappeared from behind a blue spruce like some sun-shot shadow, a flash of buckskin so natural he might have been a deer.

Far off, Pettibone heard voices. He knew Flynn heard them too. He could make no sense of them, but he recognized the grunts and gutturals of red men, and still Jared held to his course off the path. Now and then the old trapper caught a glimpse of the river and saw flashes in the sun as salmon flew upstream, hurtled the rocks and ledges like wingless beings fashioned of silver flower petals.

Pettibone had seen Flynn on the stalk before, but never at such speed. There was something about the way Flynn ran that reminded the old trapper of other hunts, other encounters with the red men. He was like a great hunting cat now, gliding soundlessly through the emerald woods, sure-footed and graceful, yet with an intensity that showed he was prepared for anything. His motion was fluid, with no wasted movements and Pettibone had the eerie feeling that Flynn could disappear in an instant, perfectly blending into his surroundings, and never be seen by man and beast. He had felt that way before, high in the mountains when they were hunting elk, keeping each other in sight. More than once Flynn had disappeared, only to reappear later in some other place. Pettibone never could figure how he had gotten there so fast, and so silently that he had not spooked the wary elk.

Pettibone heard voices now, voices strong and raised and gruffed in anger very close by. He expected Flynn to halt there and do some listening and scouting before going any farther.

Pettibone started to slow his stride.

Suddenly, Flynn leaped through the air toward a clearing where Gray Cat stood, surrounded by other Indians. One of them had him in a stranglehold and held a knife to his throat.

Before Pettibone knew what was happening, he heard a terrible, bone-rattling, spine-rippling scream that was louder and more terrifying than any savage's he had ever heard. He realized, in a split second, that no red man made that sound. Instead, the blood-curdling cry issued from Flynn's throat as he flew through the air, knife in hand, rifle held above him like a warclub.

Then all time froze. All movement seemed to stop dead in its tracks as if the Creator Himself had laid a freezing hand to the tableau before Pettibone's startled, bulging eyes.

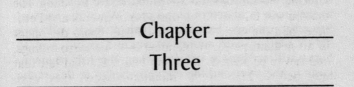

Chapter Three

McCord, in his wary and deliberate way, did not look directly into the fire as he cooked his evening meal. He ate well away from the coals, in the dark, listening intently for any sound above the monotonous tonal tapestry of the frogs grunting *gribbit, gribbit.* Afterward, he scraped away all signs of Vermeil's death with the soles of his boots, covering up the blood and obliterating the marks left when he had dragged the body to the river.

Later, he filled his pipe, lit it with a faggot from the fire, and smoked in a cluster of young cottonwood trees. He was fond of this pipe, bought from a Sioux when he worked for Dickson up the St. Peter's, the country the savages called the Wattapaw Menesotor. It was Robert Dickson, in fact, who had taught McCord the Sioux and Chippewa languages when he was an interpreter for the Michilimackinac Company. Joseph Ainse had hired Dickson. And it was Dickson who had introduced young Ramsey Crooks and McCord to the fur trade. Dickson had done well, and so, too, Ramsey

Crooks. Now it was McCord's turn. He wanted what these men had gotten for themselves, and he would have it.

He watched the bullbats flap by over the river, scouring mosquitoes that swarmed above the potholes as they rose in search of blood prey. When the fire had turned to embers, he took his bedroll there and slept lightly, alert to every sound. Wolves and coyotes sang to him until just before sunrise, when the fish began to jump in the river and the nightjars began to desert the nearby trees.

He rose just after dawn to a whippoorwill's incessant flute, built a small fire from the remaining coals, made coffee, and filled his belly with hardtack and a chunk of fried fatback. Satisfied that his cache was safe, he packed a rucksack with tobacco, beads, brass and tin trinkets, small mirrors, powder, ball, pistols, two cheap trade muskets, knives, and hatchets. He knew what the Mandans wanted. They were a lazy people, he had been told, who liked to trade for horses instead of stealing them like the Sioux. Well, he would need some horses too before this journey was over.

Before he left for the Mandan encampment, McCord lit a pipe, took one last look at his campsite. The fire was out and covered with sand, all but his own tracks smoothed away. The canoe was pulled well up on the bank, half hidden in the willows. He watched a hawk float by, following the course of the river as if reading a map. A pair of crows flew out of the trees, gave chase to the raptor and finally gave up, returning to their roosts in a cottonwood tree.

McCord shook the dottle from his pipe, crushing the sparks underfoot. Unearthing a cache, he loaded his trade goods into the canoe along with a half-dozen rifles in addition to his own, a fine .64 caliber Maryland rifle, packed with ball and ninety grains of black power. His brace of English pistols was tucked out of sight under his buckskins, but his knife and tomahawk jutted from the fringe below his waist.

When the canoe was loaded, he pushed it into the Missouri, leaping into it as it became waterborne. He picked up the paddle and turned upstream toward the mouth of the Heart River.

McCord pushed against the gentle current of the Heart, listening for any sound above the soft sob of the paddle dipping deep and slow so that the canoe sliced like a sleek knife through the flowing water. A sand crane, stately and sacerdotal on the shore of the river, lifted from its perch effortlessly, gliding upstream on silent pinions like some gray patriarch of littoral domains known only to its kind over vast eons of ancient times, holy and forgotten in the memory of men.

Before he reached the Mandan camp that afternoon, McCord could smell it. He rounded a bend, and at the end of a long stretch of water and bank, he saw the village. He paddled at the same unhurried pace, passing a few women washing clothes downstream. They eyed him curiously, and he noticed that their hair was dirty, unkempt, the dresses they wore were plain and shabby. People in the village lined the shore to watch him as he beached the canoe. Some carried crude hoes and rakes, and he saw a huge garden blooming in a clearing near the village of earthen lodges. Their huts looked like large overturned bowls. None of the women came forward, but stayed to their chores near their huts, their faces strangely blank, their eyes dull as dirty coal.

The Mandans stood their distance until McCord reached shore and stepped out of the canoe, holding up a sack of tobacco. He spoke in Sioux, signed that he came to trade. The men showed no interest, but the young boys jumped up and down shouting "Trade, trade." Some of the Mandan apparently understood him. Two braves approached and smelled the sack.

"Good, good," one said. Then others came forward and examined the tobacco. He opened the sack and let the aroma of the Virginia-grown latakia fill their nostrils.

"Let us smoke together," McCord said, and some of the men grinned.

He gestured to the two braves who had first come up, indicating that they should carry everything in the canoe with them. One man stepped forward and spoke to McCord in English. He wore a headdress of colored feathers. McCord thought they might have been dyed turkey feathers or from some bird species he didn't know. Others in the welcoming party bore less flamboyant headwear. Some feathers were fastened to the hair with leather thongs, others wore headbands made of cloth or deer hide. The men wore leggings and most were bare-chested.

"I am Shahaka. Chief. Means 'Big White.' You come. We smoke."

Shahaka and McCord led the procession to the chief's lodge. There, a woman brought out a blanket. After Shahaka and McCord were seated, the warriors laid out the trade goods, examining first the rifles and pistols, hefting the cans of black powder.

Shahaka's woman brought him a large beaded pouch. He drew a long pipe from the pouch. McCord handed him the tobacco. The chief filled the pipe and lit it from a faggot his woman brought from inside the hut. When the proper ritual of offering tobacco to the four directions was performed, the chief smoked and handed the pipe to McCord. He drew deeply. Other young men sat down on the edges of the blanket, and McCord passed the pipe to them. The pipe was decorated with various symbols and totems, painted with berry juice that had faded considerably over the years.

After they all had smoked, Shahaka put the pipe down and looked at McCord with interest.

"What you want for these goods?" he asked.

"I am looking for a man of your people to take me to the Sioux."

"Bad place."

"I am looking for a white man. He came here, traded with you."

"Many white men come to Mandan people."

"This one went to live with the Sioux. Lakota."

"Ah," Big White said. "That one."

"I must find him," McCord said. "I will give you all this and more if there is one among you who can take me to him."

"This one you seek does not want any man to find him."

"I know. But he is my friend. His name is Malcolm. Malcolm Flynn."

"He is called Iron Hawk by the Lakota."

At the name, another man spoke up, one sitting closest to Big White. "He wears a hawk made of iron on his neck," he said. "I am the one who took him into the land of the Lakota. I am called Little Owl."

"Yes, he wears such a hawk around his neck," McCord said excitedly. "Will you take me to him?"

"He is a big man. Very strong. Very brave," Little Owl said. "The Lakota believe he is a god from another tribe. He speaks the tongues of all the red men along the Missouri River."

"Why do you look for this man?" Big White asked.

"He is going to show me a river that spills into the big ocean."

"He knows of this river," Little Owl said. "He took one of our tribe to guide him there many robe seasons ago."

"Then bring me the man who took him there. I would find either this man or the river."

"I am the man who took him to the river," said

another man seated on the blanket. "I am called Black Wolf."

"I will give you many gifts," McCord said, "if you will take me to the man you call Iron Hawk. Much tobacco, a rifle, a hatchet, a knife, gold."

"You are not the brother of this man Iron Hawk?" Big White asked.

"No. I am a friend."

"That is good," Black Wolf said, nodding to the others. "Iron Hawk would kill you if you were his brother. We have seen this man too."

"What? You have seen Jared Flynn?"

"Yes," Black Wolf said. "He was here many moons ago. He took Gray Cat with him to show him where this river was, where it runs into the big water where the sun sleeps."

"Did this man ask about his brother, Iron Hawk?"

"No, he was with a man we knew. A white man."

McCord's eyes narrowed. He tried to conceal his excitement, paused so that his voice would not give him away with his next question."

"Who was this other man, this white man?" he asked.

"Pettibone," Black Wolf said. "He hunts the beaver. He knows of this river."

"Why did Gray Cat take them there?"

"He is a friend of Pettibone. He wanted to go. He wanted to be a friend of the young white man who was called Flynn."

So, Jared Flynn might already be on the Columbia River, McCord thought. It was enough to raise bumps on his arm, made the hackles on the back of his neck bristle. He wondered if Malcolm knew that his brother had passed this way. Probably not. But he would be most interested to learn that Jared had gone to the Columbia with another trapper—a man he did not know.

"Will you take me to the land of the Lakota?" McCord asked Black Wolf.

Black Wolf held a brief conversation with the others sitting on the blanket. McCord waited patiently.

"Let us see your goods," Big White said.

McCord opened the sacks, laid out powder, ball, hatchets, knives, German silver trinkets, beads, mirrors, and velvet-textured flints, all chipped square. He handed a trade musket to Big White, another to Black Wolf.

"I will give you a good rifle, Black Wolf, plenty of powder and ball, flints, a hatchet, a knife, gold to buy white man's things."

"I will take you to the land of the Lakota," Black Wolf said.

"I want to buy four horses from you, Big White," McCord said. "I will send Black Wolf back from the land of the Lakota with two of them."

"The Lakota might steal them from you," Big White said solemnly.

"Then I will walk, and you will still have two of your horses back, although I will pay you for them in gold."

Big White grunted his approval. He told the other Mandans of the trade he had struck with the white man.

"Come," Big White said. "We will look at horses. You will stay this night with the Mandan?"

"No, I want to get started right away. There is not much time."

"There is always much time," Big White said.

The men working in the tobacco fields looked up as the party of Mandans and McCord passed them on the way to where the young men watched the horses. McCord had heard that the Mandan tobacco was very bad, and only men tended to the growing of the leaves and the curing. Women were not allowed to work with such a sacred crop.

Shahaka spoke to the young men and they began separating the horses, finally leading a dozen to the place where the chiefs and McCord stood.

McCord looked at the teeth and unshod hooves of all the horses, finally selecting four by patting each in turn on the rump. Big White nodded his approval. Later, McCord presented the chief with all of the goods, and gold coins worth about ten dollars. He felt satisfied with the deal, and so, apparently, did Big White and the other chiefs.

"I will go with Black Wolf now," McCord said. "I give you my canoe that you may journey on the rivers and catch fish or game along the way." McCord made a sign with his arms and hands to augment his speech.

Big White thanked McCord in sign.

"May the spirits guide you on your way," the chief said.

There were no saddles for the horses. The bridles were made of horsehair from their manes and tails. McCord had plenty of rope to rig to the other two when they were not being ridden. Empty kegs and a basket or two would do the trick.

Before he left, McCord took Big White aside.

"There will be other white chiefs come up the river with many men and much equipment. Do you understand, Shahaka?"

"Shahaka knows what you say."

"They will build forts and give many gifts. They will speak for the great white father in Washington, a big white man's village in the east where the sun rises. They will give you many medals for you and your little chiefs."

"I have medals from the French and from the English."

"These will be from the Americans."

"That is another tribe?"

"Yes. Bigger than the others. Good fighters. Very rich. Much gold."

Shahaka laughed. "Traders?"

"Big traders." McCord wondered how much the chief understood. "Do not tell them that I was here or where I was going."

"They do not like you?"

"They are from a different tribe." McCord didn't know how else to explain it.

"When will they come?" Shahaka asked.

"Soon. In one or two summers."

"I will not tell them you were here."

McCord mounted the horse he had picked to ride. Black Wolf took the other one, grabbed the reins of the other two. They rode off from the village in silence.

It was dusk when they came to where McCord had made camp. He and Black Wolf dug up the caches and rigged the rope to carry most of the goods in packs and empty powder kegs. McCord carried cooking utensils, flour, coffee, cured meat, and various other items on his own horse. Black Wolf led the trapper to a ford where they crossed the Heart River and followed the Missouri westward into the setting sun.

"This man you look for," Black Wolf said, "Iron Hawk. Is he your brother?"

"In a way," McCord said. "A better brother than the one he has."

Black Wolf shook his head. He signed that he didn't understand.

"It's a long story," McCord said. "I will tell you all about him along the way to the land of the Lakota."

"Good. He must be a good man for you to come so far to see his face."

Good? McCord almost laughed out loud. Malcolm

Stuart Flynn was still spoken of in the East as either sinner or saint, sometimes both. Malcolm was a fierce Indian fighter when still a boy, as was his brother, Jared. Malcolm had married Randall McCord's sister, Lorna, and so, in a way, they were brothers. Lorna had been killed by Shawnee renegades. When people spoke of Malcolm, they spoke his name breathlessly, because he had tracked the Shawnees who murdered his wife and had slain them with a savagery that surprised even the Shawnee. Then he went back home, where something so terrible happened to Malcolm that he never spoke of it. Instead, he left suddenly, disappearing into the wilderness. He surfaced every so often, trapping with the French or the English, but he gained the reputation of being a loner. Then, when his younger brother Jared came into the wilderness, Malcolm vanished again. Only recently had McCord learned that Malcolm had gone to live with the Sioux.

"You hide much," Black Wolf said to McCord that night when they camped. "Many cache. Many goods. You walk alone. Where other men go?"

McCord nodded. "I carry many secrets in my heart, Black Wolf."

McCord reached into his possibles pouch. He drew out two objects, showed them to the Mandan. In his left hand he held a lead ball, in his right dangled a trade medal struck with the image of King George III of England.

"I'll give you a choice, Black Wolf. This . . ." He tossed the lead ball at Black Wolf, who caught it. ". . . or this." Black Wolf looked at the silver medal, placed it around his neck. He threw the rifle ball back to McCord.

"I keep secret," the Indian said.

"Good. Now we understand each other."

Worthless though it was, one might think McCord

had given Black Wolf riches beyond measure the way the Mandan examined it, weighing it so often in his hand, holding it up to admire.

But McCord still had the rifle ball Black Wolf had thrown back to him. He might yet have good use of it.

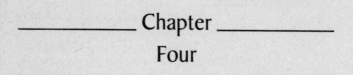

Chapter
Four

J ared Flynn leaped out of the thicket in a flash and
into the midst of the Indians, brandishing rifle and
hatchet. One of them, a short burly fellow, had Gray
Cat by the throat in an armlock. Screeching like a madman at the top of his voice, Jared knocked Gray Cat
free, hurling him to the ground. He fired his rifle into
the air, over the heads of Gray Cat's captors. The Indians ducked as the ball whined overhead. Jared shoved
the closest Indians away and put his moccasined foot
on the Mandan's chest.

"This man belongs to me," he said. "He is mine to
kill." Jared leaned downward and with his hatchet
chopped the air over Gray Cat's head as if to behead
him or split his skull.

Pettibone came running up. Out of breath, he
watched in horror as Jared stood off six bewildered Indians. They backed off from the sound of the young
man's voice, all shaking their heads, all holding their
hands open to show that they were empty of weapons.
Most of them were carrying fresh-cut poles no thicker

than a man's thumb. One or two had handfuls of horse-hair, and Pettibone thought another was carrying bone hooks. They were not painted for war, nor were they wearing their war clothes. He reckoned they meant to fish when they had come across Gray Cat looking for the cache of canoes.

"You got 'em buffaloed," Pettibone said, walking up to Jared. "They think you're plumb crazy."

"They were going to kill Gray Cat," Jared said.

"Not likely. These Injuns are friendly. Chinook, sure as shootin'."

As if to verify Pettibone's assessment, an old Indian walked out of the woods.

"I am Ma-chy-keu-etsa," said the old man. "Walking Bear in the white man's tongue. Me Tye-yea. Chief. Me Salish. Chinook. Hello, Pettibone."

"Hello, Walking Bear," Pettibone said. "It's been many a moon since I laid eyes on you. You look fit."

"I have seventy-two winters. Strong." The old chief didn't look forty. There was no fat in his flesh. He had some wrinkles in his weathered face, but his eyes crackled with youth and strength.

"This here's my friend, Jared Flynn. And that's Gray Cat a-lyin' on the ground there. Flynn thought your bunch was a-trying to kill the Mandan. He pulled him off a bluff, I reckon."

Jared took his foot off Gray Cat's chest. "Get up," he said. Gray Cat stood up. He didn't bother to wipe the dirt off his back. He seemed as puzzled as anyone there.

"You come trade," Walking Bear said. "Plenty fur."

Jared looked at the Chinooks. The men were hardy, strong-boned, with fine muscles rippling under their reddish skin. They were not as tall as Pettibone or Gray Cat, and considerably shorter than Flynn himself. Most of the men, except for Walking Bear, wore loose garments resembling blankets, which they wrapped around their bodies. These were made of small animal skins sewn together, and were painted in various colors.

Chief Walking Bear wore a robe made of sea-otter skin, beaver, weasel, and ermine. He, like the other Chinooks, wore a hat made of some kind of tough grass, with a conical crown that came to a point at the top. The hat brim was wide enough to keep rain off the shoulders. Walking Bear's hat was checkered, interwoven with the crude figures of dog and deer.

"Come," the chief said. "We will smoke and talk. We will catch some fish and eat and talk some more."

"We best get on," Jared said.

"It wouldn't be perlite to turn Walking Bear down, son. 'Sides, we may learn a thing or two. These is friendly Injuns, but farther down we might not be so lucky."

"What about our packs?"

"Gray Cat can fetch 'em."

Pettibone spoke to Gray Cat. Two of the Chinooks joined the Mandan and they set off to bring down the trappers' packs. Flynn and Pettibone followed Walking Bear and the others into the woods by a worn path. In a clearing, they joined a dozen other Chinooks, camped lazily among the trees bordering the meadow.

Jared noticed that a half dozen of the Chinooks in camp were playing some sort of game as the others looked on. Just inside the trees, they had cleared a space for their cook fire. Pots and pans lay next to the circle of stones where they built the fire. A few rifles leaned against trees.

"What are they doing?" Jared asked Pettibone as the chief and his men stopped to watch the game.

"That's *chal-e-chal*," the old trapper said. "They're gamblin' with their prized goods."

Jared saw an array of tomahawks, knives, stone clubs, and bows and arrows lying in the grass at the end of a mat that was about three feet wide and six feet long. The six players sat on either side of the mat facing each other. As Flynn watched, one man shuffled ten small palettes of polished wood, each about the size of an American dollar.

After the Indian had finished shuffling the palettes, shifting them back and forth in his hands, another gave a signal and he divided them equally into two fists and threw them out on the mat toward his opponent. He did this three times while Jared, Pettibone, and the others watched.

"I can't hardly make no sense of it, Fur Face," Jared said.

"It depends on how them little wooden cakes land and slide and such. They could go on for days until one of them wins."

All during the game, the players chanted a sonorous song in rhythm to their body movements. It reminded Jared of the voyageurs singing in time to the raising and dipping of their paddles. The singing was very loud and joyous and the game went on as Walking Bear led his party to his camping place in the trees. There the ground was bare of grass, so everyone sat on a blanket while one of the Chinooks brought pipe and tobacco to the chief. He offered tobacco to the four directions, filled the calumet. They passed the pipe and smoked.

"Why you come back, Pettibone?" Walking Bear asked.

"Jared here wants to do some tradin' and trappin'. Me too."

"There are already many white men on all the rivers. They come and they go."

More than two hundred winters ago, the old ones said, a white named Drake had come to the shores of the big water, and he had met the man called Vancouver more than ten winters ago. Since then he had seen

many white hunters, many of whom had fallen to the
knife, the club or arrow, or had been torn to pieces by
wild animals. Now, here were two more, like all the
others before them, looking for something.

Pettibone looked at Jared. He didn't want to tell
the Chinooks too much, but he didn't want to lie to
them either.

"Mostly, we're just explorin'," Jared said.

White Bear looked puzzled.

"Just lookin' around, he means," said Pettibone.

"Hmmm," the chief murmured. "Much to see.
Much game. Many deer, many goats. Many rattle-
snakes."

The other Chinooks laughed.

Jared wondered how long the Chinooks had been
upriver and whether they had seen any other white
men. But he sensed that it would be impolite to question Walking Bear. They were either his guests or his
prisoners, depending on how one looked at it. Pettibone would know what to do. He could wait to find out
what he wanted to know.

Walking Bear put the pipe down, stood up. "We
fish," he said. "Eat."

The others got up as one of their number put the
sacred pipe away. Pettibone nudged Flynn in the side
with his elbow.

"This oughter be somethin'," he whispered.

"We're goin' fishin'?"

"Looks like."

Some of the Chinooks raced ahead. By the time
Jared and Pettibone, along with Walking Bear and
three young men, reached the river, the ones who had
gone ahead were starting two separate fires by vigor-
ously rubbing barkless sticks together. Smaller sticks arranged in a cone caught fire, and soon the two fires
were going.

"Ain't they never heard of fire steel?" Jared asked.

"Their ways is just as quick as flint and steel, I reckon," Pettibone said.

Flynn snorted.

Walking Bear beckoned to Flynn. As the young trapper watched, the chief took his knife, cut a small piece of leather from a strap he had tucked in his sash. The leather snippet was about the size of a coffee bean. The other Indians were engaged in the same activity, but they waited until their chief had finished. Walking Bear removed a single strand of horsehair from his pouch, tying it around the leather bean.

"We got some Kirby hooks, tell him," Jared said to Pettibone. "Soon's Gray Cat brings us our packs."

"Let him do it his way," said the trapper. "These people been fishin' these cricks for hunnerts of years."

"Hell, they ain't no hook to that hair. How they goin' to catch fish?"

"Fish's teeth get tangled in that there spunk of leather," Pettibone said. "I seen 'em catch a passel on a good day."

The chief walked to the edge of the river, stepped over to a large rock close to the bank and squatted. He leaned over, dropped the lure into the water. Walking Bear began jerking small trout from the stream so fast that Jared's eyes could scarcely follow the action. He flicked them to the bank, where one of his men picked them up and threw them to the men tending the fires. The men skewered the fish on sharpened sticks arranged in a circle around the fire. The fish cooked slowly as the firekeepers turned the sticks gradually so that the heat was evenly distributed.

Above the chief the water boiled over large boulders, and Jared saw tiny rainbows in the spray. Farther down, the river made a flat run, its waters so clear Jared could see the pebbles and the shadowy forms of fish pushing upstream against the current. Once again he was struck by the beauty of the land and the almost mystical fabric of the universe, so unlike the world he had left, the dark past that seemed to follow him like his shadow.

The other Chinooks fished farther down and tossed their catch on the bank, where another runner picked them up and carried them to the fire. Soon the chief stood up and stepped to the shore. Jared smelled the aroma of baking fish and his stomach turned with hunger.

"Hook or no hook, by gum," he said with admiration. But he scratched his head with the puzzlement of it, just the same.

The Indians sat in a semicircle with Flynn and Pettibone in their midst, devouring fish as fast as they were roasted, swallowing them whole. Pettibone chewed the first fish he was given and Jared did the same, but he soon realized it was better to swallow them like medicine, in one gulp, without thinking about it.

Soon the kettle was boiling over one of the fires, but the Chinooks still kept throwing live fish into the boiling water. Apparently, Jared observed, the roasted fish were only the first course. Some of the Indians added tubers and greens along with handfuls of meal into the kettle, and one threw in a dried chunk of venison. One Indian stirred the contents of the pot into a thick mash.

When the kettle's contents had cooled, they all ate, dipping out handfuls of the mash and smearing the whole mess into their mouths, laughing and talking all the while. Gray Cat and the other braves joined them, dropping the trappers' packs in a pool of shadow cast by a musty blue spruce. Pettibone and Flynn ate with them until their bellies were full.

Jared went into the woods with many of the others, to answer a call of nature. When he returned, many of the Chinook braves were already asleep under trees, atop thick grasses.

"Reckon we just as well take us a nap too," said Pettibone. "We ain't goin' nowheres for a while."

"They sure take their time about gettin' to a trade blanket, don't they?" Jared asked.

"Likely, they'll get to it after we foller 'em to their main camp."

"Any idea when that'll be?"

Pettibone looked up at the sky. The sun was near its zenith. "Why, I expect afore the sun falls we'll be among the whole bunch."

Jared yawned. As he and Pettibone sat down, the old trapper looked at his young friend.

"You took quite a chance, jumpin' into them Chinooks like you did. It's a wonder they stood for your bluff."

"Who said I was bluffin'?"

"Yeahr, I reckon." But Pettibone had never seen anything so bold as when Flynn had stood off the Chinooks. He thought they might not be so much afraid of Flynn as startled by him. Like many a tribe he had lived among, the Chinooks admired bravery. But like as not, Flynn was alive this moment because he had caught the Chinook off guard and in a good mood.

He and Pettibone slept side by side. Gray Cat slept too, a short distance away. When they awoke, the sun stood at a slant, heading toward afternoon. After a couple of stretches and silent yawns, they followed the chief and his men back to the temporary camp. There, they packed up and followed him on a ten-mile trek through the forest to the main encampment of the Chinook.

Jared noticed how quietly the Indians walked, how careful they were with their tracks, leaving little sign of their passing. It felt as if he was walking through woods with a group of phantoms, so silent were they, so careful with every step that he did not hear a twig break nor see a moccasin print on the forest floor.

They crossed several small creeks, saw elk, deer, and bear sign all along the way. Jared could smell the strong scent from the bear's scat and wondered that they did not see one rise up from the underbrush to challenge them. He marked the elk beds, knew that they must be of considerable size, and noted that some of the places were fresh. Every so often he heard elk or deer walking, breaking small branches with their hooves. Then the silence filled the vacuum and he was left to follow the ghostly figures of the Chinook as they made their way back to their encampment.

Jared heard voices in the distance, and soon they were joined by two young men who emerged out of nowhere to join them. They did not speak aloud, but spoke so rapidly in sign language that Jared could not follow it. After a few minutes they emerged into a large clearing, surrounded by a meandering creek on three sides. Tall pines rose up from the meadow to rocky crags that touched the clouds.

The camp teemed with people, but Jared's eyes were drawn to the women, some of whom wore only deerskin breechcloths, six inches wide and four feet long, passing between their thighs and tied at the waist. Others wore a kind of odd skirt made of the inner rind of cedar bark twisted into threads, so it hung from their waists like long fringes. When they walked, Jared could see their private parts through the waving threads.

Several women were playing games on mats similar to the one Jared had seen the men use for their gambling, while others were weaving mats and baskets, or digging for roots along the creek and among the trees. The Chinook had built no lodges in the camp, but only large square sheds, open on the sides. In many of these Jared saw fish drying on woven racks of wood. In others, people were still napping or working at various tasks under the shade of grass roofs.

"They leave their regular villages in the spring,"

Pettibone explained, "and come to live out in the open. You'll see some of them villages when we go down the river, but don't go in none of 'em."

"Why not?"

"Full of fleas, that's why. Thick as bees."

Jared looked around him in wonder as he loosened the straps on his pack. "Why, there must be hundreds of Indians here."

"Easy," Pettibone said.

"How long are we goin' to be here?"

Pettibone shrugged.

So many people in one place made Jared nervous. They seemed strange to him, with their flattened heads and big brown eyes. The smell of drying fish was strong in the air, wafting on smoke that drifted from beneath the drying sheds.

They continued to follow the chief across the meadow toward the largest shed, but before they got there, a woman made a beeline toward them. She was carrying something in her arms and she was staring straight at Pettibone.

"Who's that?" Jared asked.

Pettibone saw the woman and halted in his tracks. Jared and Gray Cat stopped too, and waited for her to reach them.

The woman had been crying. When she saw Pettibone, she began to moan and screech, and a torrent of words spilled from her mouth.

She stopped in front of the old trapper and held out the bundle to him. She bowed her head slightly and spoke words that Jared did not understand. Pettibone backed away, and Jared saw why. In her hands, wrapped in a small woven basket, was a baby.

And the baby was stone dead.

_____ Chapter _____
Five

Black Wolf seemed wary, almost nervous, after he and McCord left the Missouri River and reached the eastern edge of the Black Hills. In the distance the hills looked dark and treeless, but the closer they approached, the greener they appeared as the trees became defined. They began to see more buffalo and antelope on the plain and browsing on the low foothills that were virtually treeless.

In all the days they had been riding, the Mandan had carefully avoided the known trails and camps of all tribes. Sometimes, when Black Wolf came across tracks, they would ride far afield to avoid any contact. They'd had to skulk from prying eyes more than once, ride into low-lying hills or take shelter in deep arroyos, put the horses into creeks to obliterate their tracks, and camp without making fire.

There were days when McCord felt the desolation of empty country, longing for some human companionship besides the laconic Black Wolf, who often did not speak for days. So it was a surprise to McCord when they approached the Black Hills to see the change in the Mandan.

"Lakota call Paha Sapa," he said. "Many spirit. We go quick."

"I want to find Malcolm Flynn."

"We go now," Black Wolf said.

They did not follow the easy valleys through the Black Hills, but kept to ridges thick with pines, which offered concealment and safety. Once, they saw a band of Lakota chasing a small herd of buffalo and they waited out of sight until the hunters and hunted vanished over a low hill. They made no smoke or dust, and when they camped each night, one or the other was always awake.

Beyond the Black Hills they lay concealed in a great basin for a full day watching a large band of Cheyenne make meat from a large herd of buffalo. The women and children and old ones soon came upon the plain to butcher the killed animals. During the night, Black Wolf led McCord well away from the Cheyenne, but when the sun dawned the next day, they rode in the open toward a distant range of mountains. Black Wolf fell silent again, only occasionally making sign to convey information to McCord.

McCord had had a lot of time to think during the long trek from the Mandan village. Time was a factor in his journey, but he knew that it would do no good to hurry in such country. A man could lose his life by indulging in needless haste. Even with the slowness of the journey overland, he knew that he was still ahead of Ramsey Crooks, Wilson Hunt, Donald McKenzie, and the others who meant to venture into the great Pacific territories now that Meriwether Lewis and Captain Clark had proved the journey feasible a scant five years before.

When McCord left Mackinac Island, Ramsey Crooks had been expected to join John Jacob Astor's

newly formed Pacific Fur Company. Wilson Hunt had
bragged about it in Montreal for weeks. When McCord
passed through St. Louis, there was word that Manuel
Lisa had formed the Missouri Fur Company, still another competitor for the newly opened fur territories
west of the Mississippi. And Astor was soon to dispatch
a ship, the *Tonquin,* a vessel of 290 tons burden, to sail
to the mouth of the Columbia River after putting to
port in the Falklands and the Sandwich Islands. So, Mr.
John Jacob Astor was launching no less than two expeditions to corner the fur trade in the Far West, one by
sea, the other by land.

And that scut Jared Flynn was ahead of everyone:
Lisa, Crooks, and Captain Jonathon Thorn of the *Tonquin.* Crooks and Robert McLellan had already traded
in furs along the Missouri for a couple of years. Lisa
had built a trading fort along the Upper Missouri. Mc-
Cord didn't know if Lisa planned to expand his trading
to include the Oregon Territory or not. But it was a
good bet he was going to protect what he had already
gained.

Jared Flynn was the real fly in the ointment, and
McCord knew that Malcolm's hatred for his brother
was beyond belief—why, nobody knew. Malcolm had
vowed to kill Jared if ever he saw him again, and Mc-
Cord knew that Malcolm Flynn had no idea that Jared
was heading for the Columbia to stake out territory for
the North-West Company. Nor did Malcolm know what
McCord's mission was, and that would have to remain a
secret for a time. But he was being well paid for his
mission, although his employer did not know about
Malcolm Flynn and the hatred that existed between the
two brothers.

McCord had a lot of time to think on the long ride
up the Missouri. The Mandan didn't talk much, and
that was good. McCord knew they were making good
time. He hadn't sat a horse for that long before, and

there were times when it felt like he was riding on the thin edge of an axe blade, but he had toughened up enough so that the horse's backbone no longer burned him or made knots in his butt. There was plenty of game, and Black Wolf was a good enough bow shot to bring food to the camp on the days when McCord didn't see anything to eat but lizards and snakes, prairie dogs and gophers. They'd had badger, rabbit, prairie chicken, and doves the Mandan had brought down with a kind of slingshot he carried in his possibles pouch. They baked the chickens in mud underneath the fire, but Black Wolf liked his half raw, so he just singed his birds on a stick.

Black Wolf skirted a large section of plain littered with the bones and skulls of buffalo. The skulls were all facing east. The Mandan seemed to hold it as some sacred place, or perhaps, McCord thought, he just didn't want to spook the horses. They were skittery enough as it was, for the smell of death still lingered on the plain, and flies clustered some of the bones.

When they reached the Powder River, the deerflies were thick, and they stung McCord where they struck bare skin. Horseflies and blowflies swarmed the banks of the river as well, and after watering the horses, McCord was happy to push on toward the Big Horn Mountains. The flies didn't seem to bother Black Wolf much, but like the horses, McCord's hide ran with blood streaks.

The closer they came to the mountains, the less the Mandan spoke. McCord had moments of apprehension, mostly when he felt swallowed up by the country and the vast blue sky, with its cottony puffs of clouds floating serene over the mountains in the distance. He wondered if he could trust the Indian to find Malcolm Flynn, and even if Black Wolf meant to, how would he find one white man in such a big stretch of country? They were eating antelope almost every day now;

bunches of them seemed to be roaming everywhere
McCord looked. They kept their distance, but Black
Wolf knew how to stalk, sometimes making them curious enough to come so close that McCord could put a
ball in a buck's heart at under a hundred yards. The
Indian would lie on the ground, stick his legs in the air,
and move them back and forth like scissors. He could
also hunch over, sidle sideways right up to a herd, and
put an arrow in an antelope's neck before the herd
knew he was upon them.

When the Big Horns loomed close, McCord
sensed still another change in Black Wolf. The Mandan
began to study the ground more carefully, and he rode
ahead for long distances and often would come back to
join McCord from a different direction. Less than a day
away they got caught in a thunderstorm, not the first of
the journey, but this one stung horses and men with
hail the size of .60 caliber pellets, and the wind blew so
hard the horses leaned a good thirty degrees from the
force. They stood in the open, Black Wolf and McCord,
and used the horses for shelter until the storm passed.
The wind blew the clouds away and the sun came out,
but the ground was washed clean of tracks. There were
only holes like doodlebugs make, filled with melting
nuggets of hail.

Black Wolf showed McCord a camp, signing that it
was made by the Lakota not long ago. There was plenty
of sign that the Lakota had been there: scraps of hide
and tanned leather, worn-out moccasins, heaps of human excrement caked by the sun, depressions where
the lodgepoles had dug into the ground, bare spots in
the yellowing grass, arrowheads, broken flints, feathers,
animal bones. The campsite was at a junction of the
Powder with another stream, no more than a creek,
McCord thought, which Black Wolf called Crazy
Woman. They did not linger there.

They crossed still another creek or river, and then

rode north in the shadow of the Big Horns. McCord felt they were getting close to wherever they were going.

"Make camp," Black Wolf said one afternoon, two days' ride from the last creek. "You stay."

"Where is the white man?" McCord asked.

Black Wolf pointed to the north, to a place somewhere in the Big Horn Mountains. "Me go. You stay."

"I don't like this much."

"Make talk. Find white man."

"When will you be back?"

Black Wolf didn't understand him. McCord pointed to the sun, made the sign for day with his right arm on his left palm arcing ninety degrees.

"Two sleeps."

"Where is the white man?" Again McCord had to sign to make himself understood.

"White man call Tongue River. *La langue.*"

So McCord made camp next to the mountains by a small stream and watched Black Wolf ride into the shadows of afternoon like some lone dark ghost he had only imagined. He looked up at the mountains behind him and wondered how many beaver might be quartered in their rocky keeps. Malcolm had told him that the beaver were thick as fleas in the Big Horns, the snows so deep a man had to use snowshoes to get back to his lodge. Better trapping than Canada, Malcolm had said, better than the Ohio, and there was no competition because the Indians were only too happy to trade their pelts for pretty baubles, weapons, utensils made of iron, mirrors, and brass tacks.

But the beaver weren't the only reason Malcolm had left the settlements, and perhaps not the real reason. Something had happened to him the time he went back home to see his mother and father, his brother and sister. Malcolm had gone there, knowing young Jared Sean had grown up and might want to work for

the North-West Company. But Malcolm had returned
to the Black Hills alone, with a long sad face and a
bitter temper that he hadn't had before. The change in
him had been remarkable, sharp-edged, as if he had
seen horror or been to war. He didn't stay long, but left
with a Frenchman, Emile Fragonard, for St. Louis.

Something had happened to Malcolm in the West
as well. For he came back one more time to see Mc-
Cord and tell him of the riches he had found, if not the
peace he sought. McCord knew that his friend was still
troubled, but he would not talk about it, no matter how
many times McCord tried to get Malcolm to open up,
tell him what had happened back in Pennsylvania when
he had gone home to see his family.

That was about the same time Robert Gillespie
was trying to put together his new fur-trading company,
XY. Gillespie wanted to buck the North-West Company, believing in Sir Alexander Mackenzie's policy of
expansion by setting up trading posts along the Pacific
Ocean shoreline. Word of all these changes in the eastern fur trade filtered down through the ranks. Big
changes were in the air, all right, and McCord meant to
cash in on them—with help from Malcolm and the
Sioux. And a very powerful man right in the middle of
it all.

McCord watched as large white clouds billowed
out of the Big Horns and floated over the plain, casting
giant shadows over the land. He wondered again why
Black Wolf had to leave him alone. Perhaps he should
have insisted on going, but then the Mandan could have
led him on a wild goose chase. McCord didn't know this
country, and he had no idea which tribe Malcolm was
living with or where they might be. So, for the time
being, he knew he had to trust Black Wolf, even though
it was his nature not to trust anyone.

He vowed to keep a sharp eye in case of treachery,
and moved his camp twice that afternoon, finally set-

tling on a knoll that was thick with pines, spruce, and juniper, where he could see without being seen. He would make no fire that night, and would keep one eye open, his ears attuned to every sound.

He took the packs from the horses, left his own bridled, and tied them on short tethers to separate trees.

He wiped out all his tracks and sat in the trees, waiting for the night and the chill to come.

Black Wolf rode to the place where the Tongue River came out of the Big Horns. There, he hid his horse in the trees, tying it to a juniper. On foot, he studied the many tracks along the river's banks, reading the story of the animals that came to drink and the comings and goings of the moccasined Lakota who walked the game path, sometimes on horseback, sometimes leading unshod ponies. He followed the Tongue up through the ravine, staying at least a hundred paces from the river, stopping every so often to listen. He made no sound as he glided through the forest on silent moccasins.

He walked until it became too dark to see, then climbed a slope, found a resting place in a small canyon just above a stone ledge. Anyone approaching from below would dislodge the stones or scrape the shale. Above his perch the slope was sheer rock, and it was unlikely anyone could come upon him without making noise. He chewed pemmican and slept until the pre-dawn chill awoke him from a shallow sleep. He climbed back down into the ravine, then continued his course upriver, even more cautiously than before.

The Mandan listened to the bird calls, the whisper of pinions as a red-tailed hawk flapped out of the sky, bucking air currents that flowed from the high snow-capped peaks. He sniffed the breeze and smelled the far-off scent of smoke and meat curing over a fire. He moved more slowly after that, and far enough from the river that he no longer heard its bubbling flow over rocks, its loud husky scrape against the banks as it twisted through the curves in its angular descent.

The smells grew stronger, and every so often he caught the sound of a metal utensil scraping against stone or flint, and scraps of voices floated to his ears like rags torn from a blanket. Black Wolf began to climb the opposite slope then, gradually gaining higher ground. He knew where the Lakota encampment would be, but he had to be sure, had to count the lodges, look at the circles to confirm which tribe summered along the Tongue. He had already seen the deep furrows worn by the heavy lodgepoles used as a travois to carry the meat to camp. He knew that these people had made meat from the buffalo and would be busy curing the hides and flesh to make robes and moccasins. But he also knew they would have scouts up- and downriver, and he did not want to be killed by mistake before he did what he had to do.

By nightfall of the second day Black Wolf was high above the camp, flat on his belly, looking down at the lodges bristling across a wide-open valley, smoke rising lazily in the air from smoke holes and open fires. The smell of cooking meat made his stomach clench with hunger. He counted the lodges and made note of their circles. These were the Hunkpapa he sought, with a few Minneconjou and Brules, cousins visiting cousins.

He crawled backward away from the camp and lay in the shade of a spruce until he made sure all sounds came from the camp and not from somewhere near him. He stood up halfway, kept his crouch, and stole a zigzag path to still higher ground, where he scouted the place he would spend the second sleep, hidden from view. He did not want the jays to call out his presence, nor flush the partridges that skulked in the grasses.

Their beating wings would announce him like drums calling warriors to the dancing circle.

He had not seen the white man this day, but this was the tribe where he lived with his Hunkpapa woman, Morning Cloud, daughter of War Shirt. The white man was permitted to live with the Lakota because he had killed Crow and counted coup on Pawnee. Black Wolf had heard that the white man was very brave and a blood brother of One Horn, son of the medicine man, Little Drum.

Before the sun came awake, Black Wolf would do what he could not do in the daylight. A Mandan could not just walk into a Lakota camp, but Black Wolf knew he must prepare the way for the white man, McCord, a name that to speak aloud twisted his tongue, to visit his white friend, the one the Hunkpapa called Iron Hawk. It might be that Iron Hawk would not want to see this McCord, and Black Wolf did not want to make any enemies. So he would have to make contact with Iron Hawk under cover of darkness.

The Mandan slept like a man floating in a river, just above the dark deepness of dream.

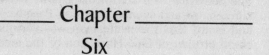

Chapter
Six

Pettibone stared dumbly at the keening woman carrying the dead baby. He took the child from the woman and shook his head.

The woman spoke and signed, scrawling little ephemeral figures in the air with her hands.

"What does she want?" Jared asked.

"She wants me to bring her baby back to life. She is offering me a horse to do it."

Jared's mouth opened but no sound came out. His throat muscles began to tighten. Unformed images swirled in his mind. He tried not to look at the child with its knotted little eyelids, its pinched face.

The Chinook woman pushed at the baby, muttering words that Flynn could not understand. He saw the pleading in her eyes, heard her pathetic cries, and something like a knife's sharp blade twisted inside him, struggling up from his subconscious. Pettibone gave the baby back to the woman and signed that he could not do what she asked.

The woman turned sadly from Pettibone and

thrust the dead baby into Jared's hands. Jared froze, trying not to look at the child's wizened and wrinkled face. Its eyes were closed, its mouth drawn up tight, and its hands were clenched into tiny fists. He looked down at the baby in horror, remembering another time and another babe, his sister's, stillborn and terribly deformed, with only one eye and a cleft palate, little stumps of hands with fingers not fully developed, its body all red and shriveled, its face pinched up as if it had died angry.

His throat constricted and he couldn't speak for several seconds. All the memories of his sister Caitlin, his older brother Malcolm, and his mother and father, came rushing back to him in a torrent. He fought against the reaction the sight of the dead baby instilled in him, the great weight on his chest, the boil of sensations in his mind, like storm clouds in a great wind.

"God," he croaked, and marveled at the lightness of the child in his hands. "No, take it. Take it away," he said, his voice a hard rasp.

Pettibone took the baby from Jared and gave it back to the woman.

"Go away," he signed. "We cannot give your child life."

The woman slumped as she took the baby, and held it tightly against her milk-heavy breasts. Tears streamed from her eyes as she turned and sadly walked away.

Jared and Pettibone stood there, watching her.

Jared swallowed hard and got back his breath. "Why does she think you can bring that dead baby back to life?" he asked.

"I doctored a child what had the croup, and they think I can do miracles with whiskey and sugar."

"Damnedest thing I ever saw."

"Well, these people set store by such things. They got more superstitions than the Romans have gods."

Pettibone pushed the woman aside and walked past her. Her weeping tore at Jared, but he knew there was nothing they could do for her. She would have to bury the child and keep her horse.

"It's gruesome," Jared said.

"Not to her," Pettibone replied. "But I wouldn't worry about it none if I was you."

Jared gave the old trapper a sharp look. "What do you mean by that?"

"Oh, nothing. Injuns get used to their chilluns dying, I reckon."

"She didn't look used to it, Fur Face. And I damn sure ain't."

Pettibone grunted and started after the chief without saying another word. Jared followed, but when he looked down at his hands, he saw they were shaking.

As they walked across the meadow, Jared noticed that many of the Chinook women seemed in high spirits. They smiled at him as they worked on weaving baskets and mats of all shapes and sizes. They seemed to be using roots, rather than bark or reeds. Some tended the fires where fish were curing, while others were stacking beaver, marten, mink, and sable pelts, removing them from willow withes. Some were singing, and sounded off-key.

Gray Cat stuck close to the two trappers, as if afraid to be captured again.

"Pretty busy here," Jared said. "Everybody hard at work."

"Well, those workin' hardest are slaves. And a lot of these women are playing games."

"Slaves?"

"Some women got two, three, four or more. Them's the one's bowin' and scrapin' and doin' all the heavy work."

Jared saw that what Pettibone had said was true.

Some of the Chinook women were followed by two or three women carrying heavy loads in their hands or on their backs. Some of the women were indeed playing games, and some had children suckling at their breasts, children that should have been weaned a year or two before.

"What game're they playin'?" Jared asked, stopping to watch a group of women sitting in the shade of tall pines. "It ain't like the one the men were playin'."

Pettibone and Gray Cat stopped too, near two women who sat face-to-face, like the men who had been playing *chal-e-chal*. Several other women sat nearby, watching the game.

"Them women is playing *omintook,*" Pettibone said.

"What's that they're throwin' on the mat? They look like dice."

"Beaver teeth," Pettibone said. "They got markings and numbers and such on one side of 'em."

One woman was shaking the beaver teeth in her cupped hands. After a long time she finally threw the teeth on the ground. She seemed to count the numbers that showed. She said the words three times, then gathered up the teeth and handed them to her opponent across the mat.

"What's the point?" Jared asked.

"Highest number wins."

Jared watched long enough to see who the winner was. Both women had bet a small bauble, a beaded thong from one, a small quilled purse from the other. The winner picked up the bauble and put it with her other winnings. Both women grinned at their audience, and another woman took the loser's place at the mat.

"We'd best get us acrost this park and find us a place to take root," Pettibone said, walking away. "We got some high tradin' to do."

"How come you know so much about these here

Chinook?" Jared asked as they walked across the meadow, Gray Cat close behind.

"Back in 'eighty-nine, Alexander Mackenzie tried to find a northwest passage. Now there was a Scot with ice in his veins. He thought he'd wind up on the Pacific Ocean, but he ended up on the Arctic. I went with him in 'ninety-three. We had a special canoe that was eight meters long from Lake Athabasca, beating the water of the Peace River against the current. Wound up in New Caledonia. We got on another river, had to cache our canoe when we couldn't run those hellish waters.

"We got lost and plenty scared, but we walked on, bought a dugout from some friendly Injuns and finally set sight on the Pacific. Mackenzie mixed up some grease and vermilion, climbed up to a granite cliff and wrote: 'Alexander Mackenzie, from Canada by land, the twenty-second of July, 1793.' I was just a boy then, but it was mighty excitin', even though the way we come wasn't worth a damn."

"But you came back another way?"

"I did, when I heard that David Thompson had found a way by comin' through the Rockies. Me and a bunch come acrost after that, and me and some others left 'em at the headwaters of the Columbia up in Canada and come right on down. I was lucky, too young to know no better. I come on this same tribe and they treated me well. I stayed a year and went back with Gray Cat and some other Mandans who knew the way, they was doin' some tradin' with the Chinook, told the Nor'westers what I seen. And here I am again."

"These Chinooks seem friendly enough."

"Likely, it'll be the last bunch of friendly Injuns we see on the Columbia, Flynn. I've heard tales."

"Tales?"

"Come on, let's get these packs off and lay out some trade blankets. Plenty of time to talk some later."

Gray Cat found a suitable camping place for the

two trappers. It was some distance away from the other lean-tos and makeshift huts, and offered both an escape route and an observation post. Jared grunted his approval. He had gotten to like the Mandan since they left the Missouri and portaged to the Snake. When their canoes had broken up, Gray Cat had helped them salvage most of their trade goods and traps. He helped them avoid contact with the more hostile tribes in the Rockies and was an asset when it came to making friends with other bands they encountered, both before the winter trapping season and afterward. He was a skilled tracker and good hunter. He seldom spoke, but he listened a lot, and Jared suspected he knew more English words than he admitted to. Often, Jared was surprised when Gray Cat laughed at some joke Pettibone was telling.

Jared laid out his bedroll and trade blanket. He began to rummage through his pack.

"No use to lay out any of the goods yet," Pettibone said. "Best not to look too eager."

Jared closed up his pack.

"Let them show us some of their winter pelfries," the old trapper said. "Then we'll dicker with 'em, find out what they want most."

"You don't trust them," Jared said.

"Chinooks don't leave you no choice. One minute they be as friendly as baby coons, next they'll put on the paint and raise holy hob. 'Sides, I think this bunch'll try to outwait us—at least for today. Likely they won't want to talk trade much until they've slept on it a night. Ain't that right, Gray Cat?"

Gray Cat, who sat stonily against a tree, nodded.

"Best see you're primed, pistol and smokepole, and keep your knife sharp, your mokkersons on."

"Maybe we shouldn't trade with this bunch," Jared said.

"They'd be right insulted now if we didn't."

Jared didn't know what to make of Pettibone's talk. One minute he seemed happy to have come upon this bunch of Chinooks, and the next he was saying they might have to fight and run from them. But ever since he'd stepped away from the Snake and gone into that meadow, he'd felt as if he was in a different world. In fact, ever since they'd come into the Rockies, things had started to change for him. Each range was slightly different than the other, each pass a road into another world. And soon he would see the Pacific Ocean, stand by the sea and sniff the salt air. Worlds within worlds, and each so far from the one he'd left. He was beginning to feel as if he'd left Pennsylvania, the graves and the remaining brother who hated him, Malcolm, and would never have to go back.

He did not think about Malcolm much, but there were times when he wished he could explain it all to his older brother and they could make peace at last. And then he thought of the rage and hatred Malcolm harbored when last they had seen each other, and he knew his brother would never change. Malcolm had taught him to hunt and trap, and Jared wished things could be as they were before those terrible events had happened, events that changed their lives forever.

They feasted that night with the chief and his family, a large one, on smoked fish, berries, venison, and *wapatoe*, a root that looked and tasted like a potato. Flynn ate several of these, declaring them the best food he'd eaten in a year or more.

Afterward, the men smoked and told stories, the highlight of which were the stories told by each brave involved in the "capture" of Gray Cat and his rescue by the wild white man, Flynn. As each man acted out the story, Flynn grew more and more embarrassed. He wanted to get up and leave, but Pettibone told him that he was the guest of honor and it would be rude if he did not let them celebrate his heroic rescue of the Mandan. The Chinook laughed long and loud after each recounting of the tale, and the tellers elaborated both their movements and their hand descriptions, bringing chuckles of admiration and wonder to the stoniest of men in the circle. The fires burned bright under the stars and, once again, Flynn felt transported into some strange magical realm far from any world he had ever known. When they were finished with their stories, he felt like a part of them somehow, as if he'd known them all their lives. Their faces gathered light from the fire, and their eyes glittered with a warmth and friendliness he had never known. He wondered how Pettibone could mistrust them, for they seemed utterly without guile. Except for their dress, they might have been a bunch of villagers gathered at the mercantile store on a Saturday night swapping hunting stories.

"I just remembered something," Jared said when the tale-telling was over.

"What's that?" Pettibone asked.

Jared grinned. "This is my birthday."

"Waahhh!" Pettibone exclaimed, slapping him on the back. He bent Jared's head over and rubbed him behind both ears before letting him straighten up.

"What'd you do that for?"

"Just wanted to see if you was dry behind the ears yet, Flynn."

Jared John Flynn was twenty-three years old on that day in 1811 when he first sighted the Columbia. He'd been trapping for the North-West Company the past five years, one of those coureurs de bois who always seemed to push beyond established frontiers with an instinct that startled and pleased their superiors.

"I guess," Jared said, "that I'm one of those old coons you keep talkin' about."

"Yep, I reckon you are, son."

Jared felt a glow inside at Pettibone's words. Now

if he could just establish the North-West Company's
foothold on the Columbia, he would feel he'd truly accomplished something.

In other parts of the camp the women were singing, and their melodious voices floated on the night air.
Some of the men at the feast began to leave, singly or in
pairs, until only the chief and the men who had been at
the river that day were left.

Walking Bear brought out the pipe again, made his
offerings. One of the braves lit it, and they all smoked
as the pipe was passed around.

"You trade fur," Walking Bear said after the pipe
was out.

"You got any?" Pettibone asked.

The chief grinned. "Me got plenty." He signed that
he had furs piled high. "You got trade?"

"We can do some tradin'."

"Good. You want slaves?"

"No, no slaves," Pettibone said. He turned to
Jared. "They deal in slaves and furs and fish," he explained. "And it's mighty complicated."

"When the sun eats the shadows on the mountain,
we trade," Walking Bear said. "You want woman?"

Pettibone blinked. Jared wondered if he'd heard
right.

"Is he offerin' to sell us a woman?" Jared asked.

"Nope. Give us each one for the night. Chinooks
buy their women, slaves and all, but they're mighty gen-
erous with 'em. Hospitality."

"Well, I'll be damned."

"You want one?"

"Hell, I'm too tired and stuffed."

"Me too." Pettibone looked at Gray Cat. The
Mandan shook his head. "Tomorry, maybe," the old
trapper told the chief. He signed that they were all
tired.

Walking Bear laughed and flexed his muscles to

show that he meant to sleep with a woman that night. He made an obscene gesture. All of the other braves laughed.

"They can have as many wives as they want," Pettibone said. "I'll bet old Walking Bear has him half a dozen."

Jared wondered at the customs of the Chinook. Their women had flattened heads, and he had seen children walking around with heads that looked as if they'd been in a fur press. The front part of their heads was somewhat higher than the back, with a wedgelike ridge raised from ear to ear. But none of the slaves had these features, none that he'd seen, anyway.

"I don't know as I'd want one of his wives," Flynn said.

"I think you could have your pick, son. When I stayed with 'em before, I got me a young'un, cute as any critter I ever seen. Fact is, I been lookin' for her, though she'd be past her prime by now, I reckon."

"I'll think about it," Jared said, yawning.

Jared, Pettibone, and Gray Cat bade farewell to Walking Bear and the other braves and left the assemblage with full bellies as the stars turned slowly in the heavens and the fires in the camp died out one by one. That night, Jared slept better than he had in months, dreamless and deep under his blanket, as the wind sighed among the evergreens and rustled the soft tanned hide of his deerskin lean-to.

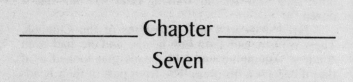

Chapter
Seven

B lack Wolf awoke well before the dawn broke, carefully making his way down the slope to the river path. In the dark, along travois and pony road, he made his signs with stones and sticks where the Lakota scouts would be sure to see it. He cut a lock of his hair and placed it under a rock. Next to the rock he drew his own sign, a pictograph of a wolf under a crescent moon.

He crept away from the Lakota camp, and when he was well out of earshot, he began to run with a steady, even gait. He found his horse and mounted it. He rode an hour, two, then the sun rose over the land and he galloped the horse for a few minutes, then rode another two at a walk. He ran the horse every so often, but never winded it. By late afternoon he left the Tongue, and the horse trotted in the shadow of the Big Horns as Black Wolf looked for any sign of the Scotsman, McCord.

McCord saw Black Wolf coming from a long way off. He waited in the shadows and looked beyond the runner to see if anyone else was coming. He felt a pang of disappointment when he saw the Mandan was alone. He had expected him to bring Malcolm Flynn back with him.

When Black Wolf drew near, McCord stepped out of the shadows, his rifle laid across his calves.

"Where's Flynn?" he asked.

"You come. We find."

"You didn't find him?"

"Come. We go quick."

McCord knew he wasn't going to get any more information out of the Mandan. He loaded his gear and they caught up the packhorses and set out for the Tongue. By late afternoon they came to the place where it left the mountains, and Black Wolf signed that they would stop there.

"Where's the Lakota?" McCord asked.

Black Wolf pointed up the canyon.

"Why aren't we going up there, damn you?"

"We wait. Make fire. They come."

"How do you know they'll come?"

"They come to fire. Smoke." Black Wolf dismounted, began to gather wood. McCord did the same after tying up his horse and the pack animals. He knew he had to trust Black Wolf, but his suspicions were aroused. They were in the open, and he didn't like the way things were going. But the Mandan struck flint to steel and made the fire blaze as the afternoon waned. He used green wood to make smoke and took a blanket and smothered the fire with it, then let the smoke billow up in little round puffs. McCord could see no pattern to the smoke, but he allowed that anyone looking could see it from a long way off.

McCord held his rifle, ready to shoot anyone threatening them, but Black Wolf seemed relaxed and patient as he squatted some distance from the fire, his blanket still smoking from being held over it. Every so often he added more green wood to the blaze, until a long column of smoke stood in the sky as the sun began to set beyond the western peaks of the Big Horns. Light sprayed through the high clouds, rimmed some with piping of shimmering silver, tinged others with a soft gild.

McCord began to pace, adding more yards to his stride as the sun continued to set. He kept looking up the canyon, but he heard nothing and saw no one. The fire slowly died away and a quietness settled over the land as the shadows began to lengthen.

Abruptly, McCord stopped. Black Wolf stood up and looked upriver. McCord stared in the direction the Mandan was looking, but he saw no sign of any movement.

"What the hell . . ."

A lone brave appeared on a painted pony, carrying lance and war shield, quiver and bow slung over his bare back. He halted his pony and stared at the two men. Then other riders joined him, and they too stared at Black Wolf. Black Wolf raised his right hand to show that he carried no weapons. The Lakota braves looked at McCord, who was carrying his rifle. The Sioux made no sign of peace. They sat their ponies, all of them armed, and waited.

The light was dimming as McCord strained his eyes to make out what the braves might do. Then they parted into two columns. Amid them rode another rider, wearing buckskins, a lone eagle feather in his hair. He was bearded and carried a rifle across the pommel of his saddle.

"Put that smokepole away, Randall, you sonofa-bitch!" the rider yelled.

Taken aback, McCord stepped back a pace or two. "That you, Malcolm?"

"It ain't no ghost," Malcolm Flynn replied. "We can talk better if you shuck that there bull thrower."

McCord walked back to his horse and sheathed his flintlock. He turned around and faced six Lakota braves and Malcolm Flynn in the fading light of day.

"How'd you find us?" McCord asked as Malcolm stepped from the saddle. "See the smoke?"

"Oh, we knew you were here. We saw your smoke too."

"How'd you know we'd be here at this spot?"

"That Mandan, Black Wolf there, left sign at the camp, moccasin mail. Didn't know who you was, but I kinda figgered it might be you. Come to trade?"

"Somethin' better—but I got goods for your friends."

Malcolm Flynn looked at the two packhorses. "Good," he said. "You still at Michimilmackinac?"

"Haw. We just call it Mackinac now. But come on, Malcolm. Me a Nor'wester? No more, laddie, no more."

"You throw in with another outfit? Hudson Bay?"

"Now why would I do that, Malcolm laddie, when I got me somethin' better?"

"Ah," Malcolm said. "Then let's get on up the river and belly up to the fire, make some smoke."

McCord looked at his friend closely. Malcolm had aged, but he seemed in good health, was still wiry and muscular, a few wrinkles around the eyes that hadn't been there before, face darkened by the sun, a few strands of gray hair in his beard and moustache. Otherwise, he looked the same.

The Lakota spoke in guttural tones among themselves. They made sign to Black Wolf, who signed back, spoke a few words of Oglala to them. He mounted his horse and caught up the packhorses as McCord and Flynn mounted up.

"You look fit, Randall. What brings you so far from home?"

"Home, aye, laddie," he said, pointing to the sky, "yon heavens are my roof, the earth is my hearth and kip; my horse feeds on untaxed grass, and I buy my meat with this fine rifle and cheap British lead."

"And where is your greengrocer, Randall McCord?"

McCord laughed. "I don't fancy Irish potatoes and dirty carrots, laddie. I get along on onions and beans."

"Out here, you'll eat roots and berries and be damned glad to get them."

"Fair enough, but I'll not tarry long enough to form a liking to such foodstuffs, for I've many leagues to go, and I'm hoping you'll go with me, beyond the bright rainbow you shelter under with your pot o' gold."

Malcolm Flynn laughed. "Well, it's true, I got tired of eatin' third table, and I'm rich enough, Randall, and living with a fine klooch and free people. It would take a lot to make me leave this country."

"I did hear you had a sleeping dictionary. What's her name?"

"Red Bead Woman. She's a Minneconjou."

"A what?"

"Another tribe of the Sioux. I'm camped with an Ogdally band. The chief is a red coon named Spotted Hawk."

They rode along behind the Lakota and the Mandan at a leisurely pace, following the course of the Tongue up into the mountains. The shadows grew thick and the darkness mingled with the mist of the river and brought a coolness to their faces.

McCord knew that Flynn was curious, but that Flynn wouldn't press him. For now, it was enough to tantalize his curiosity and let the lad wonder what it was that had brought him this far into a strange land to find him.

He had heard tales of Malcolm Flynn, back at Mackinac, and bigger ones in St. Louis, and none surprised him. He knew that Malcolm had gone up the Missouri with Lisa on a couple of expeditions, one where one of the engagés, Antoine Bissonette, deserted the brigade at the mouth of the Osage River. Lisa ordered his men to search for him and bring him back dead or alive. George Drouillard, who had been a clerk and interpreter for Lewis and Clark, tracked the deserter and shot him. He and Malcolm brought the badly wounded man back to face Lisa, who ordered him put in a boat and sent back to St. Charles. Bissonette died before the boat reached the city on the Mississippi. The next year, Drouillard was arrested and tried in a court presided over by Judge J. B. Lucas and Associate Judge Auguste Chouteau. Malcolm's testimony helped gain Drouillard an acquittal.

But Malcolm told Lisa that he was a dirty sonofabitch and that if he ever did that again to any man, he would personally kill him. Malcolm left Lisa's brigade almost the same way Bissonette had, but Lisa had sense enough not to send Drouillard or anyone else after him. Malcolm had helped him face down the Arikaras on one expedition and the Mandans on another, and Flynn was already a legend in St. Louis. Many ranked him with John Colter, another of Lewis and Clark's men, who had joined Lisa after Malcolm left the brigade.

Malcolm had trapped on his own and, through friends he'd made, gotten his furs to market in St. Louis. But like Colter, he was known as a loner. Strangely, no one knew much about Malcolm's brother, Jared, although he had been through St. Louis. He apparently didn't make much noise, and few paid him any attention. But some knew that Jared had left with a small brigade to trap the Rockies with papers from the

North-West Company, and that Pettibone, a man who knew the Columbia River better than any, had gone with him.

All of this was valuable information to Randall McCord, and he meant to make the best use of it when he spoke seriously to Malcolm. As far as he knew, Malcolm had not seen Jared in at least five years, but that hadn't diminished the man's hatred for his younger brother.

McCord and Malcolm had another tie, which was perhaps the strongest of all. At one time, Malcolm had been married to McCord's sister, Lorna, and would still have been married if the Shawnees hadn't captured and killed her. Malcolm killed her captors after hunting them down. Shortly afterward, Malcolm had gone home, only to return a bitter man, filled with an un-fathomable hatred for his brother that he'd never ex-plained. That was something he had to find out, McCord decided, before he laid it all out for Malcolm. On such an important mission, there could no longer be any secrets between them.

Darkness settled in the canyon, but the light from the stars and moon spangled the Tongue, and it served as a parallel beacon for the strange party riding toward the Lakota camp. After what seemed like hours to Mc-Cord, during which time nothing was said between him and Malcolm, two of the Lakota braves galloped ahead, leaving the others behind. McCord heard their guttural cries, heard the shouts from criers in the camp, relaying the news that the scouts had returned. In a few minutes they rode into the wide meadow where the teepees shone ghostly in the moonlight, as fires flickered in the lodges and smoke hung like a spectral pall over the camp.

Men, women, and children flowed from the lodges and formed lines on both sides of the riders, staring at

McCord and Black Wolf. Some of the young boys and girls walked up and touched McCord's leggings, then ran back into the crowd.

Spotted Hawk and other men of the tribe waited at the end of the largest circle of lodges. The riders halted and spoke to him. He made sign for all to dismount. Malcolm walked to the chief and spoke to him, then beckoned toward McCord and Black Wolf. The two came forward and exchanged greetings with Spotted Hawk.

"I have told the chief that you come as a friend and bring gifts for his people."

"I do—on both counts."

"I told him I'd take you to my lodge. The Mandan will go with one of the unmarried braves. You can pass out your gewgaws and such tomorrow."

"If these red coons don't steal my goods first."

Malcolm gave McCord a hard look. "They won't steal from you, Randy."

McCord said nothing, but he sensed the change in Malcolm Flynn. He had seen other men take up the Indian ways, but they all seemed to hold on to some part of their civilized selves. Malcolm still spoke the English language, but he seemed more comfortable with the Lakota tongue. He wore no white man's clothing. The only visible sign of his race was the hair on his face. That was all that set him apart from the Oglalas.

They turned their horses into the pony herd, and McCord, after getting his saddlebags and bedroll, followed Flynn to his lodge. The flap was open, and Malcolm ducked inside.

"Come on in, Randy."

There was a kettle on the low fire, and a young woman stood in a dark corner of the lodge. McCord smelled the food cooking and his stomach rumbled.

"This here's Red Bead." Malcolm spoke to the Indian woman, said McCord's name in English. She said something to him. "We'll have to give you a Lakota name, I guess. Red Bead says your name is too hard to pronounce."

"Is that all she said?"

Flynn laughed. McCord lay his possibles and bed-roll next to the door flap.

"She said it sounds like someone choking."

"It's a good Scot name," McCord said defensively.

"Let's put some o' them vittles in our meat traps," Flynn said. He sat down, laid his hand on the place where McCord was to sit. Red Bead woman sat across from them, but did not eat. She stared at McCord as he spooned elk meat into his mouth, along with roots and other ingredients of the stew.

"You got any tobacco, Randy?" Flynn asked when they were through. "I haven't filled my pipe since the snows melted."

"Plenty." McCord dug a sack of tobacco from his saddlebags and threw it to Malcolm. He dug his pipe from his possibles bag and filled it from a pouch. Flynn filled his pipe as Red Bead got a bowl of stew and sat away from them. She put a few more sticks on the fire for light, and left the two men to talk. She ate quietly, still studying McCord with her dark beads of eyes.

Malcolm lit their pipes with a burning stick he took from the fire.

"Well, Randy, what you got in your craw to come this far?"

"I want you to come with me to a river beyond the Rocky Mountains."

"There's lots of rivers beyond the Rockies."

"This one is called the Columbia. Named after a ship that went there sometime back."

"I've heard of it," Flynn said. "But you've come at the wrong time. We'd pay hell gettin' over the Rockies before the first snow. Sometimes we get snow in July, August."

"We can make it, travelin' light."

"How?"

"We go up the Missouri then down the Snake. I've got a map."

"We're a far piece from the Missouri."

"Not so far. Time winter comes, we'll be on the other side of the Rockies."

"I heard there's mountains clear to the Pacific Ocean."

"They peter out some. None on the coast, accordin' to my map."

"No reason for me to go way out to the ocean, Randy. I have my woman here, a warm lodge when it snows, plenty to eat, money I can't even spend."

"Bring your woman along. You won't want to come back. And there's good money in it now, and later even more."

"We would have to go through Crow and Blackfoot country. They would not take kindly to it."

McCord was growing impatient. He puffed his pipe angrily until the bowl grew hot to the touch. Malcolm kept shaking his head.

"The Crow and Blackfoot will be off hunting this time of year, Malcolm. Me and the Mandan come through hostile country and we never saw a speck of war paint."

"You were lucky."

"Black Wolf knows the way, the quick way, to the Columbia."

"You're taking him along?"

"Yes. And you're coming with me, Malcolm."

"For what reason? You got that Mandan. You don't need me."

"I need you so bad that I'm going to tell you why you're going to come with me to the Columbia. And after I've told you, you'll either come willingly with me or I'll have to kill you."

With that, McCord drew his flintlock pistol from his waistband and laid it on one leg, the barrel pointed at Flynn's heart.

Chapter
Eight

Jared Flynn heard voices. A shadow fell across his face when he opened his eyes. He saw a man standing in front of Pettibone's lean-to, speaking a strange language, and Pettibone answering in the same tongue.

Flynn sat up, rubbed his eyes.

The sun was not high, but it streamed through the trees and set a mist to rising in the meadow so that people walking, the sheds, everything he saw, seemed to be dancing above the earth, shimmering there like some painting seen through thin smoke.

"Pettibone *no. Mackouk.*"

"*Aiké,*" Pettibone said. "*Ick-etta mika mackouk?*"

"*Hi-ho etta,*" the Chinook brave replied.

"*Killemuck,*" Pettibone said. "*Thlat-away.* Pettibone *ow-low.*"

The Chinook grunted and walked away.

"What was that all about?" Jared asked.

"He come to ask if we was goin' to trade. I told him we was and asked what he had. Beaver and such. I told him to go away, that I was hungry and wanted to eat first."

"You understand all that Chinook talk?"

"Well, son, they's two kinds of Chinook, the hard kind they talk amongst themselves all the time, and the easy kind they use with the whites. I don't know enough of either one to get skittle cakes, but I guess I can understand enough to do some tradin'."

"I want you to teach it to me, Pettibone."

"Oh, likely you'll pick it up some this mornin'. Let's see to nature's business, then get our packs laid out on the tradin' blanket once we've et."

"Where's Gray Cat?"

"Oh, he got up sometime afore first light. I reckon he's prowlin' about somewheres."

Jared looked around the camp, but didn't see the Mandan. He and Pettibone found a shady spot near their lean-tos and began to lay out their trade blankets and unpack their goods.

"You didn't oncet yell out in your sleep last night, Jared," Pettibone said. "The grub must have agreed with you."

Jared turned his head the other way, as if Pettibone had revealed some dark secret. "Mind your own business, Fur Face."

"A mite techy, ain't we?"

Jared ignored the question. It was true that he had the bad dreams sometimes. He knew he cried out in his sleep, for his voice often awakened him in the middle of the night. That was something he'd probably have to live with for the rest of his life, a horror he had tried to forget but that would haunt him every minute of every day if he were not careful.

There were times when Jared wondered if it had all been worth it; times when he wished none of it had ever happened. It seemed like a nightmare still, even in the daytime, and at night he had no control over the images that surfaced in his dreams. He was constantly trying to escape the horror, trying to change things that could not be changed. When he awoke from these dreams, he was exhausted and afraid and burdened by guilt. As in his dreams, he'd been powerless to stop any of it.

He pushed these thoughts from his mind, because if he let them have free rein, all of the horror would come flooding back in on him and he would go into that dark place in his mind where it was so hard to get out of; a depression so deep he wanted to kill himself just to be rid of the thoughts, the memories.

Gray Cat walked up a few moments later.

"Big chief come soon," he said. "Many beaver."

"We'll be ready for 'em," Pettibone said. "Jared, let's get out the goods. Hand me that sack over there."

They laid out hatchets, bought for less than sixty cents apiece in Montreal. Jared remembered when they sold for thirty-three cents each, and they could sell them for ten dollars on the frontier. Soon the blankets were covered with lead for melting down and molding into rifle balls; with small trade muskets, very cheaply bought; with needles, thread, beads, mirrors, cloth of every description, knives, black powder, colored powders, small pots and tin bowls, cups, sewing awls, flint.

The Chinooks began to gather at the trading blankets, and others carried packs of beaver pelts and deerskins, pelfries of otter, mink, and marten. Pettibone examined the pelts and skins as the Chinooks picked up knives, hatchets, and muskets and talked excitedly among themselves.

"I'll take care of the negotiatin'," Pettibone said. "It gets some complicated. These Chinooks been tradin' longer'n we have. You listen and see if you can make any sense of it."

Jared soon learned that the Chinooks were trading

among themselves as well as with him and Pettibone.
For money, they used what he came to learn was called
higua, a small white shell about two inches long, but he
also saw some as long as three inches, and others as
short as a half inch, convex, and hollow inside. The
shells had the beautiful shape of a pipe stem.

"Them *higuas,*" Pettibone explained, "have a value
accordin' to how many it takes to make a fathom.
Thirty to a fathom would be worth three fathoms of
forty."

"Kind of complicated," Flynn said.

"Like I told you, son."

The *higua,* Flynn noted, was very strong and dura-
ble, but very light in weight. He watched as two Chinooks haggled over a trade musket they had bought
from Pettibone with beaver pelts. The Indian who
wanted to buy the musket laid out six shells, and the
seller shook his head. The buyer put another half shell
out, and still the seller refused the offer. Finally, the
musket sold for seven-and-a-half *higua.*

The trading went on all morning, then broke up
when the chief announced that they would go to the
river and fish. After they returned, the trading com-
menced again. Flynn watched as their store of animal
skins and pelts rose. He felt rich, for he knew what the
trade goods cost them compared to how much the
prime beaver pelts would fetch in Montreal. He wondered how they would transport such riches down to
the mouth of the Columbia, and then how they would
ship them back to the eastern markets. His job was to
establish trade with the local tribes and wait for word
from his superiors. So, none of the shipping problems
were really his worry, yet he couldn't help but try and
figure it out. If they could hold on to all the pelts and
skins and had a good winter, by the following spring
they would have something to show for it.

"We got to save some for tradin' downriver," Pettibone said to Jared late that afternoon, "but we've pretty well gotten the best pelts from these here Chinook."

"How in hell are we going to get 'em down the Columbia?"

"Gray Cat knows where the canoes be cached, and we got at least three bullboats we made ourselfs hidden a little ways from where we run into these coons."

As the sun was setting they packed away what they had left of their trade goods, put the fur packs under cover of deer hides, and joined the chief for another grand supper. Jared was worn out from the day's trading, and so full of fish from his noon meal that he could hardly eat the smoked salmon that night.

"When are we going to leave?" Jared asked when they went back to their lean-tos. "Tomorrow?"

"Not likely. Walking Bear wants to trade us some slaves for more goods."

"Slaves? What the hell would we do with slaves?"

"Might come in handy a-goin' downriver."

"And then what?"

"Trade 'em to another tribe for furs, I reckon."

Jared thought about this as Pettibone got out his pipe and filled the bowl with tobacco. Slaves. During the day, Pettibone had pointed slaves out to him. The women were far prettier than the Chinook women, and their heads had not been artificially shaped. They were dressed better than their owners. The whole idea bothered him, although he knew slavery was common. But how could one person own another? There was something wrong with it, but he wasn't sure what it was. The only way he could judge such a thing would be to put himself in the slave's place. Would he allow someone to own him? Not likely. He had seen bond servants, and they seemed content with their lot, but it seemed unfair, somehow. Now, the Chinooks wanted to trade slaves to them for goods. Once again Jared felt as if he'd entered a strange world where all that he knew could be forgotten with no loss, all that he'd learned could also be discarded, and it would make no difference to his life now, here with these people.

Later, Jared walked around the camp, watching people work, bringing fish from the river in tightly woven baskets that did not leak water. Gray Cat joined him as he stood before one of the biggest sheds he'd ever seen. He noticed, then, that the Chinooks slept under the sheds where the fish were drying. He counted several hundred beds under one of them. He stopped counting at three hundred.

"Many fish," the Mandan said.

"Do they live like this all the time?"

"Have house for winter."

"And they just leave them and come up here?"

"Many fleas in house in summer moons."

Jared and Gray Cat walked to the river to watch the men fish. They watched the fishermen for a while as they ranged up and down the river, then Gray Cat motioned for Jared to follow him. The Mandan walked downstream several hundred yards. There, the river made a wide bend and there was a deep pool where some of the Chinook women and their slaves were bathing.

Gray Cat put his fingers to his lips and led Flynn to a place where they could watch the bathers without being seen. Some of the women were very beautiful. The Chinook women were not so pretty, but the slave girls made Jared's pulse beat faster.

Then he saw her, off by herself in a place shadowed by tall spruce. She was naked and stood in the shallows as if she'd just entered the water and was adjusting to the cold. She shivered as she held her hands over her small breasts, and then she dove into the deep water like a sea otter, emerging after a few moments, breathless, her hair shining wet in the sun. She looked like some primitive forest creature bathing in sunlight and sky-blue waters, as lithe and graceful as if she had been born there only moments before and was just emerging from her watery chrysalis.

As Jared watched the girl, his thoughts turned slowly and unwillingly to a vision of his sister at that terrible moment of shame, her face scarlet with rage, standing in the shadows of her room, her flesh almost as dusky as the slave maiden's in the river. He couldn't shut out Caitlin's thin young face or the sadness of her eyes as the maiden rolled in the water and floated on her back, seemingly looking straight at him without rancor or guile, just innocence. The same innocence that Caitlin had possessed before her childhood was taken from her in brutality and blood.

As Flynn watched the girl dive and swim with froglike strokes, he forgot about the dark days he lived in the crypts of his sadness, all alone with his grief, his guilt and remorse heavy as stones in his heart.

Again the girl seemed to look directly at him, but he sat perfectly still, as if stalking game. He didn't think she saw him. Gray Cat too sat quiet and still, but he was not looking at the girl swimming alone but at another maiden, who laughed and splashed with the other slaves, an older girl, a woman perhaps, who seemed unaware that a man was spying on her like an obscene criminal.

And then Jared saw the old woman whose baby had died, squatting by the water's edge, her hands wet from dipping them in the water. He was glad that he could not see her eyes, because he thought they would be sad and filled with tears.

The girl who was alone swam to the shore and stood up in the shallows, looking down at her reflection as it wavered and settled, and then she turned toward Jared and lifted her head up. He realized that she had seen him, seen some part of him in the trees, and he felt ashamed that he'd been staring at her. She took a deep breath and held it, her small breasts standing out, and she touched herself where the dark thatch dripped with beads of clear water. Jared felt a stab of desire, a pang that afflicted his manhood, which began to stiffen with engorged blood that rang in his ears louder than the roar of the ocean in a seashell.

He wanted her then, in that moment; wanted to run down to the river and take her from it and into the woods, lay her down on soft earth under the shadows of the trees and thrust himself inside her, slake his lust in the hot broth of her sex like some animal mating in season.

Gray Cat drifted off, strolled casually to the river. Jared saw him hunker down next to a slave girl who was washing clothes in the river, laying each item on a stone, then pushing down with both hands to squeeze the water out. Gray Cat began making sign with his hands, and Jared turned away to look at the bathing girl again.

The girl waded to the shore and sat down on a grassy outcropping. She picked up a turtle-shell comb and raked it through her tresses to rid her hair of tangles. Jared walked toward her in a kind of trance. Her face was quartered in shadow as she twisted her neck back and forth while combing out the knots in her hair, and sunlight played on her neck and spine, the bumps rippling like the rib cage of a dappled fawn.

He stopped when he came upon her, knelt down so that he could see her face.

"I know you can't understand one damned word I say, pretty girl," he said, "but I want you to know I think you're the prettiest thing I ever seen in all my born days."

The girl stared at him quizzically, her eyes dull and unfathoming as cherry pits.

"I aim to find out how these Chinook court their

women, and throw my hat in the ring. I think you're plumb beautiful."

The girl did not speak, but after a moment continued to comb her hair, glancing at him every time she straightened her neck and looked back up at him.

He kept talking to her, more softly than before, and when she finished combing her hair, she stood up and smiled at him. He felt something inside him twist and melt, and he smiled back.

"You a-goin' back to camp? I'll walk you back. Wisht I knew your name. I can't keep callin' you 'pretty girl,' now, can I?

The girl stopped by a pile of clothes and wrapped herself in them as gracefully as she had bathed in the river. Jared was relieved that she was alone. He followed her through the woods, a half step behind, talking to her all the time.

He did not see the silent shadow rising out of the emerald undergrowth several yards away. Nor did he hear the muffled footfall of moccasins as the Chinook brave followed him back to camp. A shadow, nothing more, but the brave had a scowl on a face as hard and stony as flint.

"You a slave girl? I wonder who owns you. Well, if you're for sale, pretty girl, I 'spect I'll buy you from that man or woman, by God, and just take you with me to the mouth of the Columbia. Oh, I'd give a heap of goods for you, I truly would. I had me a sleepin' woman, Crow she was, when we was up in the Rocky Mountains, but she was nothin' more'n a blanket at night, dumb as a hickory stump back on the farm, didn't know more'n two words of English and never said none in Crow the whole time I knowed her."

The girl seemed to pay no attention to Jared. She walked boldly back through the woods as if she had not a care in the world, making little sound even though she held her head high and appeared not to notice where she stepped.

"Had me a pet marten, though," Jared continued. "It was more company than the Crow squaw. Cutest little thing. Broke its leg in a trap, and I got to it right after so it didn't chaw its blamed leg off or kill itself one way or another. I've seen 'em wrap themselves 'round the neck with the chain and choke to death.

"This marten, I called it Mr. Twitchell 'cause its nose was always a-twitchin'. I made little splints and set its broke leg, pet it when it was so nervous I thought it would jump out of the little pouch I kept him in so's he wouldn't run off 'til his leg healed up. I fed it, kept it warm in my own robes at night. It got to like me, got to likin' the food I fed it. Mr. Twitchell had a fine glossy coat, but I never skinned him out. When its leg was healed up, it stayed around a month or so, but at the first sign of thaw, it run off. The Crow gal left with her people and the rest of the brigade last spring, and I 'spect I'll never see her nor Mr. Twitchell again."

Jared and the slave girl reached the camp. She walked away from him quickly, disappeared in a crowd of people under one of the sheds.

"Hey, girl, I like you," he called out.

Just before she disappeared, she turned toward him. She smiled and then dipped her head.

"Well, I'll be damned," Jared said to himself. "That little colleen likes me, sure enough."

He was humming to himself when he found Pettibone engaged in finishing up a new pair of moccasins he'd started making a couple of days before.

"What are you so happy about?" the old trapper asked.

"I'm ready to trade for a certain squaw," Jared said, and he danced a little jig right in front of a dumbfounded Pettibone.

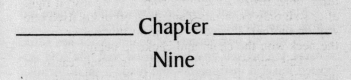

Chapter
Nine

Malcolm Flynn looked across the fire at McCord, his eyes black as bullet holes. His face appeared carved out of orange light and wavering shadows, the jawline sharp as an axe blade, the cheekbones straight as planed boards.

"You don't give a man much of a choice, McCord," he said.

"These be desperate times, Malcolm laddie, and there's more at stake here than a man's personal comfort."

"What's the Columbia River, anyway? Another place to trap? Winters are bound to be as cold, creeks as frosty as any in the Rockies. Cold, wet winter work."

"You ever hear of John Jacob Astor?"

There was a long silence in the lodge as the two men stared at each other.

"The upstart? I allow I've heard of him. Bought him a fur company, South-West I think, to compete with the North-West Company. German, is he not? A

bullheaded Prussian with a little money and big ambi-
tions."

"Aye, he's got money all right, and his American
Fur Company is most formidable—it was capitalized
with more than a million dollars."

Malcolm let out a low breathy whistle. "Where did
a little man like that get a million dollars?"

"It was his own money, Malcolm. Astor has made
a name for himself and he married well. He sold im-
ported musical instruments and made a small fortune.
He wed a shrewd woman of uncommon industry named
Sarah Todd, who has relatives in the shipping business."

"How do you know all this, Randall?"

McCord smiled thinly, but his pistol still stayed
trained on Malcolm.

"I met Mr. Astor when he came to Canada and
became acquainted with the Northwesters. I believe he
was able to arrange a partnership with them, even
though he planned to compete with them directly. A
very astute man, Astor. He does not miss a trick. He
invited me to his house on Little Dock Street in New
York because I had certain information that was valuable to him."

"And what was that information, Randy?"

"That the North-West Company planned to mo-
nopolize the fur trade in the Pacific Northwest."

"And Astor wants that too."

"He does. About four years ago he tried to reach
agreements with the Canadians for certain cooperative
ventures and enlist their support and influence in certain areas of commerce. But his partners in Canada
turned him down. A year after that, Astor was approached by no less a man than the Russian consul
general of the United States, Andrew Daschkoff.
Daschkoff asked Astor to join his interests with the
Russian American Company at New Archangel."

"And did Astor accept?"

"I told you that Astor misses no tricks. He immediately sent a ship, the *Enterprise*, under the command of John Ebbets, to explore the feasibility of such an enterprise and make contact with the Indians on the Columbia River."

"He did this without telling the Russian," Malcolm said.

"He did. Before sealing any bargain, he ventured out on his own, which seems to be one of his more formidable tactics in business, and when he could not persuade the North-West Company to join him to beat out the Russians, he hired men away from his rival. You know them. Good men all. Very professional. Very knowledgeable in the trading of furs."

"Do I know these men?" Malcolm asked, his voice low in his throat. He did not look at the pistol in McCord's lap, only at the man's face, at his eyes.

"You know 'em," McCord said. "He formed a partnership with them—all fine Scots."

"Alexander McKay," Malcolm said.

"He was one of the men, yes."

"Who were the others?"

"Duncan McDougal, Donald McKenzie, David Stuart, and David's nephew, Robert."

"Christ," Malcolm said. "The best there be."

"Aye, and by last year Astor was ready to put them all to work, setting up trading posts all along the Columbia River."

"Then Astor certainly doesn't need me. Those men know what they're doing."

"I haven't finished yet."

"I won't go with you, McCord. You can shoot me right here or walk out of here with your scalp, but I'm not throwing in with a man like Astor. He'd eat you alive. If not he, then any man jack of that Nor'west bunch."

"You haven't heard all of it, Malcolm. Sit still and listen awhile longer. I think you'll join me, all right."

"I'm listening," Malcolm said.

"Last June, Astor laid out his plans for all of us. He wanted to send two expeditions to the Pacific Ocean, one by ship under the leadership of Duncan McDougal, and another by land. He called in Wilson Price Hunt, whom you do not know, a New Jersey man, and asked him to follow the trail of Lewis and Clark and join up with McDougal's bunch at the mouth of the Columbia, which he referred to as the 'Oregon of the Spaniards.' "

"He sounds mad as a hatter."

"Maybe," McCord said. "I take him to be smarter than most men."

"Why send a boat clear around the Horn when you've got able men crossing the Rockies? Seems like a waste."

"Astor's in some hurry. He has boats standin' ready to ship out for China filled with furs and peltries, and to then invest his profits in return cargoes of beads, silks, teas, teak, pearls, jade, nankeens, and all sorts of goods in high demand."

Malcolm stretched his legs slowly, rocked backward to stretch his muscles.

"Goods for goods, eh?"

"Mr. Astor figures that would keep American specie from leaving the borders and turn the whole wide and long West into a major source of national wealth. He's got the government in a fair frenzy over such plans. They figure they'll all get rich off of Astor."

"The British might have something to say about all this, don't you think? Up in Montreal I heard the English lay claim to Oregon by virtue of prior discovery. All this settling by Astor's likely to stir 'em up, and they'll bring guns to the Columbia and give him a fight."

McCord laughed softly. "Why in hell do you think Astor's hired on the Scots? British subjects every one, practically. Oh, he's shrewd he is, Mr. John Jacob Astor. He told his critics that 'the claims of prior discovery and territorial right are claims to be settled by government only, and not by an individual.' His very words, I swear."

"What did the North-Westerns say about all this?"

"Och, laddie, they were in a fine dither, they were. They've already sent expeditions beyond the Rocky Mountains, toward New Caledonia and the north branch of the Columbia. They are a jealous lot, Malcolm, and believe in the old adage, 'Two of a trade seldom agree.' The Nor'westers are there, believe me, and that's why Astor is in a hurry to lock up the whole territory and keep the bloody Britishers out."

"You're a British subject, yourself, Randall. Have you no loyalty?"

"I've met both sides, laddie. I'll throw my lot in with Astor, thank ye kindly."

"How was Astor able to hire those men away from the North-West Company? Most of 'em were partners, were they not?"

"And that's the rub, Malcolm. Some were retired and had promises made to them which weren't met. They left in disgust, and Astor turned them to his way of thinkin'. He made them partners in his company, and now they'd like to put the sword to North-Westers' backsides, hoist them skywards and see them all squirm as he guts them on their own proverbial petard."

Malcolm let out a breath as the import of what McCord was telling him began to sink in. He knew the men Astor had hired. McKay, McKenzie, McDougall, and Stuart had all been part of Alexander Mackenzie's voyages to the North Polar Sea in 1789 and to the Pacific in 1793. These were bold, strong men of discovery and enterprise, and all had been connected in some way to the leaders of the North-West Company. Hunt and Crooks were men of vast knowledge and experience as well. And McCord himself had been on some of the expeditions.

"Are you a partner, Randall?"

"I, along with Hunt and Crooks, McLellan and Clarke, are not part of the initial joint-stock concern, but we have separate holdings, as will you. Astor has put up all the capital, in the amount of $200,000, and has divided those into a hundred shares of two thousand dollars each. He has been empowered to increase the capital to $500,000."

"And if he does?"

"Then you and I will be shareholders."

"That may never come to pass, Randall."

"There is another contingency that will give us three shares each of the original investment."

"That's six thousand dollars."

"Each," McCord said.

"What's the contingency?"

"That we intercept the Nor'westers who have gone before, those that are even now on the Columbia River, heading for its mouth to set up a trading post."

"And once we intercept these traders?"

McCord smiled. "We stop them."

"You mean kill them."

"If that is necessary," McCord said.

"So Astor wants a couple of hired assasins, is that it?"

"He didn't put it quite that way."

"You tell your Mr. Astor I'll have no part of this scheme. Even if no killing is involved. Even for six thousand dollars."

"Why not, Malcolm? You'll never get rich living with these savages. And someday this whole country will be settled by Americans. White people. And what will your Indians do then? What will you do?"

"I swear, Randall, you have no idea why I stayed here, do you?"

"It's something I've been wondering about. A great deal."

"Do you mind pointing that pistol someplace else? I've given you my answer."

"You haven't heard all of it yet, Malcolm. I still don't see what's holding you back. Astor will surely dominate the fur trade—and with his worldwide contacts, he will only get richer, and those who throw in with him will share in that great wealth."

McCord held the pistol still, the snout of it pointed directly at Malcolm Flynn.

"I left civilization a long time ago, Randall," Malcolm said. He looked beyond McCord, behaved as if he was talking only to himself. "I left and I do not want to go back. The reasons you gave me for going with you only reaffirm my desire to live with the Lakota. No such treachery as you describe exists among these people. They do not covet land, nor riches, nor domination over others. They, like I, want to be left alone, to hunt, to fish, to roam the land for buffalo. They take from the land only that which they need. They do not manufacture nor import goods for sale. They trade for what they desire and earn what they have to trade. It's a simple life, compared to yours and Astor's, but it's one that I've come to prefer."

McCord snorted in contempt. "Who do you think you're fooling with talk like that, Malcolm? Not me. I know why you left and came out here. Maybe not the exact reason, but I know it didn't have a bloody thing to do with civilization. You ran away from something you couldn't face, and living like this you think you can forget about whatever drove you away. But you can't. If you go with me, you can always come back here and live with your bloody Sioux. If you stay, you will only be

overrun someday, and will never have a damned thing
to show for it."

Malcolm's face ruddied with a sudden flush of anger. His lips tightened over his teeth and his eyes slitted
to narrow hoods out of which winked glaring blue eyes,
murderous eyes of icy depth.

"You sonofabitch," Malcolm said softly.

"Maybe you should curse me," McCord said. "Because you're coming with me, and you're going to be
rich as Croesus in spite of yourself."

"What you should have done, Randall, is mind
your own business. If you shoot me, my Lakota brothers will hack you up like buffalo meat and scatter your
bones for the wolves. Your hair will swing on some
brave's lance, and they'll put dirt in your dead mouth
and cut off your balls and cock, turn them into leather
trinkets, and make a necklace out of your teeth."

McCord didn't blink. "All for naught, Malcolm, all
for naught. You must allow me to finish, laddie. I do
not think I will have to shoot you. But if you are so set
in your ways when I have finished, and still refuse to
come with me, I will have to kill you. It's a matter of
business, you see."

"Some business." Flynn snorted.

"Mr. Astor ordered me to conduct this small expedition with the utmost secrecy, Malcolm. Any breach
could mean my own death warrant."

"I thought I knew you, Randall. But you're the
lowest scut I've come across, and I've been down the
pike and across the river."

"I think you'll change your mind about me, by-
and-by. You've just been away too long. As Mr. Astor
puts it, the very future of America may be in our hands,
yours and mine. Since Lewis and Clark mapped the
territory west of the Rockies, there are men in Washington with dreams of creating a grand empire, grand
as jolly old England and the British Isles. Why, you

could put the whole kit and kaboodle of Britain out here and it would be swallowed up."

"Astor sounds like a lunatic to me, Randy."

"Ah, but he's a powerful lunatic, and there will be none who will stop him. Not I, not you. If I don't complete my mission, why then it is of little consequence. Those who follow me will take up the flag and carry on, dear laddie. My failure will only mean a slight delay in the building of a great empire."

"I can't believe any greatness can be accomplished through murder and deceit."

"Then you have not read your history, laddie."

"Oh, I've read it, all right. That's why I prefer living here with the Lakota. They believe in things that have permanence—the earth, the mountains, the sky. But they are not so stupid as to believe even these things will last forever. Rather, they have a respect for the things that count: nature, the spirit, the bond between man and all things on earth and in heaven."

"Well, I shan't get into a philosophical discussion with you, Malcolm. There is no time for that. Speed is of the essence. I am counting on you coming with me tomorrow. Bring your woman with you, if you like. Come back when we are finished, if that's what you want. I'm betting that you will never want to return to this, ah, humble but proud life."

"Don't mock me, Randy."

"Sorry, laddie, but I'm weary from my journey and you're proving more stubborn than I expected."

"A mistake often made by your Irish countrymen."

"And now you mock me, eh? Well, no matter. I'm about finished with my plea, my urgent plea. And when I'm done, you will give me your answer, in the affirmative I trust, and we will sit and smoke for a while and you will make preparations to leave with me on the morrow."

"You know, Randy, you could probably get a ball

into me, but I'd be all over you like a panther on a rabbit, and with my dying breath I'd spit in your face."

"Now, now, laddie, let's not be predicting the future just yet. I expect this pistol will go unfired another day."

"You'd better get on with it, then. I am running out of patience, and I find your company, after all these years, most disagreeable."

"Well, now, that's better. We know, once again, where we stand, you and I. For the moment."

Flynn said nothing. He seemed to be bunching up unseen muscles, ready to spring at McCord if the man's finger so much as twitched on the trigger of the pistol in his lap.

"Very well, then, Malcolm. You got irritated at me a moment ago when I mentioned your past, so I beg you to hear me out."

"You don't know a damned thing about my past, Randy."

"Well said, laddie. And it's true, I do not know the facts of your sudden departure for the West, but I do know that it had something to do with your family."

Malcolm's teeth ground together for just a moment. "Leave my family out of this or I'll kill you with my bare hands even as you pull that damned trigger."

"Your brother, then. Jared Sean."

For a split second McCord tensed as if bracing himself for an attack. Then he relaxed and waited for his words to sink in. Malcolm sucked in a breath, held it for several heartbeats.

"Jared Sean. What about him? Spit it out, Randy, or I'll throttle you before you can swear your own name."

"Jared Flynn's the man ahead of us. He and Pettibone, remember him? They're Nor'westers, the both of them, and they think they've stolen a march on John

Jacob Astor. Astor wants us to overtake them and get them out of the way."

"You mean kill them?"

McCord nodded.

"Jesus Christ, Randy."

"Yes, Malcolm. Your own brother. He is now the enemy."

Malcolm Flynn rubbed his face in his hands. He sighed deeply and looked hard at Randall McCord. "Yes, you sonofabitch. He is the enemy. He damned sure is, that bastard son. Oh, God, Randy, how did you know?"

"When there's two people running, like you and Jared, there's got to be some big reason for it."

"You don't know the reason."

"No, but I suspect it's a family thing, and family things go deep."

Malcolm shook his head as if in a shudder. He seemed unable to speak, so McCord spoke for him.

"Then, you'll go with me tomorrow?" Randall asked softly.

Malcolm hung his head and nodded solemnly.

And the silence in the lodge swelled up around them until they could almost feel the pressure in their ears.

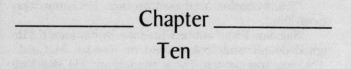

Chapter Ten

Ou-wucha." Swan.

She turned and saw the brave standing just outside the shed, his black eyes boring into hers. She recognized him, for he followed her everywhere when she was alone, watching her, never speaking. Until now.

"Essa," he said. Come here.

"Alchoya," she replied. Go away.

They called him Camux Eanux. Little Dog. She did not like him. He was like a shadow, always on her heels. Maybe that is why they named him Little Dog, she thought.

"No, Swan. You come here. I will make talk."

"I do not want to talk to you. I do not know you."

"You know who I am."

"You are Little Dog. But I do not want to make talk with you."

He walked up to her. She had never seen him so bold before. Usually he stayed away from her and just watched her. He made her very uneasy, filled her belly with the little yellow butterflies whenever she saw him. But it was not desire she felt. It was fear.

"You stay away from the Pa-she-shi-ooks," he said. "The white people are no good. *Mass-atsy.*" Bad.

"I do not know the Pa-she-shi-ooks," she said.

"That *ekass-cass,* the white boy. You stay away from him."

She laughed. "Oh, and are you my master? I do not know the white boy."

"He was watching you at the river," Little Dog said.

"And were you watching me too?"

Little Dog scowled. "I will buy you," he said stubbornly. "The white boy will not have you."

"And can you pay for me?"

"If the white boy buys you, I will kill him and take you."

"I will not go with you. Even if you buy me."

Little Dog strained not to grab the girl and shake her. His face darkened like a storm cloud and he flexed his fingers as if to bring them to her throat and choke her.

Swan saw the anger in Little Dog's face and she did not back away.

"The white boy might kill you, Little Dog. If he wants me."

"Then I will kill you both," he said.

Swan, no longer afraid of Little Dog, laughed loudly. The Chinook spun on his heels and walked away, shamed by her laughter. He turned and shook his fist at her, but she only laughed louder.

Soon she was surrounded by squealing girls wanting to know what the argument was about.

"Little Dog wants to buy me," she said. "He is afraid the white boy wants me."

"It would be better if the white boy bought you," said one girl, Cum-usack Quinum, Five Beads. "Little

Dog is no good. Bad man. He still sucks his mother's breast."

At that, the other girls laughed and the word of Swan's proposal spread throughout the camp. Little Dog could not stand all the talk and took his bow and arrows and went into the woods to get away from the humiliation. But his anger burned strong in his chest, and everyone knew he would be back and that there would be trouble between him and the white boy, Jared, whom they began to call Opitch-ach Till-cup, or White Knife.

Pettibone listened to Gray Cat, who spoke in both broken English and sign. The Mandan told him about Little Dog and the slave girl named Swan. He said that everyone expected a fight and that Little Dog would kill the young white man.

When Gray Cat was finished, Pettibone frowned. Jared Flynn walked away, leaving the men to talk. He watched the activity in camp intently. Ever since he'd come back from the river and from seeing the slave girl, Jared had been in a daze.

"Go to the river tonight," Pettibone told the Mandan. "Find the canoes. Put them close to shore. Wait for us. We will take the furs we have gotten in trade and put them farther downriver. We will pick them up on our way to the big water."

Gray Cat signed that he understood. "I know place of canoe cache," he said. "Not far."

"Good. Say no more about Little Dog. I will speak to Flynn."

"Flynn no fight?"

"I do not know," Pettibone signed.

After Gray Cat left the camp, Pettibone went to find Jared. He knew Gray Cat would not be followed. He was too wise to let that happen to him.

Jared was talking in sign to a group of women.

From the hand gestures, Pettibone knew that the young trapper was asking about the slave girl.

"Jared, when you get through jawin' with these womens, we got to make some talk right quick."

"But I found out who owns the girl. She is called Swan and I think I can trade for her."

"Come with me and let's talk first."

"Hell, what's there to talk about?"

"Are you plumb deaf, man? Blind? Can't you see that every Chinook in this camp is a-starin' at you and talkin' behind your back? They are calling you White Knife."

"What for?"

Pettibone motioned for Jared to follow him. Jared waved good-bye to the women and followed the old trapper well away from the groups that had gathered. He looked around and saw that people did seem to be watching him, talking about him. He scratched his head, wondering if he hadn't missed something.

"Jared, I done sent Gray Cat off to find that cache of canoes. Come mornin', we got to be on our way."

"Fine with me, Fur Face. First, I want to do some tradin'."

"For that slave gal?"

"Her name is Swan. In English, anyway. I got that much out of those women over there. She's owned by a Chinook name of Moluck. Elk, I think it is."

"Well, if you're bound to get in trouble, might as well get it over with. Let's go find Moluck, see what he wants for the slave gal."

Jared grinned.

"Don't get your hopes up. From what Gray Cat says, there's a Chinook named Little Dog what wants her for hisself."

"Can he buy her?"

"I don't know. But that might not make any difference to Little Dog."

"What do you mean, Pettibone?"

"I mean he might not like you a-buyin' her, and might want to sink some flint in yore chest."

"He'd fight me?"

"Likely as not. Passions run strong amongst red-skins, same as whites. You could get kilt if Little Dog has had his eye on this Swan gal. He won't want to give her up to no white man."

"But if I own her—"

Pettibone snorted. "Man has to pertect what he owns—in the wilderness same as amongst the so-called civilized."

"Well, I'm not afraid of this Little Dog, whoever in hell he is."

"No? Well, maybe you better respect him until you find out different."

"Are we going to sit here and talk all day, Fur Face? Let's go find Moluck and see what he'll take in trade for his slave."

Pettibone got up, his knee joints cracking. "Better take you something to trade, Jared. What you got in mind?"

"I've noticed the Chinooks love those metal buttons we bought, and I got a trade rifle with a sticky lock that Elk might want. Maybe some yardage."

"We're gettin' low on them buttons, no more'n a couple gross left. Offer him no more'n ten, maybe a half bolt of cloth. He might take the rifle if you can make it work."

"I can," Flynn said.

"We better take some tobacco along, just in case. Maybe a pipe. Elk will want to smoke. Don't offer him too much at first. See what he'll set still for."

Jared grunted and found a pipe and a sack of to-bacco.

They gathered the rest of the trade goods and set out in search of Moluck.

The Chinooks saw the two white men walking through camp, and several came over and spoke in pidgin to Pettibone.

"They're knowin' what we're about," said the old trapper. "They're a-showin' us the way."

"Right kindly of them," said a grinning Jared Flynn.

They followed a small bunch of young boys and girls to a big shed, where they pointed out Moluck. He was cutting fish to lay out on the drying racks. He paid the two white men no attention as they approached.

"You do the talkin'," Jared whispered.

"Likely," Pettibone said dryly.

The Chinook called Elk did not look up when the trappers stopped in front of him. Jared looked at the man closely. Elk was small of stature, wiry, muscular. His chest and forearms were scarred, his hands small and tough as boot leather. He had a round face, black hair. He reeked of fish, and his knife blade glistened with a patina of slime.

"Let us go to a place and smoke," Pettibone said in the crude Chinook dialect. "Make talk."

Elk looked up at the two men for the first time. He looked into their eyes and studied their faces. He stared at the goods the white men carried. He nodded soberly. Then he laid down his knife and wiped his oily hands on his bare chest. He grunted and strode regally out of the shed, Flynn and Pettibone following.

Elk led them to a small shelter between two pine trees.

"This is my lodge," he said, and sat down beneath the roof of pine boughs from which hung tanned deer-skins serving as walls on three sides. The lodge was quite large, and full of both men's and women's things. Pettibone figured that Elk, like many Chinooks, had more than one wife. Elk gestured that the two men should sit facing him. "We will smoke and make talk."

Pettibone glanced around the shelter. He did not like what he saw. There were iron kettles and knives no Indian had made, a tin mirror, wooden bowls, iron ladles, and pewter spoons. Elk was obviously no stranger to the white man, be he British or French or Russian.

Pettibone and Flynn set their goods down. Jared handed Elk a pipe made of pipestone, oiled to a faded pink. He gave him a pouch of tobacco as Pettibone fetched flint and steel from his possibles bag. Elk packed the bowl of the pipe full of tobacco with deliberate slowness.

Pettibone struck sparks into a small nest of tinder and blew on it until the wood crackled with flames. He lit Elk's pipe, then his own. Elk drew the smoke deep into his lungs, let out a cloud as he exhaled. His eyes twinkled as he smiled.

Jared elbowed Pettibone. "Get to it, Fur Face."

"I'm a-fixin' to. Jest let him draw a fume or two afore we talk business."

"He knows what we come for," Flynn said.

"Hias tye-yea," Pettibone began.

"Good smoke," Elk said. "I am no big chief. I speak your tongue."

"Well, I'll be damned," Pettibone said.

"Heap English," Elk said. "White man teach."

"You talk pretty good, Elk."

"Me talk good. White man teach. He no talk no more."

Pettibone swallowed. "He don't?"

"Him dead like stone. Elk kill. Chop head off." Elk grinned widely.

"Jesus," Flynn said.

"Him cheat Elk. Him talk too much maybe."

"I guess he got what was comin' to him, Elk. We come to trade. For that slave girl you got. The one called Swan."

"Me no trade to white man," said Elk.

"Why not?" Flynn blurted out the question.

"Big trouble. Little Dog kill white man."

"Are you going to sell Swan to Little Dog?" Jared asked.

Elk shook his head. "Little Dog no got trade. Little Dog got fire in heart. Want Swan heap."

Jared waved a hand across the bundles at their feet. "I will give you many good things for Swan," he said. "A fire stick. Hatchets."

"Boomgun?"

Jared unwrapped the trade rifle, picked it up. He handed it to Elk.

Elk took the rifle, looked at it. He sniffed the barrel, rubbed his hands over the stock, the iron sights, the lock. He tilted the rifle upside down and peered into the barrel, which was dark as pitch. He sighted down the barrel as if to see if it was true. He hefted it as if weighing it.

He shook it to see if the lock rattled. It did not, and Jared sighed inwardly. Then Elk cocked the hammer back.

"It don't have no flint yet, but I'll give you plenty," Flynn said quickly. "It's not good to pull the trigger."

Elk pulled the trigger anyway. The hammer came down hard without throwing a spark. The Chinook grunted. Jared couldn't tell if it was from pleasure or dissatisfaction.

"It shoots good," Jared said. Pettibone shot him a dark look.

Elk set the rifle down in front of him. He puffed on his pipe without speaking.

"Well?" Jared said.

"Heap more," Elk replied.

Pettibone and Jared showed Elk each item they had brought, and the Chinook examined them one by one. He made a pile of them as if measuring their worth. Jared set out powder and ball and a small box of chipped flint stones. He set a pair of leather patches next to the flints.

"Want knife," Elk said.

Jared grinned. He had brought two knives that he'd paid less than thirty cents for. He unwrapped them and set them before Elk.

They were big knives, but they were cheaply made in England. They had wooden handles and brass rivets.

Elk looked at them for a long time, then picked one up. He made cutting motions with it and then stabbed the air with the blade. Pettibone and Flynn leaned backward in case the Indian slashed too close to them.

"Me trade," Elk said. "Take Swan. Go. Go quick. Little Dog come back, he kill white man."

"Come on, Jared, let's get a-goin' afore he changes his mind."

"Thank you, Elk," Jared said. Pettibone gave him a sharp look of disgust. He grabbed the young man's wrist and dragged him away from the lodge.

"Wait," Elk called.

The two men stopped, looked back at the Indian. Elk had the pipe in his hand. He held it out toward them.

"Elk keep," he said.

"Yes, you keep," Pettibone said.

Jared nodded before the older trapper pulled him away again. But he caught a glimpse of the wide smile on Elk's face.

"Looks like we made us a bargain with Elk," Jared said.

"He ain't fully satisfied," Pettibone explained. "Best find that gal and light a shuck."

"I already found her," Jared said, dazed at how quickly things were happening now that Elk had agreed to the trade.

Swan stood alone several yards away in the shade

of a tall pine. She held a small bundle in her arms. It appeared she'd been watching from behind the tree the whole time the trading was going on. Jared walked over to her as Pettibone made his way back to their lodge, quick-stepping as if ready to break into a dead run.

"You belong to me now, Swan," Jared said, taking one of her hands.

She nodded shyly and went with him as he trailed after Pettibone.

Pettibone reached the shelter first and began putting things in his pack. He kept his rifle handy as he tied everything up. Jared put his clothes and loose items in his own pack, checked the powder in his pan. He adjusted the tomahawk in his belt, tapped his knife to make sure it was there. He slung his possibles pouch and powder horns over his shoulders.

"I'm ready," he said.

"Let's go, then," Pettibone said. "And wipe that goddamned grin off your face. No use rubbin' their noses in it."

"What?"

"We ain't out of it yet, young'un. Do you know what that Little Dog looks like?"

"No, I don't reckon I do."

"Me neither. But you can bet buttons to bullion he knows what you done. He'll be on our trail sure as the sun rises in the eastern sky in the mornin'."

"Aw, Pettibone. You told me they trade, buy, and sell slaves all the time amongst them."

"Not this girl they don't. Hell, old Elk there didn't even want to sell her. She's somethin' special, this one is."

"I know that," Jared said.

"Most of all, she's trouble," the old trapper grumbled as he stepped out toward the river.

"I think she's right nice," Jared said. He winked at Swan, sure that she didn't understand a word. They followed Pettibone away from the Chinook camp. Swan never looked back, but Jared could have sworn he heard one of the women cry out and set up a trilling with her tongue. The sound sent shivers up and down his spine.

Jared kept looking over his shoulder as they made their way to the Columbia River. He saw nothing, heard no alien sound. But he was apprehensive nevertheless.

When they saw the silvery waters of the Columbia, there was no sign of Gray Cat.

"Come on," Pettibone said, heading downriver.

"Do you see Gray Cat?" Jared asked.

"No, but I 'speck he'll be down a ways, waitin'. You keep your eyes peeled."

Pettibone held his rifle at the ready. Jared held onto Swan's left hand with his right, carried his rifle in his left. They caught up with Pettibone and walked right behind him.

Abruptly, Swan stopped. "There Gray Cat," she said, pointing. Both Pettibone and Jared looked at her in wonder.

"You speak English," Jared said.

"Elk teach. Elk teach good."

"Well, I guess he did," Pettibone said. "Come on, let's get in the canoes. We've got places to go, things to do."

They ran to where Gray Cat stood with three canoes. They looked to be in good shape. The furs they'd traded for were already loaded in each canoe. Jared threw his pack and rifle in one, motioned for Swan to get in. Pettibone pushed away from shore first, followed by Gray Cat. Jared was the last to shove off.

He did not see the shadowy form of Little Dog in the trees just a few yards upstream.

As soon as the three canoes were out of sight, Little Dog started running to a place where he also had a canoe waiting. He was carrying his bow, a quiver full of arrows, and one of the knives Elk had taken in trade for Swan.

Swan looked back, for some reason she could not explain. At that moment, she saw what might have been left by the passing of a shadow when sunlight shines it away and a single green leaf shimmers in the wake of its flight where only empty space had been.

She wondered what it was that she had seen, or even if she'd seen anything at all.

Chapter Eleven

Malcolm Flynn spoke softly in the Lakota tongue to his woman. "Red Bead. Do you want to come with me?"

"Where do you go, Iron Hawk?"

"To the big water where the sun sleeps."

"That is far."

"Very far," he said. "Many sleeps."

"Why do you go to this place?"

"It is a thing the white man does."

"Oh."

"Do you want to come with me?"

"You will go with the funny white man and the Mandan?"

"It is so."

"I will go with you, my husband."

"Washte," he said.

He wondered if Red Bead would have been willing to go with him if he told her the real reason he was traveling with Randall McCord. He wondered if he could even explain it to her. It was difficult to explain to himself.

There were so many feelings he had to sort through, he was glad that the distance to the Columbia River was far. He had much thinking to do. Even after all these years of thinking. Now there was more. What would he say to his younger brother? Would he say anything? Could he kill him as he had wanted?

There was good reason to kill Jared Sean Flynn. For a long time all he could think about was killing his little brother. Watching him die. Making him suffer. Yet now that he had the opportunity, he wondered if his resolve was as strong as it once was. As it was right after—right after it happened.

"I will gather for the journey," Red Bead said.

Malcolm shook his head, nodded. "Yes. I will take what I need."

But his mind refused to give up its thoughts of Jared and what had happened. Did he really know the truth of it? He did not know why Jared had done what he had, but he knew that Jared had done it. He'd killed their father. He'd murdered him in cold blood.

But was that all there was to it?

Unfortunately, his younger brother had run away before Malcolm could ask him why. Why? It hadn't made sense then, and it didn't make sense now. That Jared had done such a horrible thing was inconceivable, yet there was no doubt that he had. And more things had happened after Jared's deed that made the crime even more heinous, more vicious.

But Jared would pay for what he had done, Malcolm thought. He would pay dearly—with his life, for that was what he had taken himself—another's life. And for no known reason.

A call came from outside the lodge. "Shake a leg, Malcolm." Randall McCord.

"We're coming," Malcolm said. It was not yet

dawn, and Randall was already saddled and ready to go with Black Wolf, that damned Mandan. It was going to be a strange trip indeed, trekking into unknown territory far beyond the domain of the Lakota, the Blackfeet, the Crow.

"Hurry it up," McCord said irritatingly.

"Go tell Two Fires to get three of my best horses, Bead," Malcolm said.

"Will Nunpetapa go with us?"

"Yes. Go quick."

Two Fires was Malcolm's closest friend among the Lakota. He was about the same age, and had proven himself in battle with the Crow and the Pawnee many times. They were, in fact, blood brothers. He was a cousin of Bead, and Malcolm trusted him.

After Bead left, Malcolm carried his belongings outside the lodge. Randall and Black Wolf were standing by their horses, shadows in the darkness.

"Bead is bringing up the horses. My friend Two Fires will go with us."

"Good. The more the better. There's no turning back, Malcolm."

"I know. I just hope you know what you're doing."

"Alex Ross, bless his dear heart, gave me a map. I know exactly where we're going."

"Ross? When was he on the Columbia?"

"Last year."

"But—"

"He went for the North-West Company, but I rather think he will throw in with Astor when all's said and done."

"Astor sounds like a tyrant."

"He wants it all, but he's no tyrant. He pays, and pays well, for what he wants."

"Does he know about me?"

"He knows that I will hire help as needed, and that you will share in the bounty."

"If there is any."

"There will be," McCord said.

Malcolm didn't really care. This was his chance to find his brother and exact justice for the murder of their father. He stood there in the predawn light listening to the camp breathe, the teepees bone-white in the starlight by the river, gray and misty where they stood against the backdrop of trees. The Lakota knew he was leaving, but there were no farewells. People came and went in these camps, cousins, distant relatives, brothers, sisters, visitors with no relations. The camp was a living, breathing thing, and he listened to it with a sense of sadness.

He would miss the life among these people, but already the spirit of adventure was stirring in his breast. He would see new lands, venture into country where few white men had been, as when he first came to the land of the Lakota, full of surprises and wonders, enchantments and delights. The Lakota seemed an old and wise people to him, not at all simple, as he'd heard, but marvelously complex and fascinating. They knew things that no white man knew, cared for things of the earth and the heavens that never concerned men who lived their lives inside four walls.

Malcolm had absorbed the knowledge of the Lakota, and come to appreciate those things the white man took for granted: the earth, the sky, the trees, the rivers, the living creatures that roamed the vast spaces in the West, the buffalo, the deer, the elk, the antelope, the badger, the beaver, the marten, mink, and porcupine. And the Indian made use of every animal he took, down to its tiniest part, and from the ugliest remnants made articles of brightness and beauty, utility and comfort. They were truly a gifted and knowledgeable people, and most white men Malcolm had known looked right past them and never saw inside.

The soft pad of horses' hooves on the dewy grasses

brought him out of his reverie. Two Fires and Red Bead emerged out of the large horse shadows on foot, separated only at the last moment from the animal shapes behind them.

Malcolm didn't speak as he took the reins from Bead and mounted his horse. Bead and Two Fires climbed silently aboard the bare backs of their own horses. McCord and Black Wolf followed suit a moment later.

"The Mandan says that this is the way," McCord said. "To the big jagged mountains the French call the Grand Tetons."

"He is right," Malcolm said. "You go a hard way."

"Beyond where the Tongue springs from the mountains."

"Yes, and that is tough country, Randy. And gets tougher. And where will you go from the Tetons?"

"I will tell you tonight when we make camp."

"I won't turn back, if that's what you're thinking."

Malcolm could not see McCord's wry smile, but he knew it was there on his face.

"It will be a long ride before you see the Tetons," Malcolm said. "We still have to get through the Big Horns."

"I know."

They rode up the river canyon in silence, following the faint silver path of the Tongue as it wended its ribbony way to the plain that lay behind them.

And Malcolm thought of his father, long dead, his lean, stern face and brushy red moustache. Padraic Flynn, a quiet, brooding man of few words, fond of poteen in the old country and strong whiskey in the new land, lean, hardworking Catholic serious about God, but fearful of confession and suspicious of all priests who were not of Irish blood, and none seen in the wilderness for all that.

He thought of his mother, sharp-tongued, nagging,

and blustery with her daily issuing of commandments and homilies to each and all under her roof, with her merry blue eyes and large breasts, a surprisingly small waist and stout peasant's legs beneath her, always sewing and churning and knitting, with her family around her like dependent satellites. And their sister Caitlin, sweet, quiet, and beautiful, just budding into womanhood when she took her own life, so young, so fragile, so dark-eyed and solemn, a waif with her own dark thoughts, which he had never deciphered, never worried about, until she left them so suddenly without uttering a word of grief about their dead father. Then his mother followed her, as if chasing her loved ones' souls through the long chasm of the universe, unable to live by herself and all that death that had gone before.

Each of them had left puzzles behind them, ciphers he had never fathomed, only that one black thought that Jared Sean Flynn had murdered but one and thereby killed them all.

Tears stung his eyes, and he was glad that it was still dark in the canyon of the Tongue and that Bead could not see his grief reborn, his hatred kindled once again by thoughts of what he had lost and would never regain in this life.

They made camp on the western slope of the Big Horns late that night. They had made thirty miles and Randall was satisfied.

"We'll do better tomorrow," he said, gazing down on the dark plain below, looking strangely empty in the moonlight, like some deserted escarpment where ancient battles had been fought and the dead left behind to the worms, the buzzards, and the wolves.

"We might at that," Malcolm agreed.

"Is it all right with you if I send Two Fires up ahead to scout the first part of the day? Black Wolf can ride the last half and find a camp for us."

Malcolm spoke to Two Fires in Lakota.

"He wants to know where you are going," Flynn said.

"To the Snake. We'll follow it all the way to the Columbia."

Malcolm told Two Fires what McCord had said.

"He will guide us to the Snake. He knows the way. But he says there are many enemies along that river, and he does not know what lies beyond the big hole in the Tetons."

"I know. We'll buy or shoot our way through, God willin'."

Red Bead said something to Malcolm. He only grunted. But he looked down on the plain below and wondered what lay beyond. He had seen the Tetons once, but only from a distance, and they looked forbidding, with their sheer granite faces that towered to the sky, their jagged peaks jutting up like barriers to a forbidden place where no man should dare to go.

Malcolm wondered if his brother Jared had ridden across that same plain sometime before, like a ghost whispering in the lodges when all inside are asleep.

In his mind Malcolm heard his father as he recited Shakespeare in his taciturn, melancholy voice: "What freezings have I felt, what dark days I have seen! What old December's bareness everywhere!" He felt the chill shatter his body's heat as if a cold wind had blown over his father's grave and come to warn him of winter's, or death's, gelid touch.

"I sat in the evenings with my father," he said aloud, "when autumn had come and gone and all the vines withered in the garden, the leaves gone and brown on the ground, trees bare like skeletons stripped of flesh, and felt his uncanny sadness empty onto the porch, the dead garden and beyond, into the fields and empty trees. He would not say much, but he looked at the gray sky and seemed to cloak himself in its solemn silence and thereby render himself mute as a Trappist monk. Ah, so sad and long ago, and here we are in a summer on such an eve and I hear his quiet breathing, hear his thoughts of winter with its idleness and ruin, and wonder if he has not come here to remind me how short the seasons are, how brief the life we breathe until breath leaves us and we die, never knowing of the time and the place, the how or the why."

He said these things and did not know why he was saying them, and only one there who understood the words, if not the meaning.

"My own dear father was a bloody bastard," McCord said. "Good riddance. He died a drunkard's death in an alehouse in Glasgow, and he never spoke a word I remember for he never had anything but a curse for us all on his sodden lips."

"Did you see him die?"

"No. But I picked up his reeking body and hauled it home in a wheelbarrow."

"At least you saw him in death. All I saw was a cold grave and a wooden cross."

"Dead is dead, Malcolm."

"No, it isn't. Death is not a son's to give his father. Death is God's to give."

"By man's hand, you mean."

Malcolm cursed softly and knew he could never explain how he felt to Randall. Nor to anyone else. But he understood what McCord meant.

"And if a woman, or a girl, takes her own life, has God given that death too?"

"Aye, so that's it. You lost your whole family and you are still grievin'."

"No. Jared is still alive. Damn him. Damn him to hell."

"Aye, so that's how it is. I di'na know."

"You don't really know much, Randy," Malcolm said bitterly.

"And neither do you, laddie."

Bead spoke to Malcolm. "Come. Sleep. This talk is not a good thing."

"No. It is not a good thing," he replied.

Malcolm did not say good night to McCord. McCord watched the two climb into their blankets. He finished his pipe and sat there listening to Malcolm and Bead make love. He heard her cry out several times, and smiled to himself.

It took them five long days and half a day more to reach the Tetons, with Black Wolf and Two Fires scouting ahead, taking turns, and Malcolm strangely silent, looking for old tracks that were no longer there, and Bead just as silent, watching her man with a calm and steady eye.

They followed the Greybull, then crossed the Shoshone after following it a ways, then forded the Wind, and after that they rode down to touch the Green before forging westward to the Snake just below the big basin where the Tetons jutted toward the sky like ancient jagged towers rising from battlements no warrior could storm, no army could scale.

They descended into a low brushy valley, filled with rocks and chokecherries, and the horses fought against the rugged terrain and had to be coaxed and kicked to pass through. Then, when all seemed well, the horses spooked.

McCord's mount screamed in terror and bolted. Randall fought to stay in the saddle as the horse bucked and fishtailed, tangling his hooves in the thicket. Its eyes rolled egg-white in their sockets.

Two Fires backed his horse up, holding it under control. Bead wheeled her mount before the animal could run out from under her, kicked its ribs with her moccasined feet as it scrambled up a low boulder-strewn hill away from the danger. Her hair flopped as she bounced atop the panic-stricken horse.

Black Wolf slipped from his horse's back as it jolted to a stop, legs stiff as rods rammed into the ground. He tried to grab its mane, but gravity pulled him downward, and the horse swung away from him, running back to safety from whence they had come. The Mandan struck the ground hard, knocking his rifle loose from his grasp. He rolled down a slope and into a berry patch where the thorns nicked his bare skin in a dozen places, drawing blood.

Malcolm's horse stood its ground, snorting and pawing rocks loose when the grizzly stood up, a chokecherry vine clamped between its teeth. It wiped the vine from its mouth and growled, its arms outstretched, the black talons flexing like long, curved canine teeth.

When the bear saw the horse and rider, it let out a blaring roar and its booming voice echoed off the craggy walls of the surrounding mountains.

The grizzly's shoulders glistened in the sun as he twisted his enormous trunk to and fro like a pugilist before a fight, and Malcolm could smell the reek of the carrion the bear had been rolling in moments before as it fed on chokecherries. He felt his horse trembling beneath him, the legs quivering from shoulder to hocks, but unable to move.

The bear took a step forward as Malcolm's hand reached down to grab the butt of his rifle, sheathed in its elkskin boot, cursing himself silently for not having the weapon in his hands.

The grizzly, as if sensing the man's intent or seeing his hand move, bellowed even louder and dropped to all fours, its head swinging from side to side, feral eyes squinted to slits.

Malcolm's hand, slippery with sweat, slipped off the rifle's stock, and his horse started to move beneath him. It swung toward the bear in its turn, and Malcolm's stomach swirled with a queasy broth as fear rose up in his throat.

Then the grizzly charged, seeming to leap across the scattered boulders as if they were stepping-stones, flattening the scraggly bushes in its headlong rush to disembowel the horse and unseat its rider.

Malcolm felt himself slipping from the bare back of the horse as he reached once more for his rifle, his hand seeming to move through mud and water, so slow he knew it would never reach his weapon in time.

_____ Chapter _____
Twelve
_____

J ared fought the current, marveling at the canoe as it
swung easily at each dip of his paddle. The vessel
was a dugout, finely crafted of cedar. It appeared to
have been made by an Indian, for there were no adze
marks on its hull, and he saw that the hull was finely
shaped, but showed no signs of fire. He reasoned that
this canoe had been filled with water into which hot
rocks had been placed to soften the wood so that it
could be spread and shaped to perfection.

It was a fine craft, and he laughed as the river
doused him with spray when he bucked through white
water, scooting past treacherous rocks with all the grace
of a whitetail deer bounding over a hill. He turned to
Swan and grinned at her. She held onto the sides of the
dugout, her face a mask, her teeth clamped tightly together.

"Whooo!" Jared yelped and dug his paddle in as
the canoe shot toward a large boulder several yards
away. The craft yielded easily to his prod and skimmed

onto a calm stretch where Flynn could take a deep breath before they struck the next rapids.

Ahead of him Gray Cat deftly plied his canoe, right on the stern of Pettibone's craft, his back straight and stiff, as if he were part of the dugout. Jared wondered if the Mandan had built the canoes, for they were both made of cedar and sleek as fish as they knifed down the Columbia in perfect harmony with river, earth, and sky.

"Never such a river!" Jared cried as he shot his canoe past Pettibone, taking the lead.

"Wait!" the old trapper cried out. "There be danger ahead."

Pettibone knew that Flynn hadn't heard him, for Jared dug in his paddle and the dugout flew down a shallow, boulder-strewn drop and disappeared for a moment before popping up farther down, where the river was wide and calm. A moment later and the canoe vanished again as the river made a bend.

"Wild kid," Pettibone muttered, and bent to push his canoe through the rocky traverse of the drop-off and brace himself for the landing.

Gray Cat, his canoe just behind Pettibone's, deftly skidded through the drop-off and landed the canoe like a duck, straight and level. When Pettibone turned back to look at him, the Mandan stared at him impassively. He knew what was ahead. Bad water.

Jared became part of the river, feeling the pull of its current, the guidance of its muscular flow. He forgot about Swan sitting in the stern, as well as the load of furs and traps sitting amidships. He looked at the woods and the trees streaming past and the blue sky overhead dotted with cottony puffs of clouds. He saw the sun scintillate on the water, heard the faint hiss of the river as it coursed past the bow. The fragrance of cedar filled his nostrils, and the faint aroma of loam clung to the sides of the canoe, a reminder that it had been cached out of the weather, sleeping in the woods, waiting for him to take it to the Pacific Ocean, to take command of its cedar heart.

He floated through the calm stretch, letting the river take him to its next exhilarating destination, his muscles relaxed, his lungs steadying as his breathing returned to normal.

He remembered Swan in the back of the dugout. He turned and grinned at her, but she was scowling.

"No. Stop," she said. "Wait for Fur Face."

Jared laughed. So, she already knew the name he called Pettibone.

"Why? The river knows the way."

"Bad place. There." She pointed downriver.

"Far?"

Swan shook her head.

"Well, let's go see."

Jared pushed the paddle into the water, dug deep, and swept the blade backward with a steady thrust.

The canoe slipped into the main current and picked up speed.

The velocity of the boat surprised Jared, since the water looked the same. The canoe surged faster and faster, and he realized that the riverbed was dropping off rapidly. Yet he saw no white water ahead, only the steep walls of the banks, the blur of trees and rocks as the dugout sped by.

He tried to turn the canoe out of the main flow of the current, but was fearful of putting it into a hazardous spin. He used the paddle as a side rudder, trying to move the vessel gradually to the right, back where it might settle in one of the eddies and slow down.

The river gradually widened and Jared's canoe floated onto a glassy surface. But instead of slowing down, the craft began to move faster, as if in the grip of a strong undercurrent. Flynn, feeling something was wrong, began to turn the canoe toward shore.

"Stop," Swan shouted.

"I can't."

The girl stood up in the canoe and it began to rock.

"Sit down!" Jared yelled, trying to hold the boat steady.

"Jump, Flynn," she screamed.

He heard it then—a roaring sound ahead of them. He turned quickly to look, and saw the thin line of froth at the far edge of the flat pool. His blood quickened and he felt his stomach roil with a sudden querulous fear.

He heard Swan say something, and when he turned to look at her, she dove from the stern and disappeared under the water, sending rings of ripples coursing from the place where she'd entered the pool. The canoe, suddenly deprived of her weight, rocked more wildly and began to spin as the current caught the bow and twisted it into a sickening sidelong skid.

Frantically, Jared plunged the blade of the oar deep into the water and pulled hard against the current to take the craft out of its turn, straighten it before he lost total control.

For a fleeting moment he thought he might be able to change course and paddle back upstream, away from the jagged foam of the white water and the terrible roaring beyond. But even as the craft straightened and aligned itself with the powerful undertow, he felt himself losing way. He managed to get the bow pointed upstream, but knew, when he looked at the shore, that he was sliding backward.

The roaring grew louder, until the sound deafened him. He saw, out of the corner of his eyes, Swan's head pop up and break the surface, her arms flailing as she tried to swim out of the main current and make it to the bank.

Beyond, Pettibone rounded the bend, heading

straight for a sandy strip projecting from the bank. Jared started to stand up and dive from the canoe, but it was too late. The dugout sped toward the rim of the pond and hung up on the rocks for a moment, hurling him to the deck. The paddle clattered in the stern as it flew from his hands. Helpless, Jared felt the canoe tip, and then it was falling. He reached both hands out to grab the gunwales. He drew a deep breath and held it as the boat shot into empty space as gravity pulled it downward.

The canoe dropped like a stone, struck the water, and plunged straight down to the bottom, striking the gravel bottom with crunching force.

Flynn felt the jolt as the dugout struck, jamming his innards with such force that he thought he must have broken every bone and ruptured every organ in his body. Darkness flooded his brain then sparkled with a hundred pinpoints of light flashing on and off like miniature fireflies glowing silver in the blackness. The canoe fell away from him and the rush of water pulled him away from the craft.

He opened his eyes for a moment, and bubbles boiled around him as if he had been plunged into a boiling caldron. He held the air in his lungs, but yearned for oxygen as the current drew him away from the waterfall and into a millrace from which there seemed no escape.

The bundle of furs floated past him, a strange dark leviathan, and his rifle spun dizzily to the bottom and tumbled end over end downstream. Other things in the canoe that he could not identify floated eerily in suspension and went past him in slow motion. He saw the dugout sail by at a crazy angle as it hurtled through the turbulent narrows. He tried to swim up to the surface, but he had no control in such violent waters and his clothes weighed him down as if they were woven of lead.

His lungs began to burn as the air in them turned stale. He knew he was in a deep hole, somewhere under a waterfall, or near one, because the water was dark. He opened his eyes again and tried to see how far it was to the surface. Sunlight glimmered somewhere beyond him, and he began to swim for it although his arms felt heavy and numb.

He felt himself swept up by a rush of water, and suddenly he was somersaulting, turning over and heading back under the waterfall. He knew that if he didn't get out of that hole, he was doomed. He would just go around in a circle until his lungs burst or he let out the air and gulped in water. He twisted and kicked, struggling to free himself from the watery treadmill.

Flynn desperately kicked and stroked his arms to pull free of the clutches of the pool and the constant flow of the current streaming over the edge of the falls. He swam toward a glimmer of sunlight that seemed miles away. Again he felt the water pulling him, and he kicked harder as his lungs turned to flame, as if filled with hot lava.

He started to turn over again, and fought against it, willing himself to break free, to flow with the outward current and not be sucked back into the whorl of water that pressed against his ears until they hummed with pain.

One last kick and he was free of the tug, and then the current pushed him forward and pulled him deep below the surface. His breath threatened to burst his chest open as he struggled to rise to the bright place where there was oxygen and sun and life.

He thought he saw fish, or perhaps dark shadows that might have been tricks of the pale light, and he wondered if they were harbingers of a deeper, more final, darkness. Black messengers afloat just out of reach of his eyes, they might have been omens of a watery grave.

He began to let the air out of his lungs slowly, hoping he would not have to take in a breath while still underwater. The pressure in his lungs eased, but he felt an overwhelming desire for fresh air. He closed his eyes and climbed up through the rushing water as if on a ladder, his legs gone dead, drooping like sacks of galena.

He held the last of the air as long as he could, until he could hold it no longer. Then he let it out, knowing he was a dead man if he did not break the surface on the next slow crawl of his arms. He opened his eyes and tried to kick himself upward. His knee struck a rock and the pain coursed through him, stabbing into his brain like a saber.

His head bobbed above the water as his belly scraped on stone, and he shook his head once and drew in precious air to fill his aching lungs. He pushed himself to his knees, braced himself against the rush of the river at his back, then panted for several moments as he took in his surroundings.

He looked back and saw the sheer drop-off where he and the canoe had come over the falls. The deep pool looked calm on the surface. The river widened over shallows, then plunged on again, and just a few feet from where he knelt he saw the canoe and the furs, his other gear strewn over the shallows like ship-wrecked flotsam.

He heard someone calling his name.

Flynn stood up, his legs trembling, his knees gelatinous. He wobbled toward shore, shading his eyes with his hand as he peered upstream.

"Flynn!"

"Down here!" Jared yelled back.

He saw Gray Cat first, carrying his dugout on his back, the stern dragging. Behind him came Pettibone, lugging a pack of furs, a pair of rifles. There was no sign of Swan.

"You dumb bastard," Pettibone said. "I told you to wait."

Jared hung his head sheepishly, but he did not apologize. His legs steadied under him and he walked toward his own canoe. When he reached it, he walked around it, held it up. It did not appear to be damaged.

He dragged it ashore, went after the packs and scattered goods, his moccasined feet sopping in the shallow water. He dragged everything to shore as Gray Cat and Pettibone came up.

"We got to go back," Pettibone panted, "and portage the rest of the goods down. That wasn't the worst of the falls on this here river. You were damned lucky."

"I had a good swim," Jared said, grinning.

Pettibone scratched his head. "I don't see no bones broken."

"I reckon not. Did you see Swan?"

"Last I saw, she was swimming toward the bank. Looked like an otter."

"You ain't seen her since?"

Pettibone shook his head.

"Damn. I got to go back and look for her."

"Might be she's takin' care of personal things," the old trapper said.

"Could be."

"Or she might have drownded. Or run off. Injun women don't take much to getting dunked like that."

"Hell, it was her fault. She jumped in all by herself. I didn't push her."

"To keep from gettin' kilt, you mean."

"I didn't know I was a-goin' to run out of river."

Pettibone shrugged. He and Gray Cat walked back the way they had come, Jared following. He dreaded what he might find.

The three men climbed up the well-worn trail where others had portaged for years, and Jared looked long and hard at the waterfall, the deep pool the river had formed over the centuries. It could have been bad, he thought. He'd been lucky; mighty lucky.

Jared called out Swan's name in Mandan and in English as he began to search the shore and the other two men went on ahead. Hummingbirds flitted and zoomed past him, darted to red flowers sprouting among the grasses, tilting at all angles, reversing course, bobbing up and down on blurred wings.

"Swan," he called as he looked along the shore for tracks, for crushed grasses, footprints among the stones where the sand made little beaches. He found the place where she had crawled out of the water and felt a sense of relief.

But where was she?

He saw where she had stood up and walked into the woods. Perhaps Pettibone was right. She had gone away to take care of personal matters. But she had been gone a long time. Too long, he thought.

What had started out as a casual search for Swan had now turned deadly serious. It was true that she'd dived into the river, but her actions since she emerged from the cold waters had been anything but normal. He would have expected her to walk downstream or sit and wait for him. If she'd run off, that was another matter. But he wondered why she would wait until there was trouble before making her move. If that had been her intention, she could have run off before they set out. She would have been much closer to her people. Besides, she had packed her few belongings and seemed willing to come with him. So none of what happened a few moments before made much sense.

Jared began studying the tracks more carefully, his senses alert to any sound, any motion. He was missing something, he knew, but what? He retraced his steps to the shore. He walked up a short way and then saw it. A moccasin print that was not Swan's. And it was fresh.

Water still clung to the edges and they had not crumbled inward.

Something was very wrong. The footprint was not very deep, as if the person who made it had walked very quietly and swiftly. He looked for others and found traces where someone had walked, then slunk into the woods.

He looked upstream, wondering.

Then he heard Pettibone call his name. "Jared! Come quick!"

Jared set out on a run upriver. He saw Gray Cat and Pettibone a few moments later. They were standing next to a canoe, and it was not one of theirs. It jutted from a clump of bushes a few yards from the bank of the river.

"Whose is it?" he asked Pettibone.

"I reckon that skunk Little Dog come up behind us. You find Swan?"

"No. But I found tracks leading into the woods. Hers and another's."

"Well, sir, 'pears we got some trouble."

"I lost my rifle back there in that pool."

"You got an extry somewheres."

"I know. Is it with your goods?"

They searched Gray Cat's canoe, found the extra rifle, German-made in Delaware. Jared checked the flint, loaded it quickly, put powder in the pan.

"Nothing to do but go after her," he said. "You comin'?"

"I reckon we better," Pettibone said. "Dang it all. I knew that woman would be trouble. Maybe she run off with Little Dog all on her own."

"No. He took her," Jared said tightly. "The bastard."

"Well, let's get to huntin'," Pettibone said. He spoke to Gray Cat, who nodded. Both men picked up their rifles, which they had left under Gray Cat's canoe when they portaged.

Jared led them to the place where Swan had reached shore, showed them the tracks leading into the woods. Gray Cat went ahead of them with alacrity, hot on the trail. Pettibone gave Jared a look.

"You better hope that Injun come alone."

"I didn't see no other tracks."

"Them's the ones you got to worry about—the ones you don't see."

Jared knew what Pettibone meant. They could be walking right into an ambush.

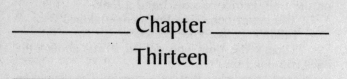

Chapter Thirteen

Malcolm's blood froze as he slid from the saddle just as the grizzly charged.

His fingers dug into the stock of his rifle and it slipped from its sheath part of the way. Then he struck the ground as the horse screamed and twisted to get out of the way of the bear. Its hooves slipped on the rocks as it scrambled for footing.

Pain shot through Malcolm's right elbow where it had glanced off a rock in his fall, and he clawed for his knife as he tried to scoot away. But there was no time to get to his feet and run. His tingling fingers wrapped around the handle of the knife and he drew it from its scabbard.

The bear looked as big as a mountain as it drew closer, its fangs bared, its hackles bristling silver in the sunlight.

Malcolm's palms slicked sweat on the knife butt as he brought it alongside him, ready to thrust. Although the blade was large and sharp, the handle of elk horn, it seemed a small weapon against such a large adversary.

The grizzly loomed huge, its hide rippling with powerful muscles, as it closed the ground between them. If it fell on him with its weight, he'd be pinned, helpless, the breath knocked from his lungs, the bear at his throat with those long yellow teeth.

In the fractions of seconds he had left, Malcolm knew that he stood no chance against the grizzly. If he'd been standing, he might have lessened the odds, but he sat there helplessly, armed only with a knife while several hundred pounds of grizzly rushed toward him.

He didn't think of McCord, Bead, Black Wolf, or Two Fires in those waning seconds, but only of the bear, of its awesome power, its fearsome jaws and teeth, its powerful muscles rolling under its fur. He felt lightheaded, almost giddy, and strangely calm inside. Since he had no choice but to defend himself, it all seemed so simple. He looked for an opening, a place to bury his knife before the bear's jaws locked onto his head or neck. He wondered if he could kill it with a single thrust to its heart, or if he should slash at its eyes or throat. These were decisions that had to be made in a split second, but they seemed suddenly complicated.

Malcolm braced himself for the crushing weight that would hit him, wondering if he would black out instantly or die a slow, agonizing death. And in that split second when eternity teetered on his mind's fulcrum, it came to him that he was involved in an ancient ritual that he had heard about at the Lakota campfires, when their brother, the grizzly bear, turned savage and violent. The Lakota thought of the grizzly as brother, as a kind of man. For he walked on two legs and he acted human. And they held the grizzly sacred and respected him.

"Brother," Malcolm murmured and rose up at the last moment and pitched forward toward the bear, his knife poised to strike straight at its throat. That sudden

movement saved his life, he thought later, for the bear
dove for his head with its arms extended, its claws
stretched to the limit of their sheaths. The bear roared
and its breath blew hot on Malcolm's face with its
stench of carrion and bittersweet berry musk. He attacked the bear at an angle, diving over the bear's
shoulder, aiming for the side of its throat.

The grizzly's left paw grazed Malcolm's shoulder,
the talons raking his flesh to the bone, drawing blood,
sending shoots of pain through his arm and neck. Malcolm twisted his body instinctively and buried his right
hand in a thicket of the beast's protective hair, wondering if there was any end to it. He felt the power surging
through his arm and hand and into the knife, knowing
that this one thrust must count, must find its target and
sink deep, deep into the bear's throat and take away its
windpipe and its air, its life.

In that last terrible moment, when he and the grizzly were locked together for a single timeless instant,
Malcolm thought he might miss the throat entirely, and
the knife be wrested from his grasp by the sheer momentum of the bear's charge. But the bear hit the
ground with its forepaws, and Malcolm felt the jolt in
the bear's shoulder as his blade stabbed into the animal's throat. Blood sprayed his face, and he followed
through with his thrust and ripped inward, then outward, trying to tear out the windpipe from behind thick
gristle, hard muscles.

Somehow, Malcolm managed to hold on to the
knife. The bear turned its shaggy head toward him, its
mouth opened wide as if to swallow him whole a foot at
a time. He felt the steaming furnace of its stinking
breath on his face, saw the huge teeth, the pink and
black gums, the tongue tucked back in that cavernous
mouth like some amphibious creature in hiding. He
pulled the knife blade back toward him, pushing it
deeper so that it sawed into the flesh, and new blood

gushed over his hand until it was slick and crimson with the pouring tide.

He knew the knife was going to slip from his grasp, and in that instant he knew also that the bear was mortally wounded and that its only thought was to crush him in its powerful embrace even if it was in its death throes. And Malcolm looked into that hideous maw of death, and felt a horrible fascination in knowing that he and the bear might die together, locking their souls together for eternity. He would be the bear and the bear would be he. In that grizzly face he saw his own visage, and it seemed he was snarling or growling low in his throat, like the bear. He knew it was his own voice, yet it was so similar to the bear's, he wondered if, in his last moment of life, he had not learned the language of all life, the language that would allow him to understand all creatures. He heard the bear's voice in his mind, but he heard his own speech also, and it was guttural and primitive and ancient, and came from all things and from just one thing that was the very spirit of the universe, the great breath that blew through all matter, all creation, like a wind from some far place that has immense power, but only whispers true things.

The grizzly twisted toward him, and in that abrupt and savage movement, Malcolm was flung away from those ghastly jaws. The knife slid from his hand and jutted from the bear's neck like a bloody stake. The bear roared and blinked its porcine eyes, and blood blew from its mouth and nose. The mighty roar became a gurgling in blood as the animal choked, its blood engorging his throat and mouth, strangling him.

Malcolm landed on his back hard and lay there stunned for a moment as the bear swung its massive body around as lightly as a dancer.

Time seemed to stand stock-still as the bear focused on its helpless enemy. It swiped a paw at the knife, and the blade sailed from its throat end over end and spanged against a rock, striking sparks that winked out before they landed on the earth.

Malcolm's knife came to rest about four or five feet from where he lay. The grizzly lurched toward him then staggered, its haunches slipping sideways. It suddenly stopped roaring and only growled. The growl was weak, almost a whining. Bubbles formed in the froth of blood around its neck, and underneath blood spewed from its throat. Malcolm knew he must have severed an artery.

Flynn started inching toward his knife. It was the only weapon that was near. He had no idea where McCord, Two Fires, and Black Wolf were. His gaze was fixed on the maddened beast lumbering slowly toward him.

He closed the distance slightly as he stretched his arm out to retrieve the knife. He scooted toward it, two inches, four inches, six. He expected the bear to charge him again at any moment. He made no sudden movement, but crept slowly toward the knife until it was but a few inches from his gasp.

The bear, summoning its strength, increased its stride, and just as Malcolm's hand darted toward the knife, it bounded forward. When its forepaws struck the ground, a fountain of blood spewed from the gaping wound in its throat. Malcolm's fingers closed around the handle of the knife and he scurried out of the bear's path, scrambling to his feet, blade in hand.

The bear, bent on tearing the man-enemy to pieces, swayed its head as it continued to stalk its prey. Malcolm, finding new strength in his legs, danced farther away in a circular movement, trying to keep the bear on the move, hoping it would bleed to death before he had to grapple with it again. He kept moving, and the bear kept changing its course, always with its head swinging from side to side, blood now foaming from its mouth, and Malcolm wondered at its immense heart, its unflagging ferocity even in the face of death.

Malcolm was struck by the bear's determination, its unyielding purpose. To the bear, he was the enemy and must be destroyed, even if he was destroyed himself. And it came to him as a blinding epiphany that he and the bear were just one thing, engaged in a dance of life and a dance of death. He had never fully understood the Lakota belief that all beings were one and the same, all part of the same mystery, but now he saw it. When a Lakota killed an animal for food, he thanked that animal and promised that he would someday be part of the grasses that would feed his descendants, all the grazing animals to come. The bear might kill him or he might kill the bear, but each must be willing to sacrifice himself to the life that was given from the Great Spirit, and each must know that the other would return in another form as part of the great circle of life that had no beginning and no end.

Malcolm was not afraid of dying, not if he fought well to preserve that gift given him by the Great Spirit, not if he died with honor according to his own nature. As the bear would die according to its nature.

The bear kept swinging in a small circle, and Malcolm glanced out of the corner of his eye and saw that a tree was in his way. He would have to make his stand there, or go back the way he'd come. He waited until the bear had completed its turn, then ran back. The bear continued to turn in the same direction, which puzzled Malcolm until he saw that it was confused, that it had lost so much blood it could not think straight. The bear kept turning and spraying blood all around him until the ground was painted like a red barn. Something like pity or compassion rose up in Malcolm and he could no longer stand to see the animal suffer.

When the bear's back was turned toward him, Malcolm raced up to it and jumped on its back, his knife

raised high overhead. He struck the bear in the center
of its back, right between its shoulder blades, burying
the knife to its hilt. He twisted and gored with it and
held onto the bear with one arm as it rose in the air and
tried to swat him away. But the grizzly could not reach
him, and it fell on all fours again and began turning,
turning in that small circle that was its last stand. Malcolm struck it again and again with the knife in the back
and the side of the neck until finally the bear grew
silent but for its wheezing as it fought to breathe
through the blood. It staggered a few feet and pitched
forward, Malcolm still attached to its back, his hand
sore from the repeated stabbing, his fingers numb and
aching, so tired they could hardly hold onto the knife
handle.

The bear collapsed on its belly, and blood continued to spurt from its wounds until Malcolm was covered in gore. He lay there atop the wounded beast,
panting for breath, full of the mystery of what he'd
done, of what he and the bear had done together. He
felt the sun on his back and saw shimmering light everywhere he looked, light that magnified and sharpened
every image: tree, rock, grass, mountain, and shaggy
bear like a mountain beneath him.

McCord found Black Wolf stunned, lying in the
berry patch, his arms covered with scratches. He dismounted and walked up to the Mandan. The Indian
looked up at him in bewilderment. McCord's face was
devoid of expression. Only in his eyes was there a
masked purpose, a cold glint that Black Wolf understood.

Randall reached down and grabbed Black Wolf by
the neck with both hands. He gave a hard twist and
snapped the Mandan's neck, killing him without a
sound. The Indian's eyes rolled in their sockets and he
slumped down, all light in them gone forever.

McCord released his hold on the Mandan's neck and stood up. "This is as far as you go," he said softly.

Then he turned and mounted his horse, rode back to the little boulder-strewn valley, and saw Two Fires sitting on his horse, watching him. He saw no sign of Malcolm's woman, Bead. The Lakota shifted his gaze back to something on the ground.

Randall rode closer and saw Malcolm lying atop the grizzly, his body soaked in blood, the bear dead.

"Looks like you had a time of it, Malcolm."

Flynn lifted his head and stared blankly at McCord, as if he was a being from another world. "Where you been?" he gasped.

"Horse run off. Been trying to calm him down. You kill that big bear all by yourself?"

Malcolm sat up, held the bloody knife up for McCord to see. He had no words for what he'd done. He felt as if he had been transported beyond the reality he now saw before him, and some part of him was in a place where only he and the bear dwelled.

They heard a noise and turned their heads to see Red Bead woman riding up, still fighting her horse. Its nostrils were flared, its ears twisting in tiny half circles.

"So, you have killed the bear," she said in Lakota. "That is good."

Malcolm got off the bear and stood on wobbly legs. He walked toward her, staggering as if drunk.

"Much food," Two Fires said in English.

Two Fires dismounted, drawing his knife. Red Bead got off her horse, tied it to a tree. The horse strained at its tether as it looked at the dead bear, with mostly the whites of its eyes showing. Red Bead drew her own knife and joined Two Fires. They pushed the bear over on its back and began to cut it open.

"We haven't got time to make meat of that grizzly," McCord said. "We've lost enough time already."

"Listen, Randy," Malcolm snapped, "I don't give a

damn about your timetable. Maybe if we'd come through here slower, we might have seen that bear before he saw us and I wouldn't have had to dance with it. But since I killed the grizzly, we're going to skin it out and take what meat we can. And I'm personally going to eat a chunk of its brave heart. And so will Two Fires. If you're smart, you and the Mandan will eat some of it too."

"You believe that eating that bear's stinking heart will give you courage?"

"I believe eating that heart will give me strength such as the bear had to live, to fight when necessary, to die when the time comes—with no fear."

McCord snorted. "You're a damned fool, Malcolm Flynn."

"You've told me that before, Randy. You might as well make yourself comfortable. We'll be here awhile."

Malcolm made no attempt to wipe the blood off his face. He cleaned his knife on his buckskin trousers while Red Bead and Two Fires cut the bear's head off, then his paws, and began to slit the fur to remove it from the carcass.

McCord dismounted, tying his horse some distance away from the bear. He sat in the small shade of an alder bush and watched the skinners at work.

Malcolm looked around him and counted the horses. He saw Black Wolf's horse standing at the edge of the little valley, browsing on tough grasses, rope reins trailing.

"Where's your Mandan, Randy?"

McCord shrugged.

"Yonder stands his horse. A man just doesn't vanish into thin air."

McCord didn't even look over at the horse. "Maybe he got scared and run off."

"You think so, Randy? The bear scared him?"

"I wouldn't know." McCord reached out and tore off an alder leaf, began to shred it slowly in his hands.

Something in McCord's demeanor sounded a warning in Malcolm's mind.

There was a cold, hard core to McCord, a pig of iron that didn't bend, did not break. Malcolm had known Randall for many years. He'd seen that hardness in him more than once, had seen how cold-blooded the man could be.

He remembered a time when they were trapping up in Canada for the North-West Company. McCord had discovered that someone was robbing his traps, so he made up his sets and sat in wait for the thief, although the ground was covered with snow and bitter cold. Malcolm had gone with McCord because he was curious about the culprit. The thief was clever covering his tracks, leaving no clear boot or moccasin print when he stole from the traps. Indeed, McCord had tried to track the man, but he never left a clear trail.

So McCord made his sets along a little stream and in beaver ponds, and he and Malcolm concealed themselves and waited at the last set. It began to snow and Malcolm wanted to give it up and build a fire. But McCord sat with his rifle at the ready and waited. They both heard the beaver spring the trap and thrash around in the water until it drowned. They waited and waited.

Malcolm had been long since ready to call it a day. They couldn't see ten feet in the thick snowfall. Four hours went by. Five. Six. Finally, an hour or two before dusk, McCord apparently heard something. He cocked his flintlock silently, and Malcolm saw the strange, hard look in his eyes.

It seemed a long long time to Malcolm that they both sat there, neither having said a word for almost seven hours.

Malcolm relaxed, thinking McCord had heard

nothing, after all. Then a small figure appeared out of the falling snow. He had four dead beavers slung over his shoulder on a piece of rope. He had no weapons that they could see, nor did the small man wear snowshoes, even though the snow was deep by then.

When the figure approached the floating stick in the pond, Malcolm saw that he was just a boy, a Chippewa, no more than ten or twelve years old. As the boy squatted by the bank of the pond and reached out for the floating stick attached to the trap, McCord brought up his rifle.

"No, don't!" Malcolm whispered. "It's just a boy."

McCord didn't reply. The boy heard Malcolm and froze. Then he turned his head to look straight at them.

The boy's eyes widened with fear.

"You don't need to shoot him," Malcolm said. "He's unarmed."

"He's a fucking thief," McCord said, and pulled the trigger.

The ball struck the boy in the chest, and he crumpled in a pool of blood that stained the snow. McCord walked over to him, jerked the rope that held the four dead beaver, kicked the boy out of the way, reached into the water and retrieved his set. Malcolm sat watching, stunned with the horror of it.

And now he had that same feeling. Deep down in his mind he knew that he would never see the Mandan again—not alive anyway.

Chapter
Fourteen

Jared had the feeling when he entered into the woods that he was once again in another world. It was all strange to him: the silence, the tall trees, the play of sunlight on the ground. Such a place could hide a thousand demons or a single Indian. He realized that his heart was pounding and that he was rushing into this new world with no clear thought, no plan. He stopped, listened, began to look for the trail. He thought of calling out Swan's name, but knew that would be useless and perhaps expose him to danger. He squatted down to think, to take his bearings. He saw two sets of moccasin prints before him in the ground. The smaller ones, he knew, belonged to Swan. They were not clearly defined; the tracks of someone being pulled by someone stronger. The others were deeper, more firmly planted.

He knew he must now imagine where Little Dog would take Swan, where he would hide and wait. Jared was sure that the Chinook meant to kill him if he tried to get Swan back.

He turned and called to Pettibone. "You and Gray Cat go on, take care of the portage. I'll catch up with you later."

"You don't want us to help you get the gal back?"

"No," he said. "Best I hunt him by myself."

Pettibone shrugged. "Suit yourself." He spoke to Gray Cat. Gray Cat looked at Flynn. The Mandan signed that there were only two sets of tracks.

"I know," Jared said. He waved good-bye to them and waited until they disappeared. When he heard them carrying the other canoe down past the falls, Jared went on with his tracking. The trail was plain, and he wondered at his good luck as he went deeper into the woods.

He brought up pictures in his mind, and with the pictures, questions. Where would Little Dog take Swan? Would he go back to his dugout or return to the Chinook camp on foot?

It was a puzzle, and there were no immediate answers. He did not know Little Dog. He did not know what was in the Indian's mind. But Little Dog had been bold enough to follow them and to capture Swan, taking her from under their noses.

Jared tracked slowly and let the new pictures form in his mind. He studied the terrain as he crept along, saw that Little Dog had come upon a low ridge that slowly rose to a higher altitude.

It was so quiet he could hear himself breathing. He came to a place where there had been some kind of struggle. The grass and bushes were trampled in a small semicircle, as if Swan had tried to break free of her captor and Little Dog had subdued her.

Jared's heart began to pound and his temples throbbed. Farther on he saw more signs that told him Swan was an unwilling hostage. A small aspen sapling was stripped of leaves, as if someone had grabbed it in passing and gripped it tightly in a fist. He picked a few leaves up, saw that they were torn and shredded, bruised and crumpled. Then he saw more signs of a brief struggle, with grass crushed underfoot, small stones overturned.

Jared felt he was getting close. He lay down, sniffed the scent of the mangled grass and watched the slight movement as some blades struggled to return to their former positions.

And still the land kept rising, ever so gradually, on the long tree-thick ridge that seemed a backbone to the forest around him. He could not see far beyond where he was, nor hear any sound from those he pursued. It was as if he'd come into this strange and silent empty world on an enigmatic quest for which there were no road maps or guideposts, no tree blazes or marker stones. He heard only softly susurrant pine needles and aspen leaves, and small, gossipy bushes rustled to speech by the soft breeze that wandered that desolate region.

He moved, then, like a praying mantis, listening intently after each step for any sound of those he tracked. He used the trees for cover, watched his back trail to make sure Little Dog hadn't circled up behind him. The trail grew steeper and the ridge broadened. He saw a set of elk antlers bleached by the sun and endless snows, shed by a bull many springs before. Every so often he discovered a bent twig and knew that Swan was marking her trail.

He no longer heard the sound of the river, and the silence in the mountain forest deepened. He made no sound himself as he climbed upward, a careful step at a time. Then he saw where Swan had fallen and Little Dog had dragged her several feet, and after that more signs that she'd fought him. Then he no longer saw her moccasin prints, only a single set of tracks, Little Dog's, and they were deeper, as if he was carrying her on his shoulders.

Jared reasoned that the Chinook must have struck her hard and knocked her out. The strides grew longer, and Jared began to marvel at the Indian's endurance. The air was getting thinner and he felt light-headed.

As he followed the trail, it occurred to Jared that Little Dog must know his destination. The climbing became more rugged, with deadfallen timber and huge boulders, outcroppings, thinner timber. He felt as if he was in an ancient ruin, a kingdom long forgotten, toppled by some gigantic cataclysm lost to memory in the mists of time. Pine needles littered the ground, and there were no aspen at that elevation. He saw neither stream nor path, and the trail became harder to follow.

There was no longer a ridge, only a vast forest atop the known world hushed as an empty cathedral, with the blue sky for a gallery, with tall pines and a sprinkling of spruce, fir, and juniper as columns for the vaulted ceiling. He lost the trail on a rocky outcropping and picked it up again where Little Dog had crawled through a carpet of dead pine needles carrying his load. The Indian's knees had created two craters where he knelt before standing upright again.

The scrapings looked fresh, and Jared moved even more cautiously as he climbed higher still. The breeze freshened in the high, thin air, and ahead he saw rimrock veined in the mountain's breast like stonework fashioned by long-dead masons. A lizard appeared on a rock, its body twitching with geometric regularity, its eyes blinking.

Little Dog, Jared reasoned, was going someplace he knew about, and he didn't want any company. The thought chilled Jared as the trail became more visible, as if the man he tracked had gotten careless or tired. He came to a place where Little Dog had sat and rested, Swan beside him, sitting as well. And then there appeared once again a pair of tracks, for Swan had begun to walk again, and Jared saw places where she'd been dragged when she faltered. He saw specks of blood on a rock and knew she must have scratched her knees. Muscles tightened in his jaw as he followed a switchback of tracks that rounded a bend. On the other side, going in the opposite direction, he saw a kind of summit that was almost all rock, with a few scrub pines bent by the wind, junipers weathered to grotesque shapes by snow and rain and knifing alpine zephyrs.

Just below the rimrock and beneath the summit, on a shelf of half grass, half stone, Jared heard a high-pitched shriek, short and piercing. He looked up through the sloping light to see if a hawk or an eagle might have uttered the startling cry, but the sky was empty of any raptor or other flying creature.

For a moment he doubted his ears, wondered if it might be a trick of the wind knifing through some crevice in the rimrock, or a sound remembered from other times when he was alone in the Rockies above the timberline, where the far-off bugles of elk were like ghostly flutes floating across the ridges of the high country.

And then he heard another shrill, a tonal keen that halted abruptly in mid-phrase, so sharply cut off that the sound hung in his memory long after his ears had gone dead and empty as a hollow horn.

The hackles rose on the back of his neck, for he recognized the cry as human. He swept the rimrock with his gaze and saw a dark hole high above him from where the anguished cry had come.

He could only see a small part of it, but he knew what it was. A cave.

Pettibone and Gray Cat finished the portage and began picking up gear scattered from Jared's dugout when he lost the boat at the falls.

"Let's try and find Flynn's rifle before we get the

rest of the goods," Pettibone said, gesturing to Gray
Cat. "Likely it's at the bottom of that pool yonder."

The old trapper began shucking off his buckskins.
Gray Cat stripped naked and was the first to enter the
water, striding into it with great dignity, like some toga-
less Roman senator at the baths, his body lean and
bronze and sculpted by centuries of breeding and an-
cestral adaptation.

Pettibone waded out near the pool, aware of the
danger of getting too close to the falls. When the water
was up to his neck, he submerged and swam to the
bottom. He saw the golden shadow of Gray Cat on the
far side of the river, paddling in slow motion like some
vagrant sea otter venturing into freshwater. Gray Cat's
eyes were wide open, his hands moving like birds that
had reverted to sea creatures, their curious silhouettes
flapping above the pebbles and boulders like coppery
terns flying against an unseen wind.

The current tugged at Pettibone and he kicked his
feet to keep from being pulled downstream. He saw the
boiling bubbles ahead of him and hoped the rifle was
not locked in some watery vault below the falls. He
swam slowly toward the deepest part of the pool, feeling the pressure against his ears.

Gray Cat swam close to the falls, then turned
toward Pettibone. He waved at the trapper and dove
down, his feet working like scissors, his hands pulling
him through the water. Pettibone dove too, and saw the
Mandan reach down for something, then pull the rifle
up with one hand. Gray Cat grinned underwater, and it
was a sight that gave Pettibone a start, all those white
teeth and bubbles leaking from between them. He
thought Gray Cat looked like some pirate raised from
Davy Jones's locker deep beneath the sea.

He waved back and turned, batting the water to
make his body surface, his lungs already feeling the
burn of used-up oxygen. He broke out of the water

seconds later and gulped in air. A moment later, although it seemed much longer, Gray Cat appeared, the rifle in his hand.

"Good, good," Pettibone said as he stood up on shore. "Hate to lose a good rifle."

Gray Cat crawled ashore, handed the rifle to Pettibone.

"You done good, Gray Cat."

"Gray Cat good."

Pettibone shook the rifle. Water ran out of the barrel and from underneath the trigger. He sat down on a large boulder and ransacked his possibles pouch. He brought out a tin of bear grease, a pewter snuff box, a rag. He set the rifle on a stone at a slant.

"Sun'll dry some of it," he said, opening the tin of bear grease. He thumbed out some of the grease, put it in the snuff box, and set that in the sun to melt.

Gray Cat retrieved the rest of the goods that had been on Jared's dugout that he could find, came back and sat down near Pettibone, watching him.

"You got a woman, Gray Cat?"

"Woman go sleep. Big sleep."

"Dead, eh? Well, that's too bad." Pettibone took the wiping stick and ran a patch through the barrel of Flynn's rifle. The patch came out dry. He greased another patch and ran it down the barrel and back. He poured the melted bear grease on the lock and trigger and wiped the pan clean. He poured light priming powder into the pan, cocked the rifle, and fired. Exploded flame surged through the touchhole. He cleaned the barrel again, loaded the rifle with patch and ball, primed the pan.

"There," he said. "Good as new."

"Good," Gray Cat said.

"You don't say much, but you know a hell of a lot, I'll bet." He signed to the Mandan. "What will we find downriver?"

"Many Salish," Gray Cat replied. "Bad. Shoot white man. Cut hair." He made all the signs and sounds, showing an arrow being shot from a bow, a man being scalped. "Bad Salish. Plenty bad. Heap bad."

Pettibone nodded. He cocked his head and looked up at the sun.

"We'll give Jared some time," he said, signing the sun crossing the horizon. "Then we best go lookin' for him."

"Little Dog bad," Gray Cat said.

Pettibone nodded. He wondered if he'd see the young trapper again. Jared was a fine tracker, a good hunter, and not afraid of a damned thing on earth. But they knew almost nothing about Little Dog, and did not know whether he had come alone or brought other men with him.

"I should never have let him go off by himself like that," Pettibone said.

Gray Cat, not understanding, sat there and grinned.

Jared trotted up the game trail that switched back along the rimrock. He heard nothing more from the cave. By the time he reached that level, he was out of breath and his side hurt. He stopped for a moment and rested until his breathing began to return to normal.

There were signs that Little Dog had dragged Swan across the rimrock, up the steep trail on the ledge. Jared loped the rest of the way to the cave and hunkered down outside to listen. He heard muffled sounds from inside. He peered around the corner, his rifle ready to bring to his shoulder. He couldn't see a thing through the pitch blackness of the cavern.

He crept around the edge of the cave on all fours, keeping as low as possible. He waited until his eyes had adjusted to the darkness. The cave was not very deep, but he could only see a few yards inside. He tried to discern shapes with what little light there was. Beyond, all was blackness.

He heard a low moan, looked in that direction, but could see nothing definable. Then he heard a guttural grunt and moved toward the sound. He held the rifle above the ground, but it was heavy and the stock dipped. He cringed when he heard it hit the stone floor of the cave. He stifled a curse and froze.

Something made a scuffling noise, and Jared's senses sharpened. He waited for someone to emerge from the Stygian blackness at the far end of the cave, braced for anything that might happen.

He heard a soft cry, then a loud smacking sound, followed by a quick, short moan. Then more scuffling. Jared crouched, ready to move forward, when he saw a figure emerge out of the coal-black innards of the cavern.

He started to stand up, then something hit him full force and he was bowled backward, his rifle kicked from his hand.

Someone fell on him and he fought to keep from being throttled as strong, lean hands reached for his throat. He kicked up with both feet, drew his knees in. He wrestled with a pair of arms, then rolled to his left to try and upend his attacker.

Strong legs clamped against his waist. He looked up as he rolled, saw an Indian's face just inches from his own, and he knew his opponent was Little Dog.

The Indian muttered something and kept rolling until he was on top of him again. Jared grabbed his wrists as he felt the tip of a knife graze his buckskins. His side began to ache again and it was hard to breathe. Little Dog was strong, and his powerful legs pinned Jared to the ground. Jared undulated his body with a mighty wrench and thrust upward with both hands.

"You sonofabitch," he said, and realized he was almost breathless.

But Little Dog fell back, and Jared tumbled with him, unwilling to release his hold on the Indian's wrists. The Chinook landed on his back and Flynn straddled him, digging his fingernails into both wrists. He slammed both of Little Dog's hands down, trying to dislodge the knife the Indian held in his right hand.

Little Dog scooted sideways, held onto the knife, and jabbed it at Flynn. Jared felt a slight prick in one of his ribs and sucked his chest out of the way of Little Dog's thrust. Little Dog wriggled sideways, trying to escape, and Jared held on tightly. Sharp rocks dug into his knees, sending needles of pain through his shins.

Little Dog forced himself up, arching his back, then dropped down suddenly, throwing Jared off guard. The Indian jerked his arms, and his wrists came free of Flynn's grip. Jared let out a breath and crabbed to the right as the Chinook's blade sliced the air inches from his throat.

He staggered to his feet, backing toward the entrance. Little Dog was on him like a cat, circling around until he was framed at the cave opening. Then he came after Jared, hunched over, the knife pointed toward Jared's belly. There was a smile of victory on Little Dog's face.

Jared stared at the Indian but was unable to see his eyes. He had nothing with which to defend himself. His rifle lay against the cave wall, six feet from him. Little Dog began the stalk, forcing Jared backward into the dark recesses of the cave.

The Indian was stark naked except for his moccasins. They sounded like the whisper of a slithering snake in the cold silence of the cave.

Chapter

Fifteen

Red Bead and Two Fires finished skinning the bear. While the Lakota brave cut out the heart and liver and removed the entrails, Bead fletched the hide of fat with a flint scraping tool. Malcolm cut the bear's haunches away until he was bathed in sweat.

McCord still sat in the shade of the alder, impatiently whittling a chunk of tree branch with his knife.

"Hurry it along, will you?"

Malcolm didn't reply.

Two Fires held out the heart to Malcolm as if it was some venerated object. *"Matahota cante,"* he said.

Malcolm took the heart and bit into it, chewing off a large chunk. He chewed it slowly and swallowed, feeling the heat of the meat as it traveled down his throat.

"Waste," he said, rubbing his belly.

He handed the heart back to Two Fires. Two Fires ate a piece of it, rubbed his belly in kind.

"Waste," he repeated. "Good."

Malcolm offered some of the grizzly's heart to Bead, but she refused. "Eat it, my husband," she said.

"Make the heart of the bear part of your own strong heart." Malcolm never loved her more than he did at that moment when she'd refused to partake in the mystical eating of the animal's heart.

He and Two Fires slowly ate the tough, fat-veined heart while the liver cooled in the shade. Red Bead cut more choice parts from the bear's carcass and trimmed them, placing them on the inner side of the grizzly's coat.

Malcolm cursed himself for agreeing to go with McCord. He was virtually a prisoner, he thought, since he was sure that McCord would kill him without batting an eye if he backed out of the expedition to the Columbia River.

Well, he would play along with McCord, up to a point, because he did have a score to settle with his brother Jared. He wasn't afraid of Randall. He just didn't trust him. There was something suspicious about that Mandan running off like that. Leaving his horse to run loose. It didn't add up. Maybe McCord knew more about that than he was telling.

Malcolm turned to Two Fires, spoke to him in Lakota. He was pretty sure McCord didn't understand the language, but he kept his voice low nonetheless.

"Did Two Fires see where the Mandan brave went?" he asked.

"No."

"There were not two bears?"

"No. There was only one, and you killed that one."

"I think that the Mandan did not run away."

"Did he vanish like a shadow when the sun dies in the sky?"

"I do not know."

"I do not see him," Two Fires said. "I see only his horse, and there is no rider sitting on him."

"That is why I think we will not see the Mandan again in this world."

"You think he is dead."

"I think he is dead," Malcolm said. "Or dying."

They finished eating the heart and wiped their hands on their buckskins.

"Let us catch up to the horses and go from this place," Malcolm said.

Two Fires grunted.

Red Bead helped them with the horses. They were still skittery from the bear smell. She rolled the bear's hide up over the meat and tied it neatly with leather thongs. She put the bundle on the back of her own horse where she could keep an eye on it. The bear meat had already attracted flies, and they swarmed over its coat.

McCord caught up to Black Wolf's horse.

"You aren't going to leave that horse here in case the Mandan comes back?" Malcolm asked.

"No use in leaving a good horse behind."

"You don't think he'll be back, then."

"No, I don't," Randall said matter-of-factly.

"I don't think he will either," Malcolm said sarcastically.

"I'll take the lead," McCord said.

"You don't want Two Fires to scout ahead?"

"Later," McCord said, a laconic flatness to his tone. "I just want to get moving, and I doubt if we're going to run into any trouble in country as bleak as this."

"No? Well, what do you call what happened here?"

"An unfortunate circumstance."

McCord rode well away from the body of Black Wolf, but Two Fires found it anyway. He spoke to Malcolm in Lakota. Malcolm and Bead rode over as McCord continued on ahead.

"Is he dead?" he asked Two Fires.

The Lakota nodded. Malcolm dismounted and

checked. He could find no marks on the Mandan's body. When he lifted his head, he heard a strange sound. When he let loose of it, it fell to one side.

"His neck is broken," Malcolm said. "Do you think he fell from his horse?"

Two Fires looked around at the terrain. The land was rugged, littered with rocks and boulders, talus from the steep slopes.

"He could have been thrown from his horse," Two Fires replied. "I do not think this happened."

"I do not think this happened either," Malcolm said.

Red Bead said nothing, but she looked at Malcolm with agate eyes, and he could read much in them.

"That sonofabitch," Malcolm said softly. He looked ahead.

McCord had stopped and turned in his saddle, looking back at them. "What you got there?" he asked.

"You know damned well what we got here, Randy. That Mandan's deader'n a stone."

"That is a shame, indeed."

"Did you do this?"

McCord laughed harshly. "I? Why would I kill my faithful scout and trusty guide? Don't be a goose, laddie. An unfortunate accident."

"Yeah, that's a good answer to just about everything."

"It will have to do," McCord said, and rode on, heading toward the pass that would take them out of that hellish hole that reeked of death.

Malcolm did not speak to McCord the rest of that day, but when they made camp that night, he could no longer remain silent. He waited until they had all eaten and Randall had taken out his pipe by the light of the campfire. Malcolm lit his own pipe, given to him by Bead's brother, made of pipestone from Minnesota.

"I think you murdered that Mandan, Randy."

"Oh, and what makes you think that, laddie?"

"His neck was broken."

"I rather think that when that grizzly scared Black Wolf's horse, he failed to keep the animal under proper restraint. Hence, he was thrown from his horse and landed on his bloody neck."

"Seems unlikely that an experienced brave like Black Wolf would be so careless."

The fire crackled between them and sent fleeting showers of sparks into the chill night air. The stars seemed close and the moon was bright, casting an eerie glow on the tall pines and spruce that surrounded their camp. The scent of balsam, pine, and spruce gave the air a pleasant headiness at that hour.

"Aye, laddie, but the lands out West are littered with the bones of the careless, don't you know? I had no reason to kill the Mandan. He meant nothing to me one way or the other."

"Except that he had served his purpose and was no longer needed."

"Are you accusing me of murdering the poor man?"

Malcolm sucked in a breath, pondered the question. Finally, after several puffs on his pipe, he replied.

"I just don't trust you very much, Randy."

"Trust? Aye now, that's a very weighty subject. What have I ever done to make you distrust me?"

Malcolm had no answer to that. He had never known McCord to go back on his word, but there were many things about the man that he didn't know.

"Why did you leave the North-West Company?" Malcolm asked, as if changing the subject. "Weren't you due for a promotion?"

"Ah, that I was, laddie. I had served my seven years and thought I had cut quite a wide swath. But, alas, I was passed over, presumably in favor of a better man."

Malcolm laughed. Indeed, McCord had been quite the gentleman in Montreal, his horse shod with silver shoes, his clothing sewn by the finest tailors. He was known as a dandy in town, a shrewd trader and skilled trapper in the woods.

"Not like Fort William, eh?"

"A wilder place, to be sure, but the Northwesters treated us lavishly, and the brawls did keep a man fit, don't you think?"

"They surely did no harm as I recall. But the promotion?"

"Alas, 'twas given to another whom you know. Promised, anyways."

"Ross?"

"None other. Alexander Ross was the man they picked to promote, and I saw no future for Randall McCord. Men were jumping back and forth from Pacific Fur to North-West, and when Pacific Fur failed, they all figured Astor was finished. All except I."

"Ross worked hard for the company."

"And he had experience on the Columbia, which I did not. So, when North-West acquired the Pacific territories and word came to Fort William, I decided it was time to leave Lake Superior and talk to Mr. Astor. I was bound to make a spoon or spoil a horn, especially when Keith and Alexander Ross made plans to open up the Columbia River to trade on behalf of North-West. Everyone there tried to dissuade them, since it was known that many a man had lost his life to the Indians on the Pacific coast, but they argued that they knew what they were doing. I believe Alex Ross's exact words were: 'Do you think we are Yankees? We will teach the Indians to respect us.' "

"That was a stupid thing to say," Malcolm said.

"I do believe Alex's heart was in the right place."

"He and Keith will be some surprised."

"To be sure, laddie. At any rate, I saw the scrawls on the wall and hied meself to New York to have a talk with Mr. Astor. That gentleman is desperate to beat the North-Westers any way he can."

"You gave him company secrets."

"Nothing he did not already know."

Malcolm had a bad taste in his mouth. It sounded to him as if McCord was trying to get even with the North-Westers for having been passed up for promotion. He knew how ambitious Randall was, but when he began this trip he never thought him capable of treachery.

"I wonder if Astor would have launched so many bold expeditions had he not known of North-West's plans."

"Laddie, laddie, there were no secrets at Fort William, or in Montreal, or in New York. As I said, men passed back and forth from Pacific Fur to North-West like ants, each carrying little tidbits of information, each loyal in his own way as long as success loomed on the horizon. There was no skulduggery in any of this."

"Well, I don't like the sound of it. And it seems to me that Astor is using you as insurance to see that he gets there first and no North-Wester gains a piece of ground along the Columbia."

"Or the entire coast, laddie. And you're part of that insurance yourself. So I hope you treat this whole thing with the respect it deserves."

The pipe smoke had begun to burn Malcolm's mouth, and he suddenly lost his taste buds, not only for the tobacco, but for Randall McCord as well. He tamped the bowl gently against the edge of his moccasin sole, spilling the hot dottle on the ground.

"I'm going to turn in," Malcolm said.

"Glad we could have this little talk, laddie."

"Does Ross know you're heading his way?"

"I doubt it. I imagine he has his hands full making those Indians bow and scrape out there along the Columbia."

Malcolm snorted at McCord's sarcasm. He did not say good night, but when he arose from the log he was sitting on, he realized how bruised and sore he was from his mauling by the grizzly.

"Sleep well, laddie," McCord said.

Red Bead was waiting for Malcolm. He groaned when he lay down.

"My husband has pain," she said.

"Some," he admitted.

"Bead will make well." She dug out something from her pouch and made Malcolm take off his shirt. She rubbed a soothing salve made from bear grease and boiled herbs over the tender spots on his arms and the deep claw wounds on his chest. The medicant had a pungent smell, and he suspected there were ingredients in the unguent that he didn't want to know about. Her hands were delicate and strong and he felt almost immediate relief from her touch.

"Does my husband feel good now?"

"I feel better. My body does not hurt so much."

She put a hand to his forehead. "In here, it still hurts," she said.

How did she know? He nodded as she slipped his buckskin shirt back over his head.

When they lay down in the blankets together, Bead spoke to him again.

"Two Fires made talk with me about the Mandan brave, Black Wolf."

"What did Two Fires say to Bead?"

"He said that he saw the white eyes near where the Mandan lay dead."

"When?"

"At the time you were fighting the bear."

"Did he see McCord kill Black Wolf?"

"No, my husband. But he says the Mandan fell from his horse and was not killed. Two Fires heard him fall and cry out. If he had broken his neck, he would have made no sound."

Malcolm considered what she had told him. "That is true, Bead."

"Two Fires believes that the white eyes broke the Mandan's neck."

"So, too, do I," Malcolm said.

"I think this white eyes has a bad face."

"I also."

"Then why do you ride his trail with him?"

"The answer," Malcolm said, "is like a tree with many branches, a river with many streams."

"He is your friend?"

"I had him in my heart as a brother once, a friend."

"Now you do not hold him in your heart?"

"No, Bead. I go with him because he would kill you and me as he did the Mandan if we did not go with him. And I go with him because I must find my true brother and call his name to answer my questions."

"You have not spoken of your true brother, my husband."

"I wish my mother had never given light to him."

"Ah, you would rub out your brother when you call his name?"

"I do not now. He deserves to die. He killed my father. And made my sister kill herself. My mother too."

"You carry much in your heart, Iron Hawk."

"Yes."

"Be careful with this white eyes. Maybe you should kill him."

Malcolm looked at Bead in the starlight. He could

not see her eyes, but he knew they were full of tenderness toward him and that she held him in her heart.

"Maybe I will kill him," he said.

That night the wolves came. The men were awakened by their howling and the horses whinnied in terror, straining against their picket ropes, fighting their hobbles.

Malcolm awoke with a start. He saw McCord sit up in his bedroll and reach for his rifle.

Two Fires was already up, speaking to the horses, trying to calm them.

Bead whimpered as she came awake.

"Stay here," Malcolm said as he picked up his rifle. McCord was already stoking the fire, adding more wood to it for light.

"What the hell," McCord muttered. "Damned wolves."

"They're hungry," Malcolm said.

And then he saw them, saw their shadows as they circled just beyond the rim of light from the fire. Great long shapes and glittering eyes, tongues lolling, and beyond, in the darkness, such a howling as he'd never heard. He saw at least a dozen wolves and knew there were more.

"We've got big trouble, laddie," McCord said.

"They're after the horses. Two Fires won't be able to hold them off."

McCord grunted and left the fire to join the Lakota with the horses. Malcolm was right behind him.

Two Fires held onto the rope of one horse's halter as the animal reared and fought to shake off its hobbles. It had already broken the rope. Wolves danced in and out of the faint light, nipping at the hamstrings of the horses. McCord waded into a small pack of them, swinging his rifle. They melted away, shadows into shadows, and when he turned, there were others, darting to and fro between the hobbled horses.

McCord swore. "There are too many of them," he shouted.

Malcolm hammered back his flintlock, drew a bead on a wolf, tracked it as it ran. He gave it a short lead and pulled the trigger. The wolf caught the ball and tumbled. Several wolves were on it, tearing at the downed brother with savage fangs. They dragged it off and several began eating it. Malcolm reloaded quickly as the horses screamed and Two Fires kicked at a wolf trying to tear out a horse's hamstring and bring it down.

McCord shot a wolf at point-blank range and backed up as three wolves came loping up and dragged the dead one away. He was reloading when one of the horses went down. A half-dozen wolves swarmed over it, ripping and slashing with long canine teeth at its neck. The horse thrashed and kicked, but could not get up.

Malcolm fired into the pack, but they ignored the shot and continued to tear at the dying horse until it kicked no more.

"Bring the horses over to the fire," Malcolm yelled at McCord. "It's our only chance."

"Christ, we're going to lose all of them," McCord said. They heard the wolves feeding on the dead horse. As they grabbed up the other horses one by one, the wolves grew bolder and more of them swarmed into the camp, clearly visible in the firelight.

Malcolm heard Bead scream and his blood froze.

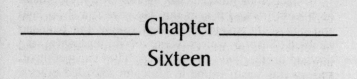

Chapter
Sixteen

Jared sucked in his belly as Little Dog slashed at his innards with the knife. Then he felt the cave wall against his back, hard and cold. He had no place to run. Little Dog was but one step away, ready to rip into him with the next swing of his blade.

Swan moaned and both men turned. Jared could not see her, but that instant of distraction gave him just enough time to step to one side and charge Little Dog. Little Dog turned back and started to jab with the knife when Jared struck him full force with a flying tackle.

The two men went down, slamming hard onto the cave floor. Jared grabbed for Little Dog's wrist, missed, then felt a knee ram into his side. He saw the gleam of the blade as Little Dog raised it to strike, but he reached out and clamped onto his attacker's wrist.

Little Dog tried to roll away, but Jared clung to him, digging his fingers into the brave's wrist until the brave yelped in pain. Jared felt fingers clawing at his face and then a sharp pain in his shoulder. He struck out, knocked Little Dog's face away. He felt teeth graze his shoulder and knew that the Indian had bitten him through his buckskin shirt.

Jared shook Little Dog's wrist, slammed it onto the cave floor until the knife fell from the Indian's hand. Both men pounced on it and the blade scooted away, twirling like a whirligig. Jared drove an elbow into the Indian's chest, knocking him sideways as he scrambled to retrieve the knife. Little Dog grunted and hurled himself at Jared's midsection, butting his head into Flynn's side.

Little Dog tried to wrestle Jared away, but Jared kicked him in the groin as his fingers closed around the butt of the blade. He kicked again as the Chinook tried to rise up and come at him. His foot caught Little Dog in the neck, bowled him onto his back.

Jared fought for air and knew Little Dog must be tiring as well. He gripped the knife, got to his feet, and backed toward the cave entrance, hoping to catch his second wind. Little Dog got to his knees, panting on all fours, waiting for another chance to kill the white man. Moments went by as both men held a silent truce, dragging in oxygen to feed starving muscles. The exertion had sapped them both of their strength. Jared's lungs burned until he thought they would crumple like smoked paper in a furnace.

Swan staggered into view. She was naked, her hair disheveled.

"Flynn," she said. "Don't kill him."

"He's trying to kill me."

"Make him go away."

"Did he hurt you?"

"Swan no hurt."

Little Dog did not turn to look at her. He stared at the knife in Jared's hand, his eyes glittering from the light outside the cave.

"He still wants to fight, I think," Jared said.

Swan said something to Little Dog in Chinook. He

shook his head. Then he charged Jared, his head down
like a battering ram.

Jared stepped to one side, clubbing Little Dog to
the ground. The Chinook fell flat on his face. Jared
jumped on his back, straddling him with his legs. He
grabbed a hunk of the brave's hair and jerked his head
backward. He put the knife blade to Little Dog's throat.

"Swan. Come here."

Swan ran over to stand by Jared's side.

"Tell him that if he goes now, I won't cut his
throat. I won't kill him."

Swan spoke to Little Dog.

"Well, I don't hear an answer," Jared said.

Swan spoke to the Chinook again. This time Little
Dog said something in reply.

"What did he say?"

"He wants me to go with him."

"You tell him you belong to me."

Swan said something in the Chinook language. It
was a long speech. Little Dog said something in return.

Jared pulled the Indian's head back still farther.
He touched Little Dog's throat with the tip of the knife,
put a slight pressure on it.

"Do not kill," Swan said. "He will go away."

"Are you sure?" He looked up at her. Swan nodded.

Jared slowly drew the knife away from the Indian's
throat. He stood up, then released his grip on Little
Dog's hair. He kept the knife ready to plunge into the
brave's stomach if he tried to fight again.

Little Dog shook his head and stood up, one hand
touching his throat where the knife point had left a
small pinprick. He said something to Swan, then walked
out of the cave without looking back.

"What did he say?" Jared asked Swan.

"It was not good."

"I want to know what he said."

"He say he kill you one day. Take me back."

Jared shook his head. "He just doesn't learn real quick, does he?"

"Him no learn quick?"

"Right, Swan. Him no learn quick." He looked at her then, wondering if Little Dog had hurt her, whether he had raped her.

"What did he do to you, Swan?"

"He hit me. He try to make baby with me."

Jared closed his eyes as memories swarmed up in his mind. "Did you let him?" he asked, rubbing his eyes with the fingers of his left hand.

"Swan fight. Swan fight good. You come. He no make baby."

Jared felt relieved, but the memories still flocked his mind like unwelcome vultures alighting in a tree. He could not look at Swan just then. His thoughts were too ugly to shed on her. He wanted to tear Little Dog apart, disembowel him, make him crawl away with his entrails trailing him. He wanted to make him suffer for trying to rape Swan. He shuddered to think of what might have happened had he not reached the cave in time, and the rage in him blazed at the thought of Swan being ravished. The way his sister had been.

Tears stung his eyes when he thought of his dead sister, and the old feelings of outrage, dead and buried for so many years, came back with full force, like those patient and ugly buzzards roosting in the tree of his mind, ready to swoop down and feed, not on the dead, but on the living.

"Let's get out of here," Jared said gruffly, his voice hoarse. He fought back the tears.

Swan looked at him for a long moment, then turned on her heel and retreated to the back of the cave. Jared waited for her, listening for any sign of Little Dog's return. Swan came back a few moments later, wearing her still-damp buckskin dress and moccasins.

"We go," she said.

Jared picked up his rifle and stuck Little Dog's knife in his belt. He and Swan walked out in the sunlight, blinking like a pair of owls. Jared squinted, looked down the trail. There was no sign of Little Dog.

"Little Dog go away," Swan said, as if reassuring him.

"We will see," Jared replied as he started down the trail.

Pettibone stood up when he saw Jared and Swan come down the portage trail by the falls.

"Well, you don't look none too worse for wear," he said when Jared came close. "I see you found your lost goods."

"And then some."

"You kill the Chinook?"

"No, I let him go. Swan wanted him to live."

"Might be the biggest mistake you ever made, Jared."

"How so?"

"If Little Dog follered you this far, a little stretch of river won't bother him none."

"If I see him again, I'll kill him," Jared replied, and there was something in his tone that made Pettibone's skin crawl. He looked at Jared and wondered if he'd ever be able to figure out what was inside him that he never let anyone see. Something bad had happened to that boy, and whatever it was had settled into a hard place deep down inside him. He pitied Little Dog or anyone else who didn't take Flynn at his word. He looked like a boy most of the time, but he was a man through and through, and a damned tough one at that. Of the entire brigade of hivernants, Jared was the only one who never complained about the snow and the cold, and when no one else wanted to hunt in waist-high drifts, Jared had gone out and made meat. It was no wonder the lad was a leader. He didn't follow anybody but himself.

"Well, we'd best make something of what's left of the day," he said. "We got a stretch to go and money to make."

Jared never looked back to see if Little Dog was following them. He almost wished the man would show up. He decided to keep a close watch on Swan from then on.

The Columbia was a grand river, and Jared fell more in love with it every day. When it widened out, they floated serenely on its waters, and when they portaged, he had respect for its wildness, the hidden currents with their age-old messages of time and timelessness, of seasons and rains and seas beyond the horizon.

They made good time and had no accidents, but he had no idea when they'd reach the Pacific Ocean. He didn't care, although he knew he had a job to do. The company was counting on him to establish an outpost at the mouth of the Columbia, and he was supposed to join up with other company men who had come by a more direct route. North-West wanted to expand westward from Fort William and beat out the competition. Well, when his brigade reported back, they would see that there were beaver and fur-bearing critters aplenty in the Rocky Mountains and from what he'd seen at the Chinook camp, no scarcity on the Pacific side of the mountain range.

But others had been here before and met with disaster. Hudson's Bay had explored the territory in 1769 and again in 1772. Sir Alexander Mackenzie, a partner in the North-West Company, had left Montreal in 1789 and gotten to the Hyperborean Sea, making it to the Pacific Ocean in 1793. Fraser and Stuart had also come this way a few years before, and then Lewis and Clark had primed the imaginations of the speculators all over again. Charters were drawn and torn up year after year, and still nobody had made a foothold on the Columbia. Jared had heard the name of Vancouver mentioned more than once, and doubtless, there were other men who had glimpsed the riches of the Northwest and dreamed of conquering it.

But Alexander Ross had taken charge now and was out to beat the competition. He'd been promised a promotion if he came to work at North-West, so he had made plans to succeed where all others had failed: Pacific Fur, Hudson's Bay, and even North-West.

Jared and Gray Cat hunted, and each night they camped well away from the river so that its sound would not cloak the approach of hostile Indians. Pettibone did not measure the distance they made each day, but by noting how the river had changed from when he was last on it, he could roughly estimate how far they had to go to reach the Pacific Ocean. That was good enough for Jared. He loved the journey, not the eventual arrival, and the country had come into him as he had come into it, growing into his consciousness like a flower in a grassy forest glade.

They stopped one afternoon to eat and take their rest along a quiet stretch of river that widened at a bend. They beached the dugouts and dragged them ashore far enough so that the sterns were out of the current.

"There's a shade tree yonder," Pettibone said, pointing to a giant blue spruce that towered above the surrounding saplings and vegetation.

"Looks good," Jared said. The spruce threw a long, wide shadow across the small glade surrounding it, where summer grasses quivered in the late morning zephyrs that played off the river.

Jared was tired. They had paddled a good long

stretch that morning, leaving their night camp just after sunup. They paddled to avoid obstacles in the river mostly, but there were times when they had to traverse stretches of comparatively calm water on shelves where the Columbia measured its bends in some mysterious geometric harmony with the earth. As soon as he stepped on shore, his tiredness seemed to drain away and his step was springy, the ache in his back only a fading memory.

"We covered some distance this morning," Pettibone said as Jared sprawled in the shade of the spruce.

"Seems so."

Gray Cat made a sign. "Listen," his hands said.

Pettibone and Jared froze in their tracks. After a few moments of intense listening, Pettibone shook his head.

"I don't hear nothin'," he whispered.

Jared was about to say something when Gray Cat signed for both of them to be quiet.

"I hear it," Jared said. "Sounds far off."

"Yeah. Me too," Pettibone said. "But what the hell is it?"

"Loon," Jared said, but he wasn't sure.

"Sounds more like a peacock."

"Man," Gray Cat said. "White man. Him hurt."

The two trappers heard the sound again. Ever so faint, the voice carried a chilling plaint in its sonorous call.

"Help me."

"Ain't far off," Jared said. "Just weak."

"Seems like."

Gray Cat pointed beyond the spruce, toward the west, downriver.

"Come on," Jared said.

"Wait, might be a trick," Pettibone said quickly.

Jared stopped in mid-stride. He fingered the lock on his rifle. Pettibone was right, he thought. What would a white man be doing all alone out here? How did he get there? Perhaps he was some captive ordered to cry out and lead them all into a trap. He stepped backward, took cover behind a pine tree. Pettibone and Gray Cat slunk off and took up positions behind cover as well, their rifles ready to bring up to their shoulders.

Then they heard the voice call out again. "Help me, please. I'm near kilt and half starved."

Jared looked over at Pettibone, shrugged. Pettibone shrugged back.

Jared signed that he was going to creep up slowly and find out what was going on. Pettibone nodded, patted his rifle to show Jared that he would cover him. He signed to Gray Cat, warning him to stay put.

Jared crept from behind the tree, making a slow, wide circle away from the place where he'd heard the voice.

"Cap'n," the man in hiding called. "I seen you come up, then I broke my leg, I think. I ain't armed. I beg your mercy."

The man's voice gave out at the last. To Jared, he sounded as if he really was hurt and needed help. Still, he didn't want to walk into an ambush. Yet something in the cracked tone of the man's plea urged him on. He increased his pace, but heard the man no more.

Jared slowed down as he drew toward the end of his half-circle approach, bringing himself up behind the man, and listened after each cautious step.

He heard nothing.

Then he stopped short of his next step. Someone was moaning softly. From where he stood, he could see Pettibone and Gray Cat as they peered out from behind the trees. The groans were very close. He scanned the underbrush. Something moved, ever so slightly, and he saw what appeared to be a man's back. Looking more closely, he glimpsed part of a torso, the tattered shirt on the man's back, and finally the top of his head.

"Don't move," Jared said. But the man looked around quickly, his eyes wide with fear, his features gaunt, emaciated.

"Lord, man, help me for the love of God."

Jared stood his ground, his eyes flickering as he took in the area surrounding the apparently injured man. "You alone?"

"As alone as a man can be—and barely alive."

"Hold on. I'll see what I can do."

Jared motioned to Pettibone and Gray Cat, beckoning for them to approach.

"You a fur trapper?" the man asked.

"A Nor'wester." Jared stepped closer, until he was looking down at the man. He saw that the man's woolen shirt was tattered and torn, the flesh showing through scratched and scabbed. The man had a thick untrimmed beard. Flynn could see his ribs and knew he was probably starving. The sight of the derelict made him shudder involuntarily. There was pain in the man's eyes, eyes that seemed too large for his thin face, eyes that had seen Death, had looked into Death's own eyes.

"Can you walk?"

"I—I think my ankle's broke."

"What's your name?"

"Donald Toomey. I'm—I was—a crewman on the *Tonquin*. Ship's carpenter."

"The *Tonquin*? Astor's ship?"

"The very same. A vessel of two hunnert and nine'y tons burden and stanch as they come. But under a stern captain, Jonathon Thorn, who left some of us for dead, me among them."

"What happened?"

"Cap'n Thorn sent four of us ashore at the mouth of the Columbia under charge of First Mate Cox, and we were beset upon by fierce savages, scattering us one and all to the Fates. I and one other managed to escape with our lives, but I have no knowledge of what happened to my mates."

Pettibone and Gray Cat came up, and Toomey cringed when he saw the Mandan.

"He won't hurt you none," Pettibone said, instantly assessing the situation."

"He's a savage, ain't he?"

"No more'n some white coons I know," Pettibone said dryly.

"Well, mister," Toomey said, "there's a pack of 'em hard astern, and I hope you can help me before they fall upon us."

"You're runnin' from Injuns?" Pettibone asked.

"I was, as hard as I could. When I seen you a-comin', I gave 'em the slip and was out of breath when I stumbled and broke my ankle."

"We'd better get him out of here," Jared said.

"And ourselves as well," Pettibone added.

Gray Cat looked off into the forest and stood like a statue before he spoke. "Many come," he said.

"Looks like the fat's in the fire," Pettibone said.

"God help us all," Toomey said. "Please don't leave me here. I seen what they done to my mate, the bloodthirsty bastards."

And then they heard the crash of bodies and the little thunder of moccasins coming toward them.

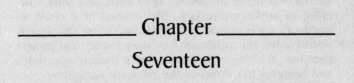

Chapter
Seventeen

Red Bead's scream hung in Malcolm's ears like the windy whispers in a seashell, and the overtones sounded over and over like a distant sea bell rocking on angry swells.

He saw the creatures prowling the night, nightmarish apparitions summoned out of a hunter's dream. Silent as wraiths, the wolves circled the horses, slunk through the trees like shadowy craft drifting from their moorings. Malcolm raced toward the sound of Bead's voice, fearing the worst. He drew his pistol, a French-made flintlock in .60 caliber, hoping it had not lost its prime.

Bead stood on a rock, naked, a firebrand clutched in her hand. A sea of dark shapes swirled around her, sharklike in the ocean of shadows and firelight pulsing like some erratic riptide in the darkness.

Malcolm yelled and charged toward his woman, but his voice sounded strangely muffled in his ears, as if the night itself had soaked up the noise, as if the wolves

had risen from the ground and trampled his tones under the threnodic tread of their footpads.

When a wolf came too close, Red Bead shook the
firebrand at it or slashed the air with it, trailing golden
sparks that made the wolves leap aside and slink cow-
ering in another direction. She turned in a circle to
ward off each attack, but Malcolm knew the beasts
would solve the riddle of her movements and swarm
over her, slashing at her ankles with their long canines
and bringing her down to the pack for slaughter.

One wolf, black as pitch and at least nine feet long,
whirled to face him, and he cocked the hammer of his
pistol. The wolf leaped at him, and Malcolm fired at it
in midair. The wolf twisted with the impact of the lead
ball but continued its flight. The animal struck Malcolm
in the chest, knocking him down.

Blood spurted from the wolf and onto Malcolm's
face, blinding him. He felt the animal wriggling, could
hear its labored breathing. He rubbed the blood from
his eyes and turned to face the wounded animal. He
shifted the pistol until he gripped it by the barrel and
stock, using it as a club. The wolf thrashed for a few
seconds and then lay still.

But other wolves quickly ran up on him, and he
heard Red Bead cry out a warning.

Malcolm scrambled to his feet and raced toward
the fire, swinging his pistol at the furry shapes that
emerged out of the darkness ahead of him. He heard
the low growls in their throats, the snarls of those who
pounced upon their slain brother, ripping and slashing
through the fur. He reached the fire, snatched up a
burning chunk of wood, turned, and hurled it at the
nearest wolf.

The pack broke off and split as he reached down
for more wood. There was only one piece left with
enough unburnt wood to allow him to grasp it. He
picked it up and held it at arm's length. The flames

warmed his hand. One wolf hunkered low, the hairs on its shoulders stiffening. It snarled at him, its yellow eyes blazing with the cunning of a skilled predator.

He knew he could not hold the wolves at bay for very long. These were slat-ribbed killers, hungry for fresh meat. He feinted with the burning faggot each time one of the beasts ventured too close, and he peripherally watched those circling, turning his head slowly to track each shifting shape.

"Can you put more fire and lead in your thunder stick?" Bead asked.

"No," Malcolm said. "It's too dark to see, and the wolves will attack if I load my thunder stick."

"They are hungry," she said, her voice never quavering. Malcolm admired her bravery.

"I know," he said. He saw the wolves tearing at the carcass of the one he had shot, but could not see the dead animal itself. He heard the snarls of the feeders, the crunch of small bones, the yelps of those bitten by the bigger, more aggressive members of the pack.

Bead was speaking softly in Lakota to the wolves holding her prisoner. He could not hear all the words, but he knew it was a kind of baby talk, a special language she used when she talked to dogs or horses.

"Little brother," she said. "Do not eat me. I am not yet ready to feed you and your family. Wait, wait. Someday I will feed your pups and their pups. Wait, wait. Someday, someday."

He stood close to the fire, so close he could smell his moccasins smoking. He didn't dare scatter the embers, for they would soon die out and the wolves would become even bolder than they were now. He looked over at Red Bead and saw that her firebrand was burning down. There were but a few flames licking the wood where it was not already ash. It would soon go out. He shut out the vision of her being torn apart by the raven-ous wolves. He could not bear to think of her small body being ravished by those long, gleaming fangs. . . .

"Randy, come quick!" he called.

But there was no answer.

He listened and heard the fight still going on around the horses. A wolf yelped and the horses whinnied in terror.

A lone wolf circled behind him, and he twisted to ward it off before it caught him by surprise. Out of one corner of his left eye he saw another crouch, ready to spring the moment he turned his back.

"Look out," Bead said.

Malcolm swung the burning chunk of pinewood, blazing a half arc around him. He charged the squatting wolf, shaking the flaming faggot in front of him. The wolf retreated, and Malcolm whirled on another wolf slinking up behind him. He kicked it, his toe striking it sharply under its jaw. The wolf yelped and scurried away, vanishing in the shadows as if it had been transformed from substance to spirit.

"Good," Bead said from her rocky perch.

Malcolm turned to look at her and saw two or three wolves, their backs lowered, bellies just scraping the ground, stalking him. He heard a soft whiffling sound, then a thunk. One of the wolves whined and then started biting at its hip. An arrow jutted from its haunch. It turned in circles, trying to pull the arrow out with its teeth. The other two wolves leaped aside as if sensing danger, then dove at the wounded wolf from either side, one going for the throat, the other for a hamstring. They both struck at the same instant and bowled the injured wolf to the ground. They pounced on their brother, teeth flashing in the darkness, shredding soft flesh without making a sound. It was over in seconds, as one wolf tore the throat open and the other crunched savage teeth through the leg bone.

Instantly, four or five more wolves appeared and

began to fight over the meat, ripping flesh and snarling, snapping their jaws at encroachers.

Malcolm drifted away from the fire very slowly while the pack was occupied with the fresh carcass, and drove three wolves away from Red Bead. She sighed as he put his arm around her waist and drew her close to him.

Two Fires stepped out of the shadows, an arrow nocked to his bowstring.

"You came at a good time," Malcolm said to the Lakota brave.

"Many wolves."

"What has happened with the horses?"

"I killed two wolves. The white eyes killed three. There is one horse dead."

Malcolm wondered where McCord was. "Is the white eyes watching the horses?"

"He is bringing them here."

The wolf pack began to break up as each member carried off a piece of carcass. Two wolves were dragging one of the dead ones away, while the others tore chunks of meat from its belly. The stench of entrails filled the air with a pungent aroma.

Malcolm heard the crack of McCord's rifle and the high-pitched yelp of a wolf as it was struck with a lead ball. The horses set up another din, and Malcolm knew McCord must have his hands full.

Two Fires watched the remaining wolves warily, his bow at the ready. Malcolm knew the Lakota brave would not kill a wolf just for the sake of killing, or in retaliation for the attack. He had to have a pretty good reason to kill an animal he considered a brother. And Two Fires, he was sure, considered all animals to be his brothers.

Malcolm threw down the burning faggot. Red Bead did the same with the smoldering firebrand. He squeezed her and let her go.

"I must help McCord with the horses," he said.

"Put fire and the soft metal in your fire stick," she said.

"Yes. Will you build the fire again?"

"I will build the fire high," she said.

"Good."

He found his rifle with his bedding and picked it up. He would load the pistol later.

McCord was wrestling with the horses, trying to calm them down.

"I'll give you a hand," Malcolm said.

"Goddamned sorry bunch."

"You lost one, Two Fires said."

"Did we? I don't know. Can't see a damned thing in this bloody darkness."

Malcolm grabbed one of the ropes from McCord, then another. He led the animals away from the others, speaking to them soothingly. They were as skittery as deer. He saw no more wolves, but heard them snarling and fighting over what he took to be the dead horse.

"We'll have to sit up all night with them, you know," McCord said.

"I expect so."

"Sonofabitch."

Malcolm wanted to laugh, but he knew it was a serious situation and McCord wouldn't appreciate any humor or lightness about it.

"We beat them," Malcolm said.

"Not if they killed one of the horses, we didn't."

"Hell, they could have killed all of us."

"Devils. Bloody devils."

Malcolm said nothing. People had funny notions about wolves. White men didn't understand them and hated them with a passion he found hard to fathom. Yet he had been the same way once. He feared them, hated them. And, he supposed, some of that was still with him, but he'd learned much from the Lakota. To them, the wolf was almost a sacred being, as were all creatures. But the wolf held a special place in the lives of the Indians. They honored him for his bravery and his cunning. They feasted him for his hunting skills. They danced to pay homage to their animal brother, they sang songs about him.

"We'd better set watches," Malcolm said. "They might come back."

"That's easy enough. It's just me and you."

"Two Fires and Bead can stand guard. That's four."

"I don't trust either one of 'em."

"Two Fires killed two or three wolves."

"He says."

"I believe him," Malcolm said quietly.

"It's my show. Two watches. You can have either first or second."

"I'll take the first."

"Why?"

"I don't trust you, Randy. You might let the wolves get all of us."

"Fair enough. Goo' night."

Malcolm tossed a wave after McCord as he turned to go to his blankets. He reloaded his pistol, checked his rifle. He told Two Fires and Red Bead to go to sleep.

"I am going to stand watch."

"I will sit with you," Two Fires said.

"Good."

"I will keep the blankets warm for my husband," Red Bead said.

Malcolm wondered if the wolves would return that night. But he didn't ask. He knew that one or two, the ones who didn't get enough food, might come back and try to get a horse, or one of them. He looked at the cold, still sky, the moon crescent sailing slowly across those dark seas and the stars winking and watching,

silver sentinals in the night; the Milky Way like distant
cities strewn across a vast prairie of unknown dimen-
sion, their lanterns and street lamps lit, their houses
silent and ghostly. He felt very small and insignificant,
as he always did when he gazed at the night sky. But, as
always, he was once again filled with the awesome mystery of those distant worlds and wondered if someone,
some person, was looking down on him as he was looking up.

The wolves were still feeding on the dead horse,
fighting among themselves over every scrap of meat
and marrow-filled bone. They could hear them snarling
and yelping like an unruly pack of dogs.

Malcolm was not sleepy, but he was tired now that
the crisis seemed to be over. He listened silently to the
blood coursing through his muscles, felt the pain running through them. Since coming to live with the
Lakota, he was more aware of his body, of what a great
instrument it was for work, for hunting, for making
love. The Sioux had taught him many things, often
without meaning to, he thought. He admired them as a
people, and he had come to think of them as friends.

Although they did not show affection in the same
ways of the whiteman, they had shown him much kind-
ness. Red Bead especially. She knew when he was
homesick, when he was sad, when he was sick. She
cared for him without demonstration or expectance of
praise or thanks. He was grateful for that, for he held
much in his heart that was not good. Memories of a
family destroyed by his brother, Jared.

There were times when he felt lost and abandoned,
and unbidden anger sprang up in him, anger at his father, at his mother, at his sister, and finally at his
brother Jared. His anger was like a rope in a wind-
storm, one end tied to him, the other lashing out
blindly at every quarter of the compass. He did not

know whom to hate, so he hated them all, for various reasons.

But he knew that such anger was harmful to him, turned him bitter when he knew it was possible to be happy—with Red Bead, with Two Fires, with his adopted Lakota family. Bead had taught him to control his anger, to let it flow out of him each morning when the sun came up, and if it arose during the day, to let it set with the evening light and sleep with the sun on the other side of the world.

Two Fires interrupted Malcolm's reverie. "A dream came to me last night, a vision. It disturbs me."

"You do not know what it means?"

"I saw a big river. It was shining, and it ran from a high mountain that was among the stars. I stepped into its waters, and the waters were warm as a mother's milk when it flows from the breast. The river carried me along and I heard men shouting at me to go back. I tried to see the men because I wanted to know who they were.

"But I could not see their faces. They were hidden in clouds and in the branches of strange trees that wiggled and shook like snakes."

Two Fires paused, and Malcolm thought that he was finished with the story of his dream.

"Why does this dream disturb Two Fires?"

"I saw a whiteman with flames on his head. His hair was aflame and the fire flowed around his face like a horse's mane when the wind blows along his neck. The man stood in the middle of the silver river and he called to me and told me to come to him."

"And did you go to him?" Malcolm asked.

"The river carried me to him. I could not turn back."

"Did you try?"

"I felt like a man whose feet had turned to stone. I

was sinking in the river, yet I was going toward the fire-haired man who had eyes as black as gunpowder."

"What happened?"

"The man lifted me from the water, and I felt the heat from his burning hair. I looked into his eyes and they turned to the color of the sky. His hands closed around my neck and squeezed hard until my breath went from me. Then he dropped me into the water, and the water was black and I saw stars floating by. I knew I was on the starpath, that my spirit had left me."

"You were dead."

"Yes. I was floating in the spirit world. And then I woke up and my skin was wet and my heart drummed like the prairie chicken's wings. I was afraid."

"What do you think this dream tells Two Fires?"

Two Fires sat silent for several moments. Malcolm could hear his breathing, knew the Lakota was deep in thought.

"I think the white eyes, Randall, is going to rub me out." He pronounced it "Wandall."

"You think Randall is going to kill you?"

"That is what my dream told me."

Malcolm didn't know what to say. The Lakota put great store in dreams, saw them as visions, as glimpses into the future. He waited, thought it through.

"What will you do?"

"There is nothing I can do. My dream told me what will be."

"Randall McCord needs you, Two Fires. I don't think he will rub you out."

"Yes. When he does not need Two Fires, he will send me to the spirit world."

Malcolm felt a cold chill crawl up the back of his neck and make the small hairs bristle. His skin broke out in goose bumps.

"I will kill McCord before he does that," he said finally.

"No, you cannot stop what will happen to me. When he kills me, it will be a good day for Two Fires to die."

In the distance a wolf howled long and mournfully, as if someone had died and he sat there by the man's grave.

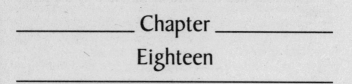

Chapter

Eighteen

Pettibone reached down for the derelict's arm.
"We've got to get the hell out of here," he said.
Jared acted quickly, taking the other arm.
Together they lifted the man to his feet.

"Swan, go get in the boat," Jared said. "Make room for this man."

"I will go," she said, and raced away on moccasined feet, swift as any young deer.

"Gray Cat, you shoot," Pettibone ordered.

The Mandan dropped to one knee, brought his rifle to his shoulder. The sounds of the approaching Indians grew louder. So close, Jared thought, they seemed to be surrounded. He and Pettibone hoisted Toomey to his feet, put his arms around their shoulders. They dragged Toomey between them, back toward the river. Toomey was unable to walk, but at least he didn't weigh much.

"They come now," Gray Cat said.

A pair of Indians crashed through the underbrush

and into the open, brandishing war clubs. Gray Cat took aim at one of them and fired his rifle.

The ball struck the Chinook in the breast and a patch of blood flowered on his chest. He stumbled and spit blood, then pitched forward. The other Indian stopped to watch his brother drop to the forest floor, then gave out a wild yell and continued his charge.

Gray Cat rose up to his feet, jerking his knife from its buckskin scabbard. With his other hand he brought up the rifle, holding it straight out to block his attacker's forward rush.

As the Chinook's momentum carried him within range, Gray Cat jabbed with the rifle. The charger struck downward with his war club, knocking the rifle to one side.

Gray Cat lunged forward then, burying the knife in his attacker's stomach.

Pettibone looked back over his shoulder just in time to see Gray Cat pull his bloody knife from the Chinook's belly. The wounded man stopped short, a look of sharp surprise on his face.

"Run, Gray Cat!" Pettibone yelled. "Come on. Quick."

Gray Cat stepped aside as the wounded Indian fell to the ground, writhing in pain, clutching his stomach.

Jared and Pettibone wrestled Toomey into Jared's dugout.

"Just stay put," Flynn said. "Sit in the middle there. Swan, you watch him."

She nodded, her lips set tight.

Pettibone turned, holding his rifle at the ready.

Gray Cat sheathed his knife and began loping their way.

"Quick, quick," Pettibone urged.

A pack of hostile Indians emerged from the woods and yelped when they saw the Mandan. Gray Cat did not look back, but began increasing his strides.

Jared heard the racket and turned to see what was going on. Pettibone was already cocking his rifle, bringing it up to his shoulder.

"Better push off, Jared," he said. "Save yourself."

"Just make sure you shoot true, Fur Face. I ain't goin' nowhere."

"Waugh! There's too many of the red coons. They'll be on us like a swarm of wet hornets."

Gray Cat was fleet of foot and he began to widen the distance between himself and his pursuers. One of the pursuing Chinooks, while on the run, threw a war club at him. It sailed just over his head, end over end. Gray Cat never broke his stride. He leaped over a bush and put on a burst of speed when he hit the ground just as another hostile stopped and hurled a spear at the fleeing Mandan.

Pettibone took steady aim at the nearest Chinook and squeezed the trigger. A puff of smoke erupted from the pan of his flintlock, followed by a sharp crack as the powder in the breech ignited through the touch-hole. A stream of bright orange flame shot out of the barrel, followed by a huge puffball of white smoke.

Jared set the cock on his rifle as Pettibone's shot claimed the lead Chinook, tearing out his throat with a startling suddenness. A rosy spray peppered the Indians behind as the man twisted grotesquely and fell to the ground.

"Get in the dugout," Jared said.

"I got to reload."

"Do it there. Gray Cat'll be here in a second or two."

Jared noticed that the Chinooks had slowed after Pettibone's kill. He took aim on another, who was the closest to Gray Cat, several yards behind the Mandan. He dropped the blade front sight on the man's chest, lined it up with the buckhorn rear sight, and caressed the trigger, giving the man a slight lead.

The flintlock, with its ninety grains of black powder, kicked Jared's shoulder as the explosion rocketed the ball from the muzzle in a spume of hot flame and flour-white smoke. The Chinook threw up his arms as the lead fractured his breastbone and smashed into his heart. He was dead before he hit the ground, a huge hole in his back where the projectile exited.

"Come on, Gray Cat."

Gray Cat dashed up a second or two later, and Jared shoved him into the dugout. Swan sat in the stern of Flynn's canoe, a paddle in her hands.

Pettibone reloaded quickly and pushed off from shore, just enough so that he could hold the boat steady for another shot before he went into the current. Gray Cat leaped into his own dugout and began to reload his rifle. Jared drew his pistol and fired one last shot at the closest Indian before he turned and pushed his dugout away from shore, climbing in as it caught the current. Swan began paddling, slowly turning the prow of the dugout downstream. He heard the whish of war clubs speeding through the air as the boat turned. One of the warriors pointed to his boat, shouted something. All of the other braves grew very excited, their voices rising to fever pitch as the dugout caught the current. Jared stared at them for a long moment, then turned to look at the derelict seaman. Toomey lay there amidships, helpless as a sack of potatoes. Swan crinkled her nose, her face a dark mask in shadow as she dug her paddle deep. Jared supposed that she was repelled by Toomey's smell. The man had obviously not bathed in days, perhaps weeks.

The Chinooks yelled insults and threw spears at the boatmen. Some picked up rocks and hurled them at the retreating trappers. Most of them landed harmlessly in the water, but Jared had to duck when one came close. He grabbed a paddle and helped Swan turn the canoe, not bothering to reload.

Pettibone lay his rifle down and paddled into the current, Gray Cat not far behind. He let out a shout as the dugout sped out of range. Jared counted a dozen Chinooks before he lost sight of the war party, but it took him several minutes before his breath returned to normal.

They ran the river for the rest of the afternoon. Jared told Toomey where he could find something to chew on and water to drink. The man groaned and complained the whole trip, and kept expressing his gratitude for being saved until Jared told him to shut up. Swan smiled without showing her teeth.

That night they pulled the dugouts onto a tiny beach surrounded by rocks, a place difficult to reach on foot from the shore. Jared and Gray Cat scouted for a half mile around the place and found no sign of Indians. They each covered a half circle through the woods.

"We'll make no fire tonight," Jared said. "And we'll have to take watches."

"Better safe than sorry," Pettibone said.

Together they carried Toomey up over the craggy rocks to the place Jared had selected for a campsite.

"He's in bad shape," Pettibone said.

"I know it. You take him in your dugout tomorrow."

"Thanks," Pettibone said sarcastically. Toomey was nothing but skin and bones, so frail they were afraid that he would break in half if they dropped him.

"I'm hungry," Toomey said. "You got any hot food?"

"Gray Cat, you got any pemmican?" Pettibone asked.

Gray Cat grunted.

"You can eat what we got," said Pettibone.

"I could eat the south end of a northbound horse," Toomey said.

"Well, I see you ain't lost your sense of humor none."

"That was a close call today. I thought we were goners."

Jared listened to the banter between the two men. Swan sat next to a tree as if deep in thought. Flynn crabbed over and sat beside her.

"You hungry?" he asked.

Swan shook her head.

"I am. Some."

"Eat."

"You don't like the man we found."

Swan shrugged.

"He's not much. Half starved. Scared."

"He will live," she said coldly.

Jared knew that something was bothering Swan. She'd been quiet, almost sullen, all afternoon. She appeared to be in a sulk just then, in fact. As for himself, he felt closed in, claustrophobic in the shadows of the huge mountains. At such times he felt very small and insignificant. Sometimes it amounted almost to a rage when he had not seen new faces for days on end.

He should welcome the sight of Toomey, he thought, but for some reason the man irritated him. And it was obvious that Swan did not like him. Pettibone never said much, but he was doing his best to ignore Toomey. Gray Cat gave the sailor some pemmican. The man ate like a savage, tearing into the pounded meat and berries like a wild carnivore.

Jared turned away. He could not stand to see a man eat like that. It was still dusk, but he wished it were night so he would not have to look at Toomey's emaciated figure, his bones visible through the torn shirt.

Toomey devoured about two day's rations of a normal man's diet of pemmican, and lay there smacking his lips.

"What's your story, Toomey?" Jared asked, just to make the man stop licking his chops like a satiated dog.

"Ain't you goin' to look at my leg? It might be broke."

"Not now. It's not broken, or you'd be screaming all the time. Stay off of it and it'll heal."

"I'm curious about how you got this far upriver," Pettibone said. "Without getting killed."

"Like I told you, I was on the *Tonquin* when she sailed from New York, a vessel of 290 tons burden. A stanch old ship, she was, but with a merciless, heartless Captain name of Jonathon Thorn. A regular navy man, he was, on leave, probably because Mr. Astor arranged it, he has that much power, and he exercised military regulations aboard ship, though we was all civilians. We were twenty-one of crew and our passengers numbered thirty-three."

"When did you leave New York?" asked Jared.

"On September the sixth, eighteen hunnerd and ten, well laden with trade goods, hunting and trapping equipment, tools and lumber for me to build a small schooner on the Columbia and for the erection of a trading post. Plus we carried seeds and such for the cultivation of food crops. We cleared the bar at Sandy Hook on September the eighth, and for some leagues were accompanied by a naval vessel to protect us against search by British cruisers.

"We sighted the Falkland Islands on December the third, reached the Pacific Ocean on December twenty-fourth and the Sandwich Islands on February eleventh, eighteen hunnerd and eleven."

"You have a good memory for dates," Jared observed dryly.

"Not much else a man can do aboard such a ship but make note of special events. We left the islands on the eighteenth of February, with twenty-four dark-skinned Sandwichers aboard, and on March the twenty-second we reached the mouth of the Columbia."

"That was a couple of months ago," Pettibone said.

"Seems a mite longer," Toomey replied. "I know I'll remember that day Cap'n Thorn sent off a boat with First Mate Fox, me, and three other luckless mates. The boat was not seaworthy, and Fox complained to Thorn and said he didn't expect to ever make it back aboard the *Tonquin*. As it turned out, none of us did."

"What happened?" Jared asked.

"First off, the boat leaked and we scuttled it before we reached shore. Had to swim for it. We lost everything, just about; rifles, powder, ball, lumber, tools. We couldn't make no fire, we were wet and cold. Hungry too. Lost all our provisions in the swell that broke up the boat. We kept hoping the captain would send a boat to pick us up, but I guess he finally realized the swells were just too big. We shivered in the night like dogs shittin' peach seeds, and in the morning the *Tonquin* was still out to sea and the breakers high as houses on the incoming tide.

"Another of our crew died the next day. He got water in his lungs when we spilled and couldn't get it out. He coughed all night, until he was coughing blood all over himself. I guess his last cough tore out what was left of his lungs."

"What did you do?" Jared asked quietly, now caught up in the story. He had begun to view Toomey in a different light, one not so harsh as before.

"A few days later we saw two more boats set out, but they turned back in the heavy surf, unable to make it to shore. It was a big disappointment, I can tell you. From where I lay, it looked like they come mighty close to founderin' in those damnable swells."

"Did the captain ever send anyone to get you back?" Pettibone asked.

"I don't know if he ever meant to, the blighter. We saw another boat set out, but it got caught in the ebb tide and was swept right out to sea. We saw it floating past the *Tonquin,* and the crew was unable to fight the swift current. We could hear them yelling for help, and then we didn't see them no more. I figure some or all of that crew drowned. The *Tonquin* sat there like a squatting duck, never pulling anchor to go to their rescue. Mr. Fox kept sayin': 'I told Captain Thorn we'd never make it, I told him.' "

"What happened after that?" Jared asked.

"Indians snuck up on us and killed Fox and the other two men in the crew. I never did learn their names good. Baldy and Squinty's what we called 'em. I barely got away. I heard 'em sneak up, and then I heard a crunching sound. There was poor Fox with his head stove in like a melon and Indians a-workin' on the other two with knives and clubs. They didn't make no sound, them Indians, and neither did none of the crew. I figured they slit their throats first, then clubbed their brains to chowder just for pure meanness."

"Did they follow you?" Pettibone asked, his voice barely above a whisper.

"I don't think they even knew I was there at first. But they probably saw my tracks. I kept on a-goin', and made a wide circle and watched where I stepped. I figured the *Tonquin* would eventually come up the river, so I waited near its mouth for a few days, so hungry I was eatin' bark and grass and ready to go after bugs. But I knew I had to keep movin' 'cause there were Indians everywhere. I seen them in their dugouts and fishin' on the shore and climbin' all around gatherin' roots and such."

"So you don't know if the *Tonquin* ever got a party ashore," Jared said.

"Oh, they did that all right. I saw her sails once after hearing a lot of musketry from ashore. But there were Indians between me and them. Finally, I had to leave, and I been runnin' ever since. I watched them Indians catch fish, and done it myself so I got some food in my belly. Threw it up at first 'cause it was raw and got a damned bone stuck in my throat. I finally swallowed some dirt to dislodge it, and the next time I kept the raw fish down. I found food at some of the camps they deserted. Camps was thick with fleas, and they ate me while I ate whatever I could find. It's been hell. I had to start running again, and went upriver, figuring they'd stay around the ocean and leave me be, but they followed me. They caught up with me this morning, and that's when I got hurt. If I hadn't run into you fellers, I'd surely be dead by now."

"We're not exactly safe yet," Pettibone said. "I reckon we'll run into some of them same savages any day now."

"But you're armed. You can defend yourselves. We lost all our weapons when our boat broke up."

"We're armed," Jared said, "but we're outnumbered. If we're to get down this river alive, we'll have to use our wits and then some."

"Where you goin'?" Toomey asked.

"Same place as the *Tonquin*," Jared said. "We're going to set up a trading post at the mouth of the Columbia same as Astor means to do."

"Well, you'll play hob settin' up any tradin' post on the ocean," Toomey said.

"Oh?"

"What with Astor's bunch bein' there, Duncan McDougal, David Stuart, and W. P. Hunt, and Indians thick as the fleas in their deserted camps, you'll have one hell of a time."

"We may at that," Flynn admitted. "But we're going to do our best to put North-West right on the Pacific Ocean. Now, you best get you some sleep. We're going to leave here before sunup tomorrow."

Jared crawled quietly over to Swan. She sat there still leaning against the tree. She looked morose.

"You should leave that man here," she said softly.

"Can't do that," Jared replied.

"Then you will all be killed."

"How do you know that?"

"I know the men chasing Toomey," she said. "They are Clatsops. They are my people."

"Clatsop? They are the ones who killed the men from the ship?"

"My people are traders. But they do not like the white people. They will kill you if they find you."

"Would they kill you?" he asked.

Swan took in a deep breath. "They would kill me for being with you," she said.

Jared felt the night descend on him and close them all off from the world they had left behind and the one that lay beyond that dark glade in the wilderness.

Chapter Nineteen

Malcolm Flynn, Randall McCord, Two Fires, and Red Bead rode the flats south to the Snake River. Two Fires led them there unerringly and without incident. They rode south of the falls, following the river.

"We would make better time if we left the horses and built canoes," Malcolm said as they gazed at the river below the falls.

"I know. But we may need these goods, and there are other reasons I want to go by horseback."

"It might be rough."

"I've been through rough before, laddie."

"I thought you were in a hurry."

"Hurry is a state of mind. We might not make as many miles, but we won't wear ourselves out paddling and portaging those many miles."

"You seem pretty sure of yourself."

"Sure as God's on my side, Malcolm."

Malcolm held his tongue. He didn't want to get into another argument with McCord. They'd come far enough that he didn't want to go back without finding his brother Jared, and he admitted to being somewhat curious about McCord's plans.

Malcolm could see how the Snake got its name. It twisted through the land like an enormous serpent, a magnificent undulating force unlike any other waterway he'd ever seen. And the river imparted a beauty to the hostile country, a coursing lifeblood, pulsing like some exposed vein or artery bringing nutrients to what might be only arid desert without its sustenance.

They saw game everywhere: deer, antelope, buffalo, birds of prey, waterfowl, doves and other wildfowl, eagles that traced the river as if following a road from on high. At times they saw Indians in canoes paddling to some unknown destination, too far away for Malcolm to determine their tribal origins, but Two Fires said they were Shoshones. Fish broke the waters in golden mornings and somnolent afternoons, feeding on winged insects floating above the winding relentless waters, unaware of the danger below.

Two Fires ranged far ahead of them, leaving signs that showed them the way. They made dry camps at night, or they built a fire to smoke the fish they caught and cook the rabbits and deer they killed. They kept the fire small and hot and smokeless, sinking it deep in a pit and surrounding it with stones so that no flame showed in the darkness.

McCord marked the passing days on a stick, notching it every night with his knife. He studied the weather each day and smelled the air as if to measure the heavens' breadth and depth and lash it to the earth with some arcane and mysterious cords of his mind's making.

As they went deeper into the barren country, they began to ride well away from the Snake to avoid contact with Indian tribes that might be hostile. Two Fires said they had crossed the path of Cheyenne and Brule, but they never saw them, and Malcolm did not know how Two Fires knew. But when they came to a cold fire, the Lakota studied the moccasin tracks and made his determination.

They passed a place where two falls broke the river in a spectacular show of force, and Malcolm sensed they were climbing in altitude after that. Because of the danger of running into a fight, they traveled a longer distance than they would have had they used canoes on the river. But McCord didn't seem to mind, as the hunting was good and the weather held for much of the time. They encountered only a few rain squalls and some high winds that slowed them only slightly.

The country began changing the farther west they rode, the river wending its way through steep bare canyons and branching off into other tributaries that seemed to flow into a no-man's-land, and there were signs that the Snake had razed the terrain in mighty floods over eons, stripping the earth of vegetation and leaving deep furrows in the rocks and soil. Some of the country reminded Malcolm of the Badlands in the land of the Lakota, a maze of canyons and gorges where a man could get lost and never find his way out.

The river seemed interminable as the four made their way across the country, and McCord's amiability finally wore off as the land stretched out ahead of them with nothing to break the gaze.

"Does that Sioux nigger know how to get to the Columbia?" McCord asked one day.

"He does."

"Well, how much farther?"

"I don't think he can answer that, Randy. He might say thirty sleeps or twenty sleeps, or he might just say many suns."

"Well, I'd like to know if we're getting anywhere."

"I'll ask him. You see the sun set every night the

same as I do, so we're going due west, and that's where the Columbia lies."

"Don't patronize me, Malcolm. I know we're headed in the right direction, but it's taking so damned long."

"It's a long way to the Pacific Ocean."

McCord broke off the conversation with a burred Gaelic curse and rode off, slapping his horse's rump savagely with the tips of his reins.

Malcolm slowed to let Red Bead catch up to him with the pack animals.

"Red Hair shows much anger," she said.

"Yes. Do not worry."

"I do not worry, my husband. I no like him speak bad words to you."

"Words don't hurt."

"They hurt the heart," she said. "And the heart can make the body sick and weak."

She was right, he knew. Words could hurt. But McCord no longer bothered him that much. It was the hard ride that bothered McCord, and Malcolm drew some perverse pleasure in that. Randy couldn't bend distance and time to suit his purposes, could not make nature succumb to his threats. So he lashed out at the only one who spoke decent English. A boiling kettle letting off steam, that's all it was. Malcolm could tolerate that as long as he was civil to Two Fires and Red Bead. But perhaps the only reason McCord was civil, he thought, was because he didn't know any insults in the Lakota tongue.

They rode long hard days, following the reptilian course of the Snake River. The packhorses had to be rubbed with bear grease every night on those places where the packs had first worn off the hair, then the hide, and finally rubbed the flesh to a state of suppuration and mortification. Red Bead never complained, but Malcolm noticed that she had lost weight and did not eat much.

"You grow thin," he said.

"It is not good to eat only meat."

"But what else is there?"

"I need to find berries and herbs. The salmon and deer meat is not enough. Red Hair does not stop. He is like the thief who runs in the night."

They had run out of dried vegetables three weeks ago, and the land was barren of edible plants, as far as Malcolm knew. Bead could find food on a flat rock, but she knew what to look for. She was right, of course. McCord didn't dawdle. He pressed on like a man obsessed, not with the journey, but with the eventual destination.

"When we come to the river that goes to the sea," Malcolm told her, "we will find the foods you need."

"That is good," she said. "But there are other things that worry me, my husband."

"What worries you, Bead?"

"I wonder about your father and why your brother killed him."

"I do not know why my brother killed my father."

"Was your father a brave man?"

Malcolm had never thought of him in that way. Cold, silent, hardened by the land and the past perhaps. But not brave.

"No, he was not brave. I don't think he was. He was a farmer. He scratched the earth and brought forth food. He was a quiet man, timid like the mouse. He did not talk much. My mother was the same. I do not know if they had love in their hearts for each other. But they did not fight or quarrel. At least I never heard them raise their voices. My father left my mother to tend to the house, cook the meals. He hunted and scratched the earth and put seeds in the ground."

"That is how it should be with the whites," she

said. "We do not put seeds in the ground, but the men
hunt and fish, and we women cook the food and make
clothing for our men and children to wear."

"My mother made clothes too. And she fixed
clothes that were worn out with a little awl and some
sinew made of cloth."

"I do not know what this sinew made of cloth is,"
she said.

"They do not use sinew from the animals, but
make thread, a kind of string, on a loom, a tool that
works like the spider when it spins its web."

"I would like to see this tool that spins like the
spider. The string could not be very strong."

"It is strong because it is not so thin as the spider's
web."

"Oh." Red Bead spent the rest of the long day
thinking of such a tool that could make strong
spiderwebs that would not break and blow away in the
wind.

And so they rode through that forbidding land like
pilgrims lost in the immensity of a desolate, uninhab-
ited planet, searching for some shining river beyond the
one they followed, staring into the sun for half a day
and burning with it at their backs for the other half.
They bathed briefly in the shallow streams they crossed,
letting the horses graze on the sparse grass and drink
from the Snake.

The June sun beat down on them like Vulcan's
forge, and at night they froze in the stiff chill winds that
blew across the dry land, sucking moisture out of every
living thing that grew in harsh soil.

McCord's disposition grew increasingly ugly, and
he took his hostility out on Two Fires—not directly,
because the Lakota brave did not understand the white
man's words. But Malcolm knew that Two Fires understood that McCord was talking about him and in a very
derogatory way.

"Red Hair is angry at the earth and the sky," Two Fires said to Malcolm in Lakota one day after they all heard McCord cursing the heat, the parched land, the river that ran past them impassive as hammered metal.

"He wants to be the bird that flies from one place to another straight as an arrow," Malcolm said.

"He has a bad heart for Two Fires."

"He has a bad heart for all things."

"I think that is true. I have seen him kick stones that have done him no harm, and he sometimes shoots at lizards and birds that he does not eat."

"That is his way," Malcolm said weakly, as if explaining the mindless antics of a child.

"Why do you ride with this Red Hair? You are better off with the Lakota. We are your family."

"What Two Fires says is true. I go with him to find my brother, whose heart is bad also. I go because Red Hair would have made trouble for me with the Lakota."

"You are afraid of this bad white man?"

"No. I do not fear him for myself. I fear what he might do to you and Bead Woman."

"You say he takes you to your brother."

"That is what I say."

"But it is we who are taking him."

Malcolm saw the truth in Two Fires's words. The Lakota brave had much wisdom.

"If we did not take him, he would still go. And I think he would kill my brother."

"Why do you not kill Red Hair, then?"

"I do not kill another man for no reason. He has done me no harm."

"Red Bead Woman says that you will kill your brother because he rubbed out your family."

"Did she say that? Yes, that is so. I might have to kill my brother. But first I want to make words with him. I want to ask him why he killed my father and caused my mother and my sister to take their own lives."

"That is very strange," Two Fires said with solemnity. "I have never known a man who wished to make talk with his enemy before he rubbed him out."

"I want to know what was in my brother's heart when he rubbed out my father."

"There was a darkness, a bad spirit, in your brother's heart?"

"Yes, Two Fires. But I must know why there was darkness in my brother's heart."

"It is all very strange, my friend," Two Fires said. "A big mystery."

Malcolm did not reply because Two Fires was right, of course. It was a big mystery.

Malcolm heard the brittle staccato of the rattlesnake's tail before he saw it strike one of the packhorses. The horse reared up and screamed in a high-pitched whinny. It began to stamp its hooves on the ground, trying to kill the rattler, but the snake struck it again and all the horses bolted, jerking the lead ropes from Malcolm's hand.

Ahead of him, McCord wheeled his horse and came riding toward him. "What the hell's going on?"

Then he heard the rattle, and his horse fought the bit and started to back down. Red Bead rode after the loose horses, clapping her heels into her mount's tender flanks. She waved one down and picked up the rope on the gallop, snubbing it around her waist as she reined to a halt.

The rattlesnake twisted and coiled, struck and recoiled, leaving wavy markings on the ground. Malcolm was about to bring his rifle to his shoulder to shoot the snake when he heard a loud report. He looked up, saw the stricken horse go down to its knees, its eyes bulged out so that they were almost pure white, and blood pouring from a hole in its neck. A plume of smoke curled from the muzzle of McCord's rifle. He was already reloading as the horse fell to its side and kicked several times while its blood pumped out through the hole. Pieces of windpipe jutted from the other side, where the ball had exited, making a hole big enough for a girl's fist.

"Best see what we can save from the packs, redistribute them to the other animals," McCord said, spitting a patch from his mouth into the palm of his hand. He sat the patch on the muzzle and placed a ball atop it. He had put the powder in so fast, Malcolm hadn't seen him tip his horn.

"We might have saved that horse, Randy."

"We haven't got time to nurse a sick horse."

The rattlesnake lay coiled, its forked tongue flicking like black lightning from its tightly pursed lips, its eyes glittering like sunken beads. Its rattle stood erect, moving so fast that the tip of its tail was blurred like a hummingbird's wings.

The horse was still kicking as McCord drew a bead on the snake's head. Blood pooled up on the ground from the severed artery in the horse's neck.

Red Bead watched the Scotsman in fascination, and the horse on the rope finally calmed. Randall drew a breath, held it, then gently squeezed the trigger. The rifle bucked against his shoulder, and a split second later the snake's head flew off like a popped champagne cork, its body wriggled as if alive, the rattles chilling Malcolm's blood.

Malcolm looked at McCord as he brought the rifle down to reload it from the saddle. The expression on his face hadn't changed one whit. Not even a smile of satisfaction broke his even features.

"Can that goddamned Injun gal catch up those horses or do I have to do that too?" McCord said as he poured a measure of powder down his rifle barrel.

"Watch your tongue, Randy."

"She's just sitting there like a stump. Tell her to get the horses and start repacking."

"Who in hell are you to order her about like she's some lackey?"

"I'm the leader of this expedition, that's who I am, Mr. Flynn, and we've wasted enough time as it is. Now get down and start shaking off those goods from that dead horse."

Malcolm felt bile rise up in his throat. He gagged and swallowed it back down before it strangled him.

"Do it yourself, you sonofabitch," Malcolm said, laying his rifle on a direct line with McCord, the muzzle pointing straight at Randall's belly. "I ain't your coon."

McCord did not hurry the reloading. He finished ramming the ball down the barrel with the wiping stick and put the rifle back in its boot.

"You catch the horses, then, and bring them over here. It's plain to see that redskin bitch isn't going to do it."

"One more curse about Bead, Randy, and I'll blow your guts to porridge and watch you kick like that horse there."

"Do you have the nerve, laddie? Do you? Can you shoot a man down in cold blood like your brother Jared did? Can you watch a man die slowly from being gut-shot? It's a damned sight harder than watching a horse give up the ghost."

Malcolm blinked his eyes at the rage that boiled up in him like blazing lava from an exploding volcano. His finger crimped around the trigger of his rifle. For a long moment he thought about cocking the rifle and letting a ball fly square into McCord's gut. He hadn't decided whether he would kill Randall while his blood was still boiling mad, the rage in him surging hot as a furnace.

"You're seven kinds of sonofabitch, McCord. I

ought to blow some of that hell out of you right here and now."

"You have the advantage," McCord said coolly. "You'll probably never have a better chance."

There was a long silence as McCord and Flynn stared at each other across the eternal short space between life and death, with neither flinching from the slow tick of fortune's clock that boomed in their ears with a solemn cadence.

Malcolm heard the hammer slide back and the sear engage in the lock, and it sounded like the last tick of that terrible timepiece of death and destiny.

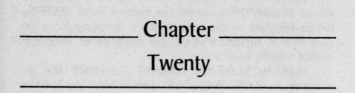

_____ Chapter _____
Twenty

Just before dawn broke over the Columbia River, Jared heard a sound that jolted him out of a deep sleep, shooting a gelid electric current through his spine, making the hairs on his head stiffen and crackle. He bolted up, tossing Swan aside as if she was just another of the robes covering him.

Toomey was screaming at the top of his voice register. Screaming as if the devil himself was piercing his flesh with a fiery trident.

Pettibone, who was on the morning watch, came running up out of the darkness. Gray Cat lifted a sleepy head, and Jared saw a knife in his hand, ready to strike the nearest attacker.

Jared bounded to where Toomey lay shrieking and clamped a hand over his mouth, shutting the scream down to cottony muffles.

"Shut up, Toomey," Jared whispered. "You want to get us all killed?"

Toomey struggled, clawing at Jared's hand.

"What's the matter with him?" Pettibone asked. "Bad dream?"

"I don't know. Toomey, if you want me to let go and don't want to get knocked cold with a rifle butt, shut your mouth and keep it shut."

"Mmmmmfffff," said Toomey, but he nodded in agreement.

Jared slowly released his hand from across the sailor's mouth.

"My foot," he said. "My leg. It's killing me."

"It's swollen is all," Jared replied.

"No, no, it's worse. I can't stand the pain. I can feel a bone move."

Pettibone squatted beside Flynn and Toomey. "Too dark to see," he said.

"Can you walk at all?" Jared asked.

"No, it's really bad. The pain woke me up. God, what pain. Worst I ever had."

Gray Cat emerged from his robes. Swan joined them. They all stared at the injured man, a shadow lying in the predawn darkness.

"Can't do a damn thing until it gets light," Pettibone said.

"You got to do something now. I think my ankle's broke."

"Hell," Jared said, "we can't see and I'm damned sure not going to light a fire. You want a stick to bite on?"

"You got any rum? Any whiskey?"

"No," Jared said. "You've already made enough racket to wake the dead. We've got to get the hell out of here."

"Oh, God, I can't move."

"We can leave you here, pilgrim," Pettibone said. "But we're going on while we still got our hair. Sound carries far, and I'm not going to fight off a pack of Injuns just 'cause you got a twisted ankle."

"It's broke," Toomey said.

"Maybe we better feel it," Jared said.

"Toomey, you change your mind about chewin' on that stick? If your foot hurts as bad as you say, you're goin' to need something in that mouth of yours so's you won't scream and bring us unwanted company."

"God, I don't want you to touch it."

"Well, if it's broke," the old trapper said, "we're goin' to have to set the bone and slap a splint on it. Ain't no way we can do all that 'thout causin' you pain."

Toomey began to moan and curse to himself while the others looked on. Jared looked up at the sky. He couldn't see a hint of morning, although he knew it wouldn't be long before sunup.

"Well," Flynn said, "we can't just stay here and wait for trouble. We've got to get on that river."

"Every minute goes by I get nervouser," Pettibone said.

"We can hold him down," Jared said. "Put a gag in his mouth."

"No—No, don't do that," Toomey begged.

"You got to keep your mouth shut," Pettibone told him. "And one of us has got to feel that ankle to see if you got a bone broke."

Sweat broke out on Toomey's face. Jared could smell its sour tang mingled with the scent of pine needles wet with dew and the aroma of balsam. He was running out of patience with Toomey. The man might even cost them their lives if he screamed again.

"Make up your mind, Toomey," Jared said curtly. "We either leave you here or you let us take a look at your foot."

Toomey hesitated for a long time before he replied.

"A-All right, g-go ahead. B-But you better give me something to bite on. It hurts so bad now I want to scream."

"You scream again," Flynn said, "and I'll shoot you dead."

Pettibone felt around for a stick to put in Toomey's mouth. Swan handed him one. So, she had heard and understood every word they had said, Jared thought.

"Here's you a chunk of pine," Pettibone said. "They's bark and sap on it, but neither one'll hurt you none. You bite down on that whilst I take a look at your foot."

Pettibone rammed the stick between Toomey's teeth.

"Jared, you better hold him down, just in case. Gray Cat, get you a hachet and club him with the flat side if he screams."

Gray Cat scooted closer, holding a tomahawk ready to brain Toomey if he made a sound. Jared was sure the Mandan was grinning, but he couldn't see him that well in the dark. Jared put both hands on Toomey's shoulders and pressed downward. If the man broke that hold, Jared was prepared to strangle him with an arm-lock.

Toomey flinched when Pettibone touched his leg, just above the ankle.

"Take it easy," the old trapper said. "I'll go slow, try and be as careful as I can. You just bite down on that stick real hard if the pain makes you want to holler."

Toomey said something that sounded like "Aarmphunnn."

"Hurry it up, Fur Face," Jared said. "It's going to be light soon." He saw a paling in the sky to the east, and a few stars faded away at the low edge of the horizon. He heard the far-off call of a great horned owl, and then the silence of the forest rose up in a predawn hush.

Pettibone moved his fingers down toward Toomey's ankle, gently touching the flesh. When he reached the ankle itself, Toomey threw his head back, crunched down on the stick between his teeth, and whined between them as he tried to stifle a scream. Jared pushed down on the hurt man's shoulders, pinning him so he couldn't rise up and spit the stick out of his mouth.

"Jesus God," Pettibone said.

"What you got?" Jared asked.

"Bone done broke through the skin, sticking out big as you can please. I can feel fresh blood too."

A muffled sound from Toomey.

"Is it bad?" Jared asked.

"Bad as it can get," Pettibone replied. "Bone's splintered, sharp as a knife. I don't think I can set it like that. Toomey here'd pass out if I did, or we'd have to knock him senseless. It's a wonder he didn't scream more'n he did."

"You hold on, Toomey," Jared said. "We're going to have to get you down to the dugout and put some distance between us and those Clatsops. We'll look at your leg in the daylight and see what we can do."

More muffled sounds from Toomey.

"Just keep a-bitin' on that stick," Pettibone said. "It ain't goin' to get no better."

Jared lifted his weight from Toomey's shoulders. "You just lie there. Me and Gray Cat will carry you to the boat. Just try not to move much so it doesn't get worse."

"Aaagh," Toomey moaned, which Jared took for an affirmative reply.

"Gray Cat, you get his shoulders," Jared said. "I'll lift his legs."

"Swan will help."

Jared turned to Swan. It was light enough by then to see her face.

"You get the blankets and such, carry 'em down to the river."

"Swan will do," she said.

Gray Cat moved around to Toomey's head, put his hands underneath after tucking his tomahawk in his belt. Jared grabbed Toomey's calves with both hands and nodded to Gray Cat. They lifted the man in a single motion. Toomey twisted in agony and mumbled something unintelligible. They could hear his teeth grinding into the pine stick. Gray Cat swung around so that he and Jared could both face the river and walk toward it carrying their injured cargo. Pettibone grabbed his bedding and the rifles. He and Swan managed to lug all the stuff they'd had in camp, which wasn't much. The sky began to get lighter as they walked to the river.

"Better let me and Swan climb down to the boats first," Pettibone said. "Then we can be down on the bank when you get Toomey there."

"Good idea," Jared said. "It's pretty steep. We might drop him."

Pettibone started to say something, but changed his mind. Jared wanted to say the same thing. A look passed between them.

For all his fragility, Toomey seemed heavy to Jared, probably because he was writhing in pain and wriggling like a worm. He wanted to drop him from a high cliff, but knew the man couldn't help his plight. As long as Toomey obeyed orders, Jared would do everything he could to give him comfort and aid.

Gray Cat and Jared lay Toomey on the ground while Swan and Pettibone clambered down the steep slope. The dugouts were still there, untouched.

"Swan," Pettibone said, "just stand over there. I think I can handle him."

Swan stood to Pettibone's left and slightly behind him on the spot he'd indicated. The river surged past, iron-gray in the dim light, black where the trees shrouded it with shadows. The stillness pounded in Jared's ears as he picked Toomey up again. Gray Cat lifted the sailor's feet and moved him perpendicular to the slope. Jared handed Toomey to Pettibone, his head down and knees bent so that he squatted low, bearing the weight for as long as he could.

Pettibone grabbed Toomey under his shoulders and backed up while Jared slid down the slope. Toomey groaned and twisted in agony, making their task more difficult. Gray Cat followed Flynn's example and together they got the afflicted man down the slope.

"Now, if we can just get him into the boat," Pettibone said, panting from the effort.

"Let's take a look at his leg first," Jared said. "See if we can't fix it up."

They all looked up at the sky, which had lightened considerably in the past several minutes.

"I reckon we can see the damage," Pettibone said. They lay Toomey down, and Jared rolled up his pants leg. He gave a low whistle when he saw the jagged bone sticking out, blood oozing from the fissure in the skin.

"It looks bad," Jared said.

"Might have to chop off his foot," Pettibone said quietly.

Toomey started to rise up, and Jared pushed him back down. "Look, Toomey," he said. "You've got a bone sticking out of your leg, and the wound looks like it's starting to fester. We can either wait and see if it gets any better and try and push it back in tight enough to mend, or cut it off and pack it with mud."

Toomey removed the stick from his mouth. His face was ashen and bathed in sweat. There was a look of fear in his wide eyes. "God, man, don't cripple me up."

"Might not have no choice," Pettibone said. "That wound gets any worse and you'll get the gangrene. Know what that is?"

Toomey nodded. Every sailor feared it.

"We had a man this past winter got gangrene,"

Jared said. "He got frostbit on his toes. He wouldn't let us cut them off and it ran right up his leg, ate all his meat, and killed him."

Toomey shuddered. "I seen it before too."

"Well, what will it be, Toomey?"

"See if you can set it. If it starts to go bad, I—I guess you'll have to cut off my foot. Jesus God."

"Either way, the pain is going to be so bad you're going to pass out or scream until your lungs go flat."

"I—I know. It hurts so damned bad now, I want to shoot myself."

"Well, we can do that too," Pettibone said.

Jared looked at the old trapper and scowled. "Better put that stick back in your mouth," he said. "Pettibone, get some cloth to wrap this up. Gray Cat, find some sticks or flat stones. Swan, you help hold him down. Lie on him if you have to."

"Swan hold man down," she said. Her command of English continued to surprise Jared. She seemed to understand every word he said, and she didn't talk too badly either.

Jared looked at the wound again. It didn't look right to him. The bone seemed to come from the foot, up through the ankle. How would a man gain such a wound in such a place?

"You had a bad ankle when you come up on us," Jared said. "How come it's broken like that? Were you struck by one of those Clatsops?"

"They threw spears and war clubs at me. I was so scared and running so fast, I didn't feel anything at first. Then my ankle went bad on me. I don't know what happened last night to make it like this."

Toomey was scared, Jared knew. His voice shook when he spoke and he was sweating even more profusely than before. His face had turned waxen from fear, bloodless as a corpse. Jared didn't blame him. Anyone would be afraid in such a situation. Many a man died through carelessness, he knew, but this one had been terror-stricken for days, and it was a wonder that he had stayed alive as long as he had. But the worst was probably yet to come. No matter what they did with him, Toomey would lose a foot, maybe a leg. And he might still die, either from the shock or from gangrene that they wouldn't be able to see until it was too late.

He pulled up Toomey's pants leg and looked all around for a telltale streak of blue that might show the poison was already at work. He saw nothing, but the man's leg was black and blue from bruises. He might have missed it.

"I've got an idea," he told Pettibone.

"Eh? What's that?"

"That water's plumb freezing this time of morning. Let's get him down to the river and put this bad foot in it. I'll work underwater and try to set the bone. The cold might numb it some so it won't hurt him so bad."

"Hmm, sounds like it might work," Pettibone said. "Toomey, you grit down real hard on that there stick, 'cause if you jump out of my hands, you'll drown right quick." The trapper had a handful of cloth and leather scraps he'd been accumulating for months. He set them down near the bank.

Toomey nodded and put the stick back in his mouth. It was pretty well chewed up but ought to serve its purpose, Jared thought.

Pettibone and Jared lifted Toomey up, turned him around, and carried him down to the water's edge. Gray Cat returned with two pieces of pine he'd shaved nearly flat on both sides. Jared saw the splints and nodded. "Set them down on the bank there, next to that pile of cloth and leather," he told the Mandan.

"Make hurry," Swan said.

Jared looked up at the Indian maiden. She was glancing around furtively.

"Can't hurry something like this," Jared said.

"We go, we go," Swan said. "Quick. Make quick."

Jared saw her pacing about, peering everywhere. He listened but heard nothing.

"We'll lay him on the bank so his feet can dangle in the water," Jared said.

He set Toomey down where he wanted him and told Pettibone to keep him there. "I'm going to find out if this is going to work," he said.

"Need any help, you just holler."

"Likely it'll be Toomey doing all the hollering."

Jared pulled the bad ankle into the water, submerging it as Pettibone peered over Toomey's shoulder. Gray Cat squatted down to look at what the young trapper was doing. Swan seemed agitated and kept looking around and pacing back and forth between the bank and the dugouts.

"Hurry, hurry," she said.

"Be quiet, Swan," Jared told her.

Jared looked at Toomey's foot, felt the broken bones.

"You must have felt the blow that fractured your foot," he said to the sailor. "I can see a bruise there. It feels as if all of the little bones near the ankle were shattered."

"Bone must have worked up through the skin while he was a-sleepin'," Pettibone said.

"Hmm, could be."

Jared reached down and pushed on the bones. Toomey bucked from the pain and nearly wrenched loose from Pettibone's grip on his shoulders.

"Swan, get ready to hand me a wide piece of cloth from that pile there."

"Me do," Gray Cat said. Swan was back against the bank, trying to peer over it.

Jared traced the broken bone with his finger, pushed it back through the fissure in Toomey's flesh. It oozed blood that swirled in the water, floating down-

stream. He heard the bone squeak as it slid back
through the wound. He pressed downward after the tip
disappeared and reached for the swatch of cloth in
Gray Cat's hand.

He quickly wrapped the wound with the cloth, as
tightly as he could. He began to figure how he would
bind the injured foot so that the bone would stay in
place. He made several wraps, then tore the tail end of
the cloth in half for about eight inches. He then
wrapped each end around the foot and tied it at the
top.

"Now, the splints, Gray Cat."

Gray Cat handed Jared the two pieces of pine.
Jared put one on the sole of Toomey's foot, the other
on the arch. Gray Cat, seeing what Flynn was doing,
handed him another piece of cloth. Jared wrapped the
splints tightly and tied them securely. Then he took
bands of leather and wrapped those over the cloth.
With his knife he pierced holes in the leather and then
ran thongs through the holes and tied those off.

"It doesn't look pretty, but it might hold," he said
when he was finished. He looked up to see Toomey's
reaction.

"He's done passed out," Pettibone said softly.

"Good. I knew it must have hurt him a lot."

As he got to his knees to stand up, Jared was
nearly knocked down by Swan. She pounded on his
back.

"Must go, must go now," she said.

He turned around, grabbed her arms, pushed her
away as he got to his feet. "All right, Swan. We're going."

"Gray Cat, help me get this man into Jared's dugout," Pettibone said.

Swan continued to struggle, trying to break free of
Jared's grip.

"What's the matter, Swan?" Jared asked. "Did you see something? Hear something?"

He released her and she nearly fell backward. "Men coming. Men coming."

"Where?"

She looked all around, wild-eyed.

Jared could see that she was distressed, but he didn't know why.

She pointed to Toomey's foot as Pettibone and Gray Cat loaded the unconscious man into the canoe.

"Clatsop break bone so they catch you."

"What?"

Swan repeated what she had said.

"You hear that, Pettibone?"

"Makes sense. Slowed us down. That bunch that chased Toomey could be close by." He grunted as he and Gray Cat lay the wounded man in the bottom of the dugout. "We better hightail it right quick."

As Gray Cat climbed out of the dugout they heard a sound. Jared looked upriver and saw the canoes coming, three of them, no doubt filled with the same Clatsop braves that had pursued Toomey for so many miles.

And then Swan was pulling him into the dugout.

"Let's go," Pettibone said, leaping from the shore to his own canoe.

But as Jared pushed off from the bank, reaching with one hand for his rifle, he felt as if he was moving in slow motion and that it would be too late for them to get away.

Chapter
Twenty-one

Malcolm's finger lingered on the trigger for an interminable moment. McCord's lips curled slowly into a faint trace of a sneer, as if daring him to shoot. Yet the Scot made no move to defend himself. He made no move at all, as if he was stone or bullet-proof. Malcolm hated him for that. Randy was so damned sure of himself, so smug, so arrogant and self-righteous.

"Well, laddie, are you going to shoot me or just stare a bloody hole through me?"

"I ought to end it right here," Malcolm said. "Leave your carcass for the wolves and the buzzards."

"Now, why would you go and do such a thing? When we're so close. Haven't you been paying attention for the past week or more, laddie boy? Don't you miss that torturous ride through the devil's own country? Don't you see that we're on the downhill slope, figuratively speaking, of course. Why, the Columbia's just an hour or so away by my calculations. Maybe even closer."

The truth was that Malcolm hadn't been paying much attention to the distances they'd traveled, nor did he know how far it was to the Columbia River. It seemed to him that they'd been riding for months on end, through land broken by time and the raging weathers of countless seasons, country so rugged they seldom saw game and had not glimpsed sight of another human being in weeks. The days had blurred past him, folding one into another so that he scarcely marked their passing, nor knew one from the next.

But the country had been gradually changing, almost imperceptibly, and there was even a different smell to the air, as if the wind carried the scent of a distant sea on its zephyrs, mingled with the elusive scent of balsam and pine, cedar, spruce, and fir from another country, a land he could not see with his eyes and that might be only a deception in the coils of his memory, a vague whisper in some far dark corner of his mind.

Here, the country seemed much the same as the northern plains of the Lakotas, only harsher, more damaged, more inhospitable. Or was that too a caper of his mind, a coloration his homesickness gave to the things he saw? As he began to reason the thing, he noticed subtle differences. Even the Snake seemed bent on forging down a different corridor on some mysterious leg of an unknown journey, gathering its forces for one last twist through uncharted shoals of land before it mingled its waters with another unseen tributary beyond its borders.

"Two Fires should be back, then," said Malcolm. "If he found the Columbia."

"Oh, he's found it by now, bucko, and he'll be riding up soon to tell us about it."

"How do you know we're so close?"

"I can read maps and tell time, that's how."

That arrogance again. That sneer on Randy's face.

It would almost be worth it to pull the trigger and see it wiped out all of a sudden, Malcolm thought, to see McCord's look of surprise as the lead ball tore through his gut and cracked his spine. Let him smirk then. Let him gloat evermore in hell, the sonofabitch.

Something caught Malcolm's eye, and then he heard Red Bead's voice.

"Two Fires returns," she said. "His horse is wet."

Malcolm sat up, shaded his eyes. McCord did not move. He just widened his smile to a full smirk and sat on his horse as though he had no concern at all about Two Fires or any of them.

"Two Fires is wet too," Malcolm said in Lakota.

"So, the Columbia is closer than I figured," Mc-Cord said. "I knew it couldn't be far. Now, my fine friend, we have some decisions to make."

"I'm still trying to make up my mind whether to kill you or not."

"Oh, I think you've already made up your mind on that, Malcolm. We're right on the heels of that scalawag brother of yours, and I don't think you want to face him alone."

"What makes you think that?"

"Your conscience, for one thing. You'd have to live with yourself afterward, when you do kill him and you want someone who can defend your honor."

"I don't need any justification for what I do."

"If you ever want to go back to civilization, you do. Come now, laddie, put the rifle down and let's get on with the rest of the journey."

"Do not shoot him now," Red Bead said.

"Why should I not?"

"This is not a fight. It would be a killing without honor, my husband."

Malcolm eased the hammer back down. She was right. And maybe Randy was right too. Perhaps he did have a conscience. He wondered, though, if he would come to regret not killing McCord when he had the chance.

"That's better. Let's see what Two Fires has to say and then make our way to the Columbia. Oh, it won't be long now before you face your brother and come to terms with the brutal deaths of your loved ones."

"Shut up, Randy. I don't need any goading from you."

"Fine, now that that's settled, let us speak to our red friend and see what he has found."

Malcolm lay the rifle across the pommel of his saddle. McCord's eyes narrowed just before he turned away to look at Two Fires. There was a grim set to his jaw that neither Malcolm nor Red Bead could see.

Two Fires rode up slowly, his horse sleek and shiny wet. The Lakota's own breechclout was soaked through and his skin glistened with water. He signed to Malcolm before he stopped his horse and spoke to his white friend in Lakota.

"The big shining river is down there," he said. "That is where the Snake gives its water to the river you look for."

"That is good. Did you see anyone?"

"No. There is much sign. Many moccasin tracks and many tracks of deer and elk and birds and mice. It is a big river now that the Snake has come to it."

"We will go down it to the big water," Malcolm said.

"Did you have trouble with Red Hair?"

"We made some talk. There is no trouble."

"He looks two ways," said Two Fires. "His heart is bad."

"I know. He will not be with us for many more sleeps."

"Good."

They set out for the river, and when they came to it, McCord didn't even stop, but kept following its course. Malcolm wondered if his brother had come that way, if Jared had looked at these same waters. The river was wide and deep and appeared navigable by vessels with more draft than a canoe or dugout. Suddenly, Malcolm began to understand why the fur companies would want to explore this territory and set up trading posts. Here was a mighty river in the West where they could bring in men and supplies and load furs aboard for the world markets.

He imagined that the Columbia must have been a grand sight to Lewis and Clark on their expedition. As the waters from the Snake mingled with those of the Columbia, swirling whirlpools and antic eddies boiled on the surface, and Malcolm could almost feel the power in the river's depths, the surge and flex of its robust muscles beneath the surface.

He turned to Bead and saw that she was looking at the river too.

"Big," she said.

"Pretty," he replied, and she smiled.

"Perhaps we will find berries here," she said.

"Farther down we may find them."

He wondered, then, if McCord was ever going to stop so they could rest and enjoy this small victory after so long a journey. Two Fires was no longer ranging ahead but was riding wide on their right flank, several yards behind McCord. Red Bead followed behind Malcolm, leading the packhorses.

"When you are tired, I will take the packhorses," he told her.

"They are no trouble, but they want to drink. They keep trying to get to the river."

"I will talk to McCord."

Red Bead made a sound in her throat. It sounded almost like a growl.

McCord slowed his horse so that Malcolm could catch up to him. "We probably should think about building dugouts and going downriver on them," he said.

"What about the horses?"

"Two Fires and Bead can bring the horses overland."

"No. Where I go, Bead goes. The same goes for Two Fires."

"I was afraid you'd be that way. Well, it will take us a lot longer, but I suppose it can be done."

"It will have to be done."

"Then done it is," McCord said, almost cheerily.

"The horses are thirsty."

"By-and-by we will all drink."

He rode on ahead, and Malcolm wondered why the Scot hadn't kicked up more of a fuss. He usually wanted his way and got it. Randall was not one to back down from a wish or a whim. It had been too easy. Hardly any argument at all. No bitter words, no retort. He'd just given in. And that caused Malcolm to worry over what McCord had on his mind.

Red Bead Woman rode well ahead of McCord's small expedition, leaving her horse tied in their path so that she could forage on foot until they caught up with her. She found many of the plants she wanted and put them in a large deerskin bag she had brought along for that purpose. She wandered along a low ridge and saw a berry patch growing on a hillside. The bears had been into the brambles, but she managed to find many that had been overlooked or ripened since the last visit. She gathered the small blackberries until she filled her bag, then returned to where she'd staked her horse.

Malcolm was sitting in the shade of an alder when she walked up on him, his horse feeding next to hers with the packhorses. He did not get up when she approached.

"I found berries and sweet grasses and wild on-

ions," she said. "The grasses and onions will taste good
in my stew when I cook after the sun goes to sleep."

"Good. Does your heart soar?"

"It soars and sings," she said. "Like the lark on the
hillside."

"My heart is happy for you, Bead."

"Where is Red Hair and Two Fires?"

"They rode that way to find a place to camp." Malcolm pointed downriver.

"My heart would soar if we could stay here, you
and me."

"It would make Red Hair worry."

"I do not care about that man."

"Two Fires would come back for us."

"We could send him away."

Malcolm laughed. There was no wearing away at
Red Bead's logic. "We could do that."

She gave a little cry and then sighed as she sat
down next to him. She put her arm inside his and nes-
tled close to his side. He touched her hand, stroked it.

"Will we stay here?"

"For a while. There is no hurry. Two Fires said he
was going to catch some fish, and Red Hair said he
would hunt. They will wait for us."

She doubled up a fist and struck him on the arm.
"You tease Red Bead Woman."

"Only a little teasing," he said.

"I want you to tease me some more."

"What if I do not want to tease you?"

"Then I will tease you, Iron Hawk."

She withdrew her arm and began to tickle him. He
doubled over and began laughing. Then he tickled her,
and soon they were tumbling away from the tree, rolling in the grasses. Their laughter made the horses
twitch their ears and floated over the meadow like
shimmering bright streamers plucked from a rainbow.

Bead wriggled out of her buckskin dress, squirming away from Malcolm in seductive undulations. He crawled after her, his throat empty of laughter, taut with desire. She jumped up and ran into the trees like some wood nymph, her body golden in the sunlight, her dark hair glistening like a raven's wing down her back.

"Find me," she taunted, and Malcolm took up the chase, stripping out of his buckskin shirt, loosening the sash around his waist. He trailed clothing all the way to the trees, until he was clad only in moccasins.

"Where are you, Red Bead?" he asked in the silence of the grove.

She made a little sound in her throat, and his blood throbbed in his temples. He chased after the sound, but she was not there. He heard the patter of her feet on the ground, and turned to see her flash between the trees, lithe as a yearling fawn, her hair bouncing on her bare back like a lady's fine cloak of prime beaver. She trailed laughter behind her as he raced to cut her off in flight.

When he reached the spot where he thought she'd be, she was nowhere in sight. He paused to listen, but heard nothing. Then he heard what sounded like a dove cooing and turned to see her feet flying away, her body concealed by the underbrush.

"Wait," he called, and began to run after her.

"Catch me," she said, and disappeared behind the trees.

Malcolm ran after her and then saw her again, racing ever faster away from him.

"I'll catch you," he said, and bounded through the underbrush in hot pursuit.

Bead made a sharp turn, and Malcolm turned with her. She turned once again and he leaped forward, catching her on the run. She collapsed in his arms and let her body fall to the ground. Malcolm took up her weight and felt himself falling. She landed first, and he braced himself so that he would not crush her.

"Take me, take me," she whispered, her voice a soft husk. He felt the desire in him turn to a rush of flame, and he looked down into her eyes. They were glistening with lust, almost feral in their intensity.

"Yes," he said, and folded her in his arms, came down softly on top of her.

She opened to him and grabbed his manhood, jutting from his loins, guiding him to the thicket between her legs, opened to him like a flower, and he descended into her where their twin heats joined and enflamed them both. She cried soft sounds of bliss into his ears and her fingers clawed his back without the nails breaking the skin. He arched his back with the pleasure of her touch.

"It is good, my man," she breathed.

"Is is good, little bright Bead."

Her voice grew husky as he plumbed her depths, taking her slow and long through uncharted valleys of delight. She made little animal sounds in her throat, and he growled with her as the intensity of his passion rose like thunder out of the sacred Lakota hills inside him, his blood pounding in his ears and in his manhood until he was deafened by the awesome sound of it.

Sunlight streamed through the trees and long gauzy shadows stood in slanted pillars on his back as Malcolm covered Bead in the little glade where they mated like wild creatures in a timeless corner of the universe. Red Bead rose up against him, her body melding with his until they were just one being caught out of time with eternity blazing like a distant fire in the regions of their minds.

She rose up to meet him on that lofty pinnacle where only gods dwell, and they met there and fused until his seed exploded from its vessel and poured into her and she shuddered with the wondrous joy of it, caught up in the mindless splendor of a single burning moment that would last forever.

Malcolm shuddered too as his seed burst forth like creation's own and he became a god again, released from mortal bonds that stretched backward in time to Eden's lush gardens. In that one glorious split second of eternity there was no beginning and no end and all things were in harmony and always would be.

And finally the god spent himself and came down from the eternal mountain and was mortal once again.

Red Bead descended with him and they fell onto each other in wonder at where they had been and how high they had flown. She quivered in delicious after-spasms and clasped him inside her, leaving eternity in her wake, became some being washed up on the shore of a daydream, helpless and weak as a newborn child, but with the thunder of her man still throbbing between her legs like the echoes of deep-throated drums.

They lay there in the wash of the tide that had swept them to this forested shore and listened to the soft murmurs of their minds, dumbstruck with the awe-some grandeur of their secret illuminations.

McCord sat on a grassy sward near the Columbia River, a large stone for a backrest, watching Two Fires chipping a flint fishhook to make it sharper. The Lakota brave had his back turned to Randall as he hunched over with an elk antler in his hand, the fishhook on a flat rock. He held the hook down with his left hand and scraped small flakes of flint from the point.

The horses fed on grass a few yards away, switching their tails at flies.

McCord was glad that Red Bead had picked that day to go berry picking and that Malcolm had waited upstream for her. It gave him time to think things through. Watching Two Fires prepare to catch some fish had given him the answer he had been looking for over the past few days. The Sioux had already outlived his usefulness, and Randall wanted to keep cutting Malcolm's ties to the Lakota, bit by bit.

McCord smiled. He had already figured out how he was going to kill Two Fires and leave no trace of his deed.

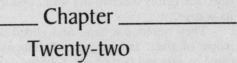

_____ Chapter _____
Twenty-two

J ared swung his rifle around as the dugout settled
into the current, its prow headed downstream.

"Get down," he yelled to Swan as he aimed the
rifle from his hip.

The lead Clatstop boat carried three braves, only
one of whom was paddling. The other two had arrows
nocked to their bowstrings and were pulling back to
shoot. The paddler sat in the prow. Jared figured he
would get the dugout closer, then swing the bow slightly
to give the other two a shot at him broadside.

Behind that dugout, four more craft raced to catch
up, two braves paddling in each one.

Jared knew his only hope was somehow to stop
that first boat by killing the paddler, gaining, he hoped,
enough time to reload. Otherwise he'd have to use his
pistol and the range would have to be very close for him
to hit a moving target when he himself was moving. His
dugout would not stay on a straight course for long
without his guidance.

"Can you load a rifle?" he asked Swan.

She shook her head.

"Try and keep the boat straight," he said. "But stay down."

A tall order, he knew. To his surprise, Swan picked up a paddle and, still hunched over, stuck it over the side. She gently touched the water and the boat held to its course.

They rounded a bend and glided into a wide expanse of river. Behind him, the dugouts in the rear came on fast and fanned out, forming a single line of six canoes, all bearing down on him with alarming speed.

He saw an arrow float toward him, deceptively slow, for it had great force behind it. It whizzed close enough for him to duck, and a lump of fear formed in his throat as he realized that he could die without being able to fire a shot. They were badly outnumbered, and the Clatsops seemed to be skilled oarsmen. He saw their sinewed arms bend and flex as they dipped their oars into the water with precision and perfect form.

More arrows flew toward them, one landing in the dugout, just barely missing Toomey, who cursed when he saw the arrow sticking out of a bundle of furs.

Swan sat up straight in the boat and began to paddle, but Jared knew it was too late. She couldn't outrun the pursuing dugouts.

"Swan, duck your head," he yelled, but she ignored him.

Jared cocked his rifle and waited until the nearest canoe was only a few yards away, then swung his rifle a few inches and squeezed the trigger as one of the oarsmen dissected his imaginary line of sight. The ball struck the brave in the side and he crumpled over, dropping his oar into the water. The Clatsop dugout swung partially off course and struck the bow of another, knocking it slightly out of line. But both canoes recovered quickly, even the one with but a single oarsman, which glided as silently and unerringly as a snake and began to close the distance.

Jared set his empty rifle down and drew one of his pistols from his belt. He brought the pistol up and fired at the nearest Clatsop from point-blank range. A dark stain spread across the Indian's bare chest and he fell backward, dropping his bow into the boat.

Two dugouts flanked them on both sides, and Jared drew his knife from its scabbard. Swan stood up and he saw an arrow sprout from her chest as if it had grown out of it. She looked at him one last time, a sadness on her face, a mist in her eyes, then pitched over the side of the dugout and disappeared beneath the water, trailing streamers of blood behind her that twisted in the water like coils of red ribbon. A Clatsop leaped into the boat and swung his war club in a downward arc. Jared flinched when he heard the stone strike Toomey's skull and crunch it to a bloody pulp. It sounded like a melon struck by a sixteen-pound maul. The bile rose in Jared's throat as he saw Toomey's brains leaking out of his skull like pudding boiling out of a kettle. Toomey had no face, only a mashed nose and a torn, twisted mouth that could no longer scream.

Jared grappled with one brave as another scrambled to grab him from behind. He and both of the braves fell into the water as he gulped in lungsful of air. He gripped the knife tightly in his hand as the cold water sent shivers through his flesh.

He felt the pull of the undercurrent, and when he opened his eyes he saw the two Clatsops flailing their arms underwater as they fought to climb to the surface. Jared swam for the nearest one and caught him by surprise. He shoved the knife into his belly, once, twice, and watched the dark blood spew out, the Indian writhing in pain and doubling over until he began to sink like a stone.

Jared kicked away from the dying man and swam

with the current, propelling himself away from the dark
underbellies of the dugouts and the spidery shadow of
the other Indian in the water. He held his breath as he
skimmed away just below the surface, then broke the
water, gulped in a deep breath, and dove under. He saw
at least three arrows streaking toward him in that brief
instant.

And, too, he saw the dugouts, the Clatsops
backpaddling to hold back. Circling like wolves, he
thought. Arrows nocked to bows, spears held like ancient javelins ready to hurl, the men all knew their prey
was underwater and would have to come up to breathe
or else drown.

Jared stopped swimming and drifted with the current. He wondered if the Clatsops could see him. He
did not move his arms or legs, but floated like a jellyfish
downstream, just below the surface. He vowed to make
them work at killing him. He would not make it easy for
them.

He drifted upward, tipping his head back. He
pushed up so that his face just barely emerged from the
water, letting the air out of his lungs and breathing
deeply before he ducked down and kicked away. He
heard a muffled shout just as he submerged, saw the
water boil as arrows knifed through the aqueous fabric,
lost momentum, and floated aimlessly away from him.
He swam with the current, across the stream to the
other side, making small kicks and pulling himself
through the water, expending little energy. He knew he
could not keep this pattern up for very long. But he
would keep them guessing and looking for him.

He saw a dark shadow pass above him, blocking
off the sunlight, and he followed beneath it, invisible to
those above. The dugout moved faster than he could,
though, and he soon lost his cover. But he saw the opposite bank, and knew he would have to draw in more
air.

Jared kicked away gently, turned belly up, and let his body float upward. When he was close to the surface, he lifted his head until it broke the water. He expelled the breath in his lungs and drew in fresh air. He had made hardly a sound, and now he sank again and twisted slowly in the water until he turned over on his stomach. He kicked and pulled himself down into the depths of the river and started toward the opposite bank, letting the current do most of the work so that his lungs didn't burn the oxygen so fast.

He saw the shadow of the last dugout pass over him as he hung there, paddling to slow himself down. He knew that those above could not see him, but his lungs were starting to burn again, and he couldn't make another traverse of the river before drawing in a fresh breath.

He waited as long as he could stand it, then surfaced, blowing out dead air before inhaling again. He saw the stern of one of the dugouts disappear downstream and felt some relief. Still, knowing he wasn't out of danger yet, he arched his back and dove under, his eyes still open for any sight that spelled danger.

That's when he saw Swan float toward him from upstream, her eyes strangely open, an arrow sticking from her breast, her mouth smiling in rictus, chilling him to the bone. Her arms and legs moved as if she were alive, and Jared stared at her, transfixed, visions of his sister oddly superimposed over the floating figure of Swan.

But when his sister died, she hadn't moved and there had been no smile on her face. Only shadows under the closed eyes, lips tightly shut as if she was still in agony. It was almost too much to bear, seeing Swan float past him like some blood-drained wraith and thinking of his sister dead so young, gone forever from the world, but never from his heart. For a moment he forgot the danger, that he was being hunted by men who wanted to kill him, and how he wanted to strike out blindly at each one and smash them as they came for him, whether he go down to death or emerge triumphant in blood drawn from their torn bodies.

He almost choked underwater and rose to the surface again. This time he took several breaths before he submerged again, but could not blot out the image of Swan, and when he went under, he looked for her, as if she might still be alive and just waiting for him to swim alongside her. The temptation to join her was so strong, he considered letting his lungs empty out and then breathing in the water, breathing it in until he joined the darkness of the deep and floated with her to wherever her young body would find rest.

He saw her body again, not far away, as if she'd waited for him, and once more he felt a chill at the sight as she began to turn slowly in the current until she faced him. He felt as if his chest was bound in iron straps as claustrophobia overcame him. He could no longer look at Swan, with her grinning face and her eyes wide open as if in accusation. She'd been in his care and now she was dead. He felt responsible, as if he hadn't done enough to preserve her life. He'd taken her away from her people, albeit her captors, and now she was dead. He fought the water, flailing to propel himself to the surface, and as he swam upward, he felt the powerful pull of the current, as if the river wanted him to join Swan in her watery tomb. Panic gripped him as his claustrophobia strengthened. He shot to the surface, spat out water and stale air, filled his lungs deeply. The pines and spruce swam in a dizzying circle as he swirled in a half circle as though trying to leap from the water and escape its clutches.

He swam hard for shore then, weighed down by his buckskins, and when he reached the bank, his muscles throbbed and he was breathing hard. He crawled up out of the water, a sodden creature, the panic in him subsiding slowly as he reached firm ground.

Light-headed, giddy, it took Jared several moments to get his bearings. He lay facedown until his head cleared, then he turned over and slowly looked around. He tilted his head, gazed up at the sky, and saw the rainclouds gathering as they had almost every afternoon on the western horizon. He stared down at the flowing river, shuddered at the thought of Swan floating beneath the surface. It seemed like a dream as he sat in the sunlight, watching the birds fly overhead and disappear in the trees. Fish broke water, salmon, he supposed, and his thoughts were jarred as he thought of her body slowly decomposing, teeth sawing at her mortified flesh, fish and muskrats, other creatures, tearing her apart bit by bit until there was nothing left of her but bones turned to dusty silt.

Jared knew, without thinking it through, that he could not leave Swan down there in the river. She deserved better, and he'd hoped to make a good life for her, learn from her, teach her. He might even in time have grown to love her, and she might have come to love him. But there was more to it than that. Swan represented something else to him, he was sure of that. She was his lost sister, the woman she might have become had she lived, and she was his own small child to raise as a father would raise. Yes, he had tasted her, made love to her, but that was only part of it. From the moment he first saw her, he knew that Swan meant something more than a sleeping dictionary, a woman to warm his blankets. He saw her as a young girl on the threshold of womanhood. He saw a chance to change the past in a small way, create something alive and beautiful out of death and ugliness.

Now she too was gone. Like his sister, like his mother. And somehow he felt responsible for all their deaths. He should have been able to see far enough ahead to prevent each of them from dying, he thought. He would have been able to save them had he not been so wrapped up in himself, so blind to what might happen.

It took but a moment for these thoughts to race through his mind, and then Jared was in the river again, diving down, searching with burning eyes for Swan's body, hoping he was not too late. Caught in between his thoughts was a nagging hope that she was still alive, that he'd been wrong, that he would find her and be able to bring her back to life.

He fought against the urge to see if he could breathe underwater, and he knew the thought was connected to Swan, a wild and insane belief that she could breathe like a fish.

He saw her then, underwater, caught on brush that grew out of the bank, and his heart sank like a stone. Her body swayed back and forth in the current, slack and limp, her dress clinging to her, that accursed arrow protruding from her chest. He swam toward her quickly, tore her from the branch, and bore her in his arms to the surface, gulping air as he kicked himself toward the bank. She seemed so light in the water, and he tried to keep her head up, knowing it was an insane thing to do, but wanting to give her every chance to breathe in air, to come alive again, as if his will could force her to come back and laugh in his face and smile a real smile at him, not that hideous false grin that was only something death had given her, some final mocking irony meant to torment him, to taunt him for letting her die, for failing to save her life, even if he had to give up his own.

He struggled to get her up on the bank, and finally laid her there. He crawled up beside her and lifted her torso, pushing the arrow through her body with one hard shove with the palm of his hand. He took her away, beyond the river and into the trees, to a spot none could see from the Columbia, only the hawks and eagles as they hunted along the river.

He lay her beneath a stately pine and touched his belt. His knife was still in its scabbard. He knelt down and closed her eyes, pushed her lips over her teeth until she appeared to be sleeping. He smoothed her hair and wiped her face dry until he began to weep. Biting back the tears, Jared turned away from her so that he could do what had to be done, so that he could find Pettibone and Gray Cat and regain what was left of his sanity.

Jared marked out a square plot of earth with the point of his knife and began digging. He chopped at the soil and the grass and scraped out a shallow grave, piling earth at the sides and ends until it was deep enough to hold Swan's body. He sat and rested for a time, then turned to look at her one last time. Rigor had begun to freeze her features, and she appeared to be sleeping peacefully.

"Swan. Good-bye. Rest in peace, good woman."

With that, Jared picked her up and placed her in the grave. He started putting the soil on her, beginning at her feet. When he got to her face, his throat tightened up and he felt tears sting his eyes. He clamped his teeth tightly and gently poured soil over her face until it disappeared. When he used up all the dirt and grass that he'd dug up, he began piling rocks atop the mound of soil. When the grave was completely covered, he cut spruce boughs and placed these over the rocks until he could no longer see any stone showing through, only green bowers covering Swan's final resting place. He thought it was the most beautiful grave he'd ever seen.

He didn't place any headstone, nor blaze a tree to mark the spot where he'd buried Swan. He wanted to remember it, but he never wanted to come back to this place of death again. Swan belonged now to the earth and the sky, to the heavens where he hoped her spirit would go, where perhaps one day he would rejoin her.

He bowed his head and said a simple prayer, as if to assure that her spirit would not die even though she was not a Christian, as if to give her the best possible chance in the next world.

"God, if you're there, take this young innocent woman's soul and keep it safe in heaven. She was took too young and she deserves better. Amen."

Jared did not look back, but walked to the river and headed downstream. He didn't care if he encountered the Clatsops, he'd had enough of running. He was ready to fight if need be, with bare hands, his knife, whatever it took to kill the men who had killed Swan.

Sunlight played on the softly boiling waters of the Columbia as he walked next to it, watching it eddy and swim seaward, flat and featureless on a wide bend. When he rounded the bend, he heard gunfire and saw canoes overturning way downstream. He saw men in the water swimming for shore, and a large boat filled with riflemen shooting. Jared could hear the shouts of white men, the shrieks of Indians.

Jared began to run, and he could feel his heart in his chest and the wind threading his hair. He wanted to fly to that place and draw blood and praise those men in the boat who had put the Clatsops to rout and begun to avenge Swan's death, to exact an eye for an eye, a tooth for a tooth. But he could only run and curse the distance that kept him from exulting in the deaths of those who had killed Swan and clubbed Toomey to death.

"I'm coming," he yelled. "Save some of the bastards for me!"

Jared saw Pettibone stand up in the dugout and take aim with his rifle. He tracked the path of the ball with his eyes, and when he saw a Clatsop on the bank throw up his hands and pitch forward, Jared yelled in triumph and raised a victory fist in the air as if he himself had done the deed. He knew all would be well, that

Swan's death would not go unanswered. In that moment, he saw her smile as she had while alive, and his heart began to swell until he could hear it pounding in his ears like a primitive drum. Then he realized that he was hearing another sound. It was the sea, and when he looked beyond the boat on the river, he saw the Pacific all a-dazzle in the sunlight, even as the dark clouds pushed in and began to close down the light as the rifles kept popping and white clouds of smoke billowed from a dozen guns and the water around Pettibone's and Gray Cat's dugouts ran crimson with blood.

_____ Chapter _____
Twenty-three

M alcolm stood before the tree and read the legend that had been carved into the bark. The impressions were new, no more than a few days old. The gashes had not yet lost their pristine look. Fresh sap oozed from the slashes, and they were not discolored.

JARED FLYNN and underneath: _Apr 1811_.

McCord looked at the blaze too, and made a noise in his throat.

"My brother was here. Just days ago by the freshness of the cuts."

"We're not far behind," McCord said.

"What do the talking marks say?" Red Bead asked in Lakota.

"My brother's name and the month he was here," Malcolm replied. "A few sleeps ago."

"That is good," she said. "Soon you will find him."

"Yes."

"Be a lot quicker if we stopped and built a couple of dugouts. Plenty of cedar here." McCord gave Malcolm a piercing look. "We could catch up with him in jig time."

"Whatever you say," Malcolm replied. A strange feeling came over him when he looked at Jared's blaze again. He put his hand on the lettering and felt the grooves. This was the first contact he'd had with his brother in years. It was as if Jared was trying to reach out to him, and he could almost feel his presence as his fingers touched where the knife had cut out his name.

He stepped back from the tree and looked at his brother's name again. So you were here, he thought. A week ago, or less. It seemed to Malcolm that Jared had branded the tree to taunt him, to let him know that he knew his brother would catch up to him someday and exact payment in kind for the deaths of his father, mother, and sister. "Well, little brother," Malcolm whispered to himself, "you're going to get your wish."

"How long do you figure it will take to make a couple of dugouts?" he asked McCord.

"Three days at the most. Having the boats will save us a couple of weeks."

"I'll help you on one condition," Malcolm said.

"I'll consider it."

"We leave the horses, take what we can with us. Bead goes with me, you take Two Fires with you."

"I suppose we could cache the goods we can't take with us. Or we could build big-enough dugouts to take it all."

"I would go along with that, Randy."

"I've brought along felling axes and adzes. If we got started now, we'd be on the river by this time in seventy-two hours."

"Let's have at it, then."

"To be sure, laddie. Pick out your tree. I'll do the same for my boat."

"No cottonwoods here."

"The cedar are pretty thick. Probably better than pine."

"I've built pine dugouts before."

"So have I," McCord said, "but I rather think the indigenous Indians use the cedar."

"How do you know that?" Malcolm asked.

"Perhaps I heard it somewhere," McCord said cryptically. Actually, he had learned of cedar dugouts in St. Louis from trappers who'd crossed the Rockies and visited the native Salish tribes. They spoke of cedar canoes that were easy to make.

The two men unpacked bundles and dug out axes and adzes. They each selected a large tree-felling axe and set out with rifles slung over their shoulders to explore the forest. Malcolm explained to Red Bead what they were going to do and told her to set up camp with Two Fires and wait for them. They would come back for the horses and drag the felled trees to the camp so they'd be near the river when they finished their work.

"I will catch fish for supper," Two Fires said. He pointed to a place upstream where the water ran fast over boulders and pooled out below. "I see a good spot up there."

"Good," Malcolm said. "After you help Bead set up camp."

Two Fires snorted. "Woman's work."

"We all do what must be done," Malcolm said, as he had many times before. "Just help her unload what we need. She can put up the tents and build the cook fire."

"I will do this," Two Fires said, but he did not seem happy about his concession.

"Let's get to it," McCord said impatiently. The two men walked into the forest and separated.

Malcolm did not have to go far before he found a large, tall cedar. He walked around it, going over the procedure in his mind, determining the work he'd have to do before it was ready to drag back to camp. The tree was uniform in size, which would make it easier to work with, its girth well-rounded for a considerable length. It had many branches growing close to the ground, so he began to trim at its base. When he stopped, he heard the ring of McCord's axe somewhere farther on.

He selected a location to fell the tree so it would land cleanly and be easy to hook up to the horses. When he was finished with the trimming, he made his notches, then, after removing his buckskin shirt, began to wield the axe. The work made him feel good as he cut into the soft cedar bark, gouging out chunks of wood, exposing the red heart beneath. The tree seemed enormously thick, and the deeper he cut into it, the more he knew he'd made a good selection. They would have a good-sized dugout when he was finished with it, and could carry considerable weight inside its hull.

He made sure to make his prime cut even, and gradually deepened it at a good angle so it would fall cleanly and not kick out when it gave way over the previously cut notch on the opposite side. His muscles seemed to sing as he swung the axe, and soon he was gleaming with sweat. He listened to McCord's axe bites and made a silent and private contest out of it. He timed McCord's strokes with his own and tried to increase his speed to beat the Scotsman in felling his tree. The game made the work more enjoyable to him.

When the cut was very deep, he heard the tree groan, and he knew it would not take many more strokes to bring it down. He rested for a few moments and realized the woods had grown quiet. He knew McCord was resting too, for he hadn't heard his tree crash to the ground. Malcolm hefted the axe once again and put his full weight behind the swing. The axe bit deeper and deeper, and then the tree swayed toward the opposite notch. Malcolm stepped back and waited.

The tree did not fall, although it had begun to
lean. He wiped his hands on his buckskin trousers until
they were dry and then looked at his cut. One more
swing ought to do it, he figured. He found the precise
spot to make the last bite, and swung the axe as far
back as it would go, then hurled himself into the final
blow, inward and downward. The axe smashed into the
tree, then the tree groaned as if in agony, beginning to
lean. Malcolm stepped back and to the side, in case it
kicked out when it broke at the cut. The tree began to
fall toward the ground. He looked up at its top and saw
it start to pick up speed, leaning more and more as its
weight shifted and gravity exerted its pull.

The huge cedar did not kick out, but broke perfectly at the notch. Malcolm stepped back even farther
to watch the death of the giant and felt his heart jump
when it crashed to the ground, sending up a cloud of
dust, its branches smashing into the earth and cracking
under the impact. He knew McCord would be able to
hear its thunder, and he smiled.

The tree settled and was silent. Malcolm walked its
length proudly and then took up the axe and began to
trim the branches from the bottom upward. He knew
he'd have to hook up the horses and roll it to get the
branches underneath, but he worked quickly, walking
up the trunk, taking off branches cleanly until the trunk
grew smooth behind him.

Halfway up the tree's length, he heard McCord's
tree go down with a resounding crash. Then the woods
were silent for a time. He waited until he heard Mc-
Cord begin trimming, then turned back to his own task,
striding up the trunk with the axe, still sharp enough for
that work, taking off the branches at the bark.

When he'd gone high enough, Malcolm jumped
down from the tree and walked up one side, taking off
branches as close to the ground as possible, then he did
the same back down the other side. He stepped back to

survey his work, and the tiredness in his muscles became evident. The axe weighed heavy in his hands when he set it down, and he sat under a tree to rest for a few moments before attacking the top end of the tree to separate it from the part he would need for the dugout.

The sun was falling off in the sky, and he wondered if he could finish such a daunting task before dark. Probably not, he decided. But he'd do as much as he could, then bring the horses up early in the morning. Two Fires could help him, and then they could go after McCord's tree.

Malcolm heard footsteps and looked up. "Speak of the devil," he said.

"Were you talking about me?" McCord asked, the familiar half smile on his face.

"Thinking of you."

"Have you quit, laddie?"

"No, just resting before I top that sonofabitch."

"Hmmm." McCord walked around the tree as if inspecting Malcolm's work. Then he returned.

Malcolm stood up, grabbing the handle of his axe. "Well?" he asked. "Does the tree meet with your approval."

"It will do," McCord said. "Think you can finish topping it before dark?"

"I'm going to try. How are you doing?"

"Still trimming away. Not far to go. I think we'll have two dugouts big enough to carry all the goods downriver with us."

"I don't believe I've ever seen a cedar grow this big," Malcolm said.

"I'm sure there are some bigger."

"I thought I'd bring the horses up early in the morning, haul this one back to camp, then come and help you finish up."

"I should be ready by the time you finish doing that."

"Well, back to work."

McCord said nothing and left. Malcolm was glad to see him go. He was sure that his cedar was bigger than Randy's, and it gave him a feeling of perverse pleasure to know he'd bested the Scotsman.

Malcolm stood away from the tree and swung the axe downward. This would be the hardest part of all, he knew. He would have to make a cut wide enough so his axe wouldn't get caught in the crack. It was harder to attack it from top to bottom rather than with a side swing.

He cut two sides for his notch at an eighty-degree angle, which allowed him a clean downward swing. The top would be the hardest, he knew, but he'd try and cut into two sides deep enough first. If necessary, he'd have to drive a wedge into the bottom part to break the tree in two where it rested on the ground.

It was hard work, the hardest of the day, and Malcolm took only brief rests to catch his breath. He went as far as he could on one side, then walked around to the other. He wished he had a good crosscut saw and another man on one end of it. The work would have gone much faster. In fact, it would already have been done. Mindlessly, he delivered blow after blow to the new side until he had cut as deep as he could. The chunks were not coming out as easily as before, and he knew it was time to climb up on the log again and attack from the top down. By then he would have to drive a wedge to separate the top from the trimmed trunk.

His cut on the top was considerably wider, double the width of the axe blade, but it could not be helped. He still had enough tree left to make a good, long, deep dugout. He was blessedly tired as the forest began to darken, and he knew the sun would set before he finished. But he was far enough along, he thought, so that it should not take more than an hour to finish the next morning.

Malcolm picked up his rifle and slung it over his shoulder, leaving the axe leaning against the felled tree. The light began to fade quickly as he walked back to the river, but the sky was smeared with daubs of salmon and purple and he stopped to look at it, feeling, as always, an inner peace within himself. He heard no other sound as he walked back through the woods, and wondered if McCord had already gone back to camp.

McCord did not go directly to camp, but headed upstream, walking quietly, rifle in hand. He left long before the sun began to set, for he had something to do. When he caught sight of the river, he hunkered down and began to step very carefully so as to make no sound.

Two Fires sat next to the river, dangling a line with a flint hook, a piece of bright cloth attached to it. He was intent on the fishing and did not hear McCord come up behind him. Several small salmon lay on a bed of cut grasses behind him, each gutted, their rainbow colors fading.

McCord took the last few steps and was very close to Two Fires when the Lakota landed a salmon. The fish bolted and jerked the line taut. Two Fires pulled back and then turned at the sound Randall made as he stood up. Just as Two Fires saw him, McCord smashed the butt of his gun into the Lakota's mouth. There was a loud crunching sound as Two Fires's teeth broke and his nose caved in. Blood spurted from his face. McCord dropped the rifle and closed on Two Fires with his bare hands.

The Scotsman grabbed Two Fires by the throat and shut off the air in his windpipe. He bent him over backward and twisted him around until he straddled his waist at the back. He forced the Indian's head down-

ward into the water, holding it under as Two Fires
fought for his life. But McCord was powerful, and he
had the advantage of his weight pinning the Indian
down. Two Fires struggled for a few moments and then
stopped kicking. McCord held his head underwater for
several additional seconds to make sure, then released
his grip and sat back on the Indian's buttocks. Two
Fires did not move. His head rocked gently in the water. He was no longer bleeding.

McCord got to his feet, grabbed Two Fires by the
collar, and shoved him into the river. He watched as the
body floated downstream, sinking as it went. He knew it
would float past the camp, since there were no rocks to
impede it. With luck, it would wash downstream and
never be found.

He washed his hands in the river and retrieved his
rifle. Then he walked back into the woods and took
another path to the camp. Malcolm was there with Red
Bead when he arrived, just as the sun was setting. The
fire put an orange glow on Malcolm's face.

"What took you so long?" Malcolm asked.

"I worked until I could no longer see."

"About finished?"

"About. You?"

"I've almost got the top separated. Finish in the
morning."

"Good. What's for supper?"

"Two Fires is catching some fish. He should be
back any minute now."

Red Bead had set a kettle of water on to boil, and
steam rose from it. She had another smaller kettle filled
with herbs and roots sitting on rocks inside the fire ring.
In a skillet, she had made a kind of bannock that was
warming on the side.

"Two Fires should be here now," Red Bead said to
Malcolm.

"Maybe I should go to look for him."

"No. I will go. You are tired, my husband."

"I might smoke a pipe. Tell him to come back."

"I will do that," she said.

Red Bead left the campground and headed upstream.

"Where's she going?" McCord asked.

"To bring Two Fires back." Malcolm got out his pipe and tobacco pouch. He offered some to McCord, who shook his head.

McCord sat down some distance from the fire but did not look into it. He kept his rifle close by his side. They did not speak after Malcolm lighted his pipe. Soon they heard the sound of Red Bead returning, on the run. Malcolm sat up straight, peered into the darkness beyond the fire.

Red Bead had several salmon in her skirt, which she dumped by the fire.

"Two Fires is gone," she said in Lakota, slightly out of breath.

"What?"

"He is not fishing by the river. I found these. Something has happened to him."

"What's going on?" McCord asked innocently.

Malcolm gave him a sharp look. "Bead says Two Fires is not there."

"What do you mean—not there?"

"He's gone. Vanished. Those are the fish he caught."

"Well, we'd better go looking for him."

"McCord, do you know anything about this?"

McCord drew himself up straight and looked at Malcolm indignantly.

"How dare you, sir!"

"It's mighty funny. We'd never find him in the dark."

"Perhaps he had an accident," McCord offered. "Fell in the river."

"He was too smart for that."

"Well, I'm at a loss. We can either wait for him or look for him. You tell me."

Malcolm spoke to Red Bead for several moments in Lakota, while McCord kept silent.

"I do not trust Red Hair," she said.

"I do not trust him either. Do you think he killed Two Fires?"

"I do not know. Two Fires is not here. I did not hear any sound from a thunder stick. I did not see any sign that there was a fight. Just the fish by the river. I did not find his hook or his string."

"We will look for him in the morning if he does not come back."

"Yes. There is nothing we can do now. I will cook the fishes and we will eat. Do not argue with Red Hair. Just watch him. He might have rubbed out Two Fires and he might rub you out."

"Tomorrow, we will go to the place where Two Fires was catching fish and see if we can tell what happened to him. Do you think he could have fallen into the river?"

"No," Red Bead said. "No more than I think that he flew away like a bird."

"I think you are right," Malcolm replied.

The tobacco no longer tasted good to him, and he put out his pipe to save the remainder for later.

"Well, what did you and your squaw decide?" McCord asked.

"She ain't no squaw, McCord. She's going to cook our supper and we'll look for signs of Two Fires in the morning, when we can see."

"You do not think he will return before then?"

Malcolm's eyes narrowed to slits as he looked at the Scotsman.

"No, Randy. I don't think Two Fires will ever return. And neither do you."

Chapter Twenty-four

Jared looked at the dead bodies floating in the river, the ones on shore. Pettibone, his face blackened by powder blowback, grinned at him as he set the dugout to shore.

Gulls wheeled in the sky overhead, and from a distance he heard the scree-cries of shore birds. Buzzards had already begun to flock on the horizon, riding the air currents toward the human carrion lying on the bank and floating in the river.

"I want to look at the bodies of the dead Indians," Jared said.

"Why?"

"There's something I have to know."

"We can come back later today. I want to make some smoke with our saviors first."

"I guess we owe them some thanks, all right."

"Climb in, son. You missed a hell of a fight."

"So I see. Who's in the boat?"

"Alex Ross, some of the other men. Looky yonder. The *Tonquin*'s a-settin' in harbor, ready to sail tomorry."

"Tomorrow?"

"That's what they say. Come on. Where's Swan?"

"She's dead. Toomey too."

"Damn. Mighty sorry, Jared. We wondered what had happened. Didn't see your canoe, and then these others come down and we got into a scrap. Thought you might have gotten kilt up yonder."

"I was lucky."

"Lost your rifle, eh?"

"Damned near everything."

Jared climbed into the dugout. Gray Cat sat in the middle, reloading his rifle.

"So, Astor's bunch are here already?"

"Know what date this is?"

"No."

"The thirty-first of May in the year of our Lord eighteen hunnert and eleven."

"We made good time."

"I reckon."

They paddled over to the boat, a small sloop like a bullboat, with a center mast. The name *Dolly* was painted on the sides of the hull. The men in the boat cheered as Jared waved to them, beckoned for them to follow them back to the mouth of the Columbia.

"How are they doing?" Jared asked.

"I don't know. They look pretty wore out to me. We didn't have much time to talk. Them Clatsops were fair frettin' for a fight, and these boys were ready for 'em. Saw me and them others and came sailin' up to us, rifles spoutin' smoke. A sight to see."

"Well, we can sort it all out."

He saw the *Tonquin* at harbor a few moments later when they beached. He saw signs that some building had been going on and an indication of more to come. There was a log fort set on a foundation that seemed not quite finished, but serviceable, kegs and barrels scattered everywhere, tents set up. Men were still unloading cargo from the *Tonquin,* sending the empty boat back as another arrived. Other men were dragging timber in from the thick woods. These men were haggard and drooping. He heard the ring of axes from within the forest, and angry curses floated on the air. The men he saw looked morose, and he wondered why. He noticed they were all armed and seemed wary of him and Pettibone, but especially of Gray Cat.

"Do you know Ross?" Pettibone asked.

"I've heard of him. Don't know him. What's he doing here?"

"I haven't had a chance to speak to him, but saw him during the fight. Capable man, Ross."

"That's what I heard."

"Let's go make some smoke with him."

"Gray Cat, you stay close to us," Jared said.

"What do you know about Ross?" Pettibone asked as they approached the boat where Alexander Ross was disembarking.

"I know he used to be a schoolteacher. Well-educated."

"Yes, he taught in Canada. He's with Astor now."

Ross waved to them as they came up on him. "Pettibone? Is that you?"

"Howdy, Alexander. Thanks for saving our hides."

"We're getting pretty used to Indian fighting here at Astoria."

"Astoria?"

Ross laughed dryly. He was a small, wiry man who seemed very neat and fastidious. He had wiped his face and neatened his hair after the battle and was now straightening his clothes as if entering a rich man's parlor. Jared almost laughed, but understood the man's need to maintain dignity. A schoolteacher. But apparently a fighter as well.

"So, you named this place after Astor," Pettibone said.

"And who's this young lad?"

"Jared Flynn, Alex."

Ross and Flynn shook hands.

"Let's find a place where we can talk. Where did you come from?"

"We come in at the Snake," Pettibone said as they walked to a little hillock overlooking the new fort, which itself was on a risen point of land overlooking the harbor. Jared estimated that the passage through the inlet was about twelve miles from where they were. He could see the breakers foaming at the bar in the distance. Seabirds filled the sky, and sandpipers, killdeer, and other shorebirds raced along on spindly legs at the water's edge.

"Surprised you didn't run into any of us along the way. Some of us just got back around mid-month."

"We did run into one of you," Jared said. "A carpenter named Toomey."

"Toomey? Lord, he was one of the first to land at this terrible place. We never found the bodies of any of the others."

"Well, Toomey's dead too," Jared said. "Killed just this morning."

"Ah, it's been that kind of a trip," Ross said, sitting down on a tuft of sawgrass. Jared, Pettibone, and Gray Cat sat down nearby, where they could all see their host. Hundreds of hummingbirds flitted around them, trying to drink from the red beads and porcupine quills on their buckskins and possibles pouches. Gray Cat wore an amused grin on his face.

"Fraught with perils at every turn."

"You've come a far piece," Pettibone said.

"The *Tonquin*'s log shows more than twenty-one thousand miles from New York. I gather you're trappers. From Montreal?"

"We're Nor'westers," Jared proclaimed proudly.

"Well, that's to be expected, I suppose. It's a wonder you weren't killed by the Chinooks. We've had our fill of them, lost several men the other day. A treacherous lot."

"We traded with 'em," Pettibone said. "Didn't have no trouble. Them was Clatsops what chased us down to your boat."

"Well, none is to be trusted."

"When did you get here?" Jared asked, curious about this quiet, scholarly man who seemed to fit well into the wilderness.

"Those of us here disembarked on the twelfth of April, thirty-three persons, all British subjects excepting three. Some were Sandwich Islanders. We were relieved to be ashore after that long and tedious voyage, and to escape from the tyranny of Captain Thorn, a sullen and despotic man. But that day we landed was not one of pleasure, but of labor. The misfortune we had in crossing the fatal bar had deadened our sensibilities and cast a melancholy gloom over our most sanguine expectations.

"We cleared away brush and rotten driftwood for a spot to encamp on. Duncan McDougal, an old Nor'wester whom you may know, assumed command in the absence of Mr. Hunt."

"Duncan McDougal's an ass," Jared said.

"Not fit to lead any man," Pettibone said.

"True, true. A most ordinary man, with an irritable, peevish temper. I was most depressed that Mr. Hunt, whom Mr. Astor holds in the highest confidence, was not our leader. Can you imagine how it was? Look out there at those rocky shores, those breakers on the bar rolling in wild confusion, closing our view on the west, and to the east it's as wild and uncommon a land as I've ever beheld. And look toward the south to that grand and magnificent forest stretching for miles upon miles. It seemed a most inauspicious place to settle, even though it's on a point of land having a very good harbor, where vessels not exceeding two hundred tons burden might anchor within fifty yards of shore. We call it Point George."

Jared followed Ross's arm as it swept the surrounding country.

"It looks powerful rough," Jared said. "Big trees in there."

"Some of them are fifty feet in girth, and grow so close together and mingled with rocks, it made our labors difficult. We worked with axe in one hand and gun in the other, the former for attacking the woods, the latter for defense against the savage hordes that were constantly prowling about. We toiled from sunrise till sunset, from Monday till Saturday; and during the nights, we kept watch without intermission."

"You had fights with the Indians?" Jared asked.

"Not at first. The natives seemed most friendly, no doubt because we gave them trifling presents from time to time. Later we were to discover that they were sly and treacherous, not to be trusted."

"What did you do after you cleared a place to camp?" Jared asked.

"The frame of a coasting vessel to be named the *Dolly* was brought out on board the *Tonquin,* and we brought her ashore, set her in the clearing. The carpenters worked to fit her up for immediate service; the smallness of her size, only thirty tons, rendered her useless for any purpose but that of navigating the Columbia."

"That was the boat you were on?"

Ross nodded. "It took us nearly two months of hard labor to clear less than an acre of ground, during which time three of our men were killed by natives, two more wounded by the felling of trees, and one had his hand blown off by gunpowder."

" 'Pears to me you had a bad time of it," Pettibone

said, pulling his pipe from his possibles pouch. He offered tobacco to Ross, who brought out his own pipe.

"Thank you, Pettibone," Ross said, taking the tobacco and filling his bowl. Jared took out his own pipe and offered tobacco to Gray Cat, who took some, offering a portion to the four directions before filling his own small clay pipe.

"I must get back to work," Ross said, "but I will tell you while I smoke my pipe that it wasn't the labor that tried us. We were prepared for that and knew it would be hard in such a land. No, it was the neglect and ill-treatment that we bore that aroused our feelings, set them in full revolt against the conditions we were forced to undergo."

"You mean McDougal?" Jared asked, holding the magnifying glass to his pipe.

"McDougal, yes, but we suffered greatly from the humidity. Those Sandwich Islanders you see down there are used to a drier atmosphere than this. They buckled under at the intense damp heat that saturated our bodies, our clothes, our very minds. And the fogs that rolled in hugged the shore, dampened our locks, our powder, our tools, our souls. Fogs and sleet were frequent, and if they were not enough to fill our hearts with despair, there has been the constant rain, every other day, at least."

"We had rain near most ever' day," Jared admitted, pulling on his pipe. The others had gotten their pipes to smoke despite the high humidity of the afternoon. "I never seen so much wetness."

"Aye," Ross said, "and we had no tents or shelter for some time. The food was terrible. We subsisted solely on boiled fish and wild roots. We had no salt and had to depend on the natives for our daily supply, which was far from being regular. Half of our men were constantly on the sick list, and more than once I have seen the whole party so ill that scarcely one could help the other."

"You should have had better rations than those," Jared said. "There is plenty of game in this country, and you must have brought provisions from New York, or at least from the Sandwich Islands."

"I lay a great deal of the blame on the conduct of Mr. Astor. Firstly, he did not send out a medical man with the expedition, and secondly, by choosing that great pasha, McDougal, as head of his affairs."

"Mighty niggardly of him, I'd say," Pettibone said, expelling a cloud of blue smoke into the heavy damp air. It seemed to hang there like a mist even after it broke up on the sea zephyrs that plied the coast.

"I probably shouldn't be telling you all these things, you being the competition, but it's a relief to get some of this off my chest. I trust you will keep what I tell you in confidence."

"Of course we will," Jared said. Hummingbirds darted about them like bullets. Gray Cat tried to catch one or two, then gave up. They were just too fast for him.

"We were forced to stand watch by night, do hard labor by day, and such was the state of affairs that we were reduced by sickness and discontent to a ragged gaggle of men constantly plotting and planning how to escape from this hell and cross the continent overland."

"You would have found it hard going," Pettibone said.

"Aye, I'm quite sure of that. I tell you this so that you will know how it has been with us. Some of the men formed a party and confronted McDougal, begging for relief. They were rebuffed, even though they had hoped they would be able to open his eyes to our plight. Rather, things got worse. A second deputation proved equally unsuccessful. At last four men deserted and had proceeded eighty miles upriver when they were laid hold of by the Indians and kept in a tent; nor would the stern and crafty chief of the tribe deliver them up until he had received a ransom for them."

"Did McDougal then realize the seriousness of your situation?" Jared asked.

Ross shook his head. "It was not until six more men deserted and were captured by the friendly chief Comecomly, who, realizing that there was gain to be had, attached himself to our small settlement. After a suitable ransom was paid and the deserters returned, McDougal began to see the error of his ways. He had been a tyrant and suddenly changed for the better. He saw to it that tents were distributed among the sick and more attention was paid to their diet."

"Still, you had no medical officer," Pettibone said.

"Aye, that is sadly true," Ross replied, blowing smoke at a hovering hummingbird eyeing a red feather in his cap. "Mr. Astor was most derelict in not providing a medical officer either for his ship or his infant colony."

"But things got better," Jared said.

"On the surface, but there were still feuds and petty grievances among ourselves, arising from the hardships, but we began to feel a sense of common danger and we realized that unless we stopped bickering and joined forces, we would be unable to oppose a common enemy."

"Sounds to me like you was the enemy," Pettibone said.

"Aye, that we were. It was then that we began to hear rumors from every quarter and suspicious appearances by strange Indians who promptly disappeared began to work their toll. We thought that perhaps the distant tribes had gotten word of us and were forming some dark design of cutting us off."

"Where did these rumors come from?" Jared asked.

Ross laughed. "Well, to be truthful, they came to us daily in the form of messages from Chief Comecomly and his people."

"I'm surprised you believed them," Jared said bluntly.

"We didn't wholeheartedly," Ross replied. "We established a regular patrol of six men, which further diminished our body of laborers. But self-preservation obliged us to adopt every precaution."

"Did you have any trouble, then?" Pettibone asked.

"We sent for Comecomly and questioned him thoroughly, but all we could learn from him was that the hostile tribes were a very bad people and ill-disposed toward the whites. We believed him since Comecomly and his people were the only ones who would regularly trade with us."

"Sounds as if the old chief was trying to scare hell out of you," Jared said.

"To be sure, we were anxious to ascertain the cause of this rupture between us and the distant tribes. We had traded with some of them for sea and land otter and had done nothing to offend them."

"Maybe Comecomly was the one who caused the hostiles to mistrust you," Pettibone said.

"Aye, that is what we determined ourselves after learning enough of the language to converse with the natives. We sent Alexander McKay, accompanied by Mr. Robert Stuart, up the Columbia to make peace with the distant tribes. They returned in twelve days with a favorable report. Thinking all was well, I myself ventured up to the cascades with Stuart and five men. It seems the Chinooks had managed to undo all that McKay and Stuart had accomplished, for upon our approach, the Indians flew to arms and made signs for us to keep our distance. We offered them presents, but they would not listen to us. They began to gather forces, and we feared that we were in extreme danger. We knew that the longer we stayed, the more likely it became that we would become surrounded. We began to make plans for a hasty retreat."

"Did they attack, then?" Jared asked.

"Just at the last moment, a sympathetic Indian arrived and explained that we were friendly, not at all the hostile white men the Chinooks had portrayed. In fact, when they compared the prices we paid with that which the Chinooks were in the habit of giving them, they put their hands on their mouths in astonishment and strongly urged us to return, saying they would never more trade with the one-eyed chief, Comecomly. But it was a narrow escape for us."

Ross put out his pipe and stood up. "I must be getting back," he said. "I see, Mr. Flynn, that you have no rifle. That is dangerous in this country. Might I provide one for you?"

"I have another in Pettibone's canoe," Jared said. "I will arm myself and go upriver. I want to look at those dead Clatsops before the buzzards get to them."

Ross shuddered. "Well, then, I trust you have enough information to proceed cautiously on your own. This part of the Columbia is claimed by Mr. Astor."

"Yes," Jared said. "Thank you. We will establish our posts well upriver. I expect other Nor'westers will join us presently. There should be trade enough for all."

"Not to Mr. Astor's mind, I fear. Well, good luck to you. Pettibone, a pleasure to see you again."

"You too, Ross. Watch yore topknot."

Ross smiled and then he was gone.

"Why do you have to go and look at a bunch of dead Indians, Jared?" Pettibone asked.

"There's something I have to know."

"I'll come with you. Gray Cat, you'd better come with us. Might not be safe for you to stay around here."

Gray Cat nodded.

Jared dug out another rifle from the goods in Pettibone's canoe and they paddled upstream to where the
battle with the Clatsops had taken place.

They dragged the dead Indians in the river up on
shore and laid them out with the other bodies. Jared
looked at each dead man's face intently. Pettibone and
Gray Cat stood well away and watched him as men will
watch someone who has gone around the bend minus
an oar or two.

Jared turned around and walked to where the two
men stood.

"Satisfied? They all plumb dead?"

"Yes," Jared said. "That last one there is Little
Dog."

"Why, he's a Chinook."

"I know. I wondered why those Clatsops came after us like that. Little Dog, it seems, was just as schem-
ing as Ross's one-eyed chief, Comecomly, treacherous
as a blind snake."

"Well, I'll be damned. You sure?"

"Dead sure," Jared said.

"Now what? We going back down to Point
George?"

"No," Jared said. "We've seen the ocean. That's
enough. I saw a place upriver that would make a dandy
site for a Nor'wester trading post."

"How far up?" Pettibone asked suspiciously.

"Far enough to stay out of Astor's hair, and close
enough to give him fits," Jared replied, grinning.

Chapter
Twenty-five

Malcolm found no sign of Two Fires the next morning. He and Red Bead searched up and down the river. All they found was his line and lure. They returned to camp dejected. McCord was sitting on a rock, drinking coffee as hummingbirds darted all around him like rainbow-colored bees.

"I gather you did not find your Sioux friend."

"You know damned well I didn't, Randy."

"Perhaps. I gathered that since he was not with you, he had run off."

"Run off? Why would he do that?"

McCord shrugged, threw out the grounds, and shook his cup. He snatched a handful of grass, wiped the cup clean, and set it on the ground. "Maybe he went for a swim and the current took him."

Malcolm glared at McCord. For a long moment he was tempted to walk up to him and lash out with both fists. The smugness of the arrogant Scot irritated him.

"Do not fight with Red Hair," Red Bead said softly in Lakota.

"I think he killed Two Fires."

"I know he killed him," she said, "but you cannot beat him now. He is ready for you."

Malcolm looked at McCord. The man seemed very calm, but his pistol was within easy reach in his sash. Malcolm knew that he would not get two steps before McCord drew it and shot him dead in his tracks.

"Let's go finish off the canoes, McCord. Damn you."

"No need to be surly about it, laddie. Actually, I've been giving that issue some thought while you and the squaw were gone."

"I told you not to call Bead a squaw." Malcolm doubled up his fists. Red Bead touched his arm, and he flexed his fingers. She was right. Now was not the time.

"Very well. Your 'woman.'"

"What is it you've been mulling over, then? Certainly it was nothing that concerned my friend, Two Fires."

"I'm a realist, Malcolm. I knew that when the Indian did not return, he had either run off or some accident had befallen him. No, I was thinking that our work will be considerably lessened now. We will only need one canoe. I believe you are well ahead of me in that regard, so we shall both finish the one you felled. Does that make sense?"

"I suppose. What about the horses?"

"We will turn them loose when we're finished with the canoe. I believe we can carry most of our goods, cache the rest, and return later on, if need be. The important thing is to reach the ocean and establish contact with those of Astor's company who sailed on the *Tonquin.* Do you agree?"

"The sooner this is over with, the better."

"And the sooner we will find your long-lost brother, eh?"

Malcolm said nothing. His hatred for McCord was

seething inside him, and he didn't know if he would be able to control himself much longer.

"Well, then," McCord said, "let's be off. Bring as many horses as you think we'll need to haul off that log of yours. Bring plenty of strong rope. I'll fetch my axe and meet you at the cedar you felled. It looks like a good day to work."

Malcolm spoke to Red Bead in her native tongue, telling her to wait for them but to be on her guard.

"Red Hair will not rub me out so easily," she said. "I will wait for you. I will bring you food when the sun stands over my head in the sky."

"You keep a rifle loaded. If McCord comes back by himself, you shoot him."

"I will shoot him if you are not with him."

"Good."

Malcolm took out three coils of strong manila hemp rope and caught up three horses. He rode one of them, leading the other two to the place where he'd felled the big cedar. Mist rose up from the forest floor. The rising sun had not yet caught the treetops, and it was still dark in the woods. He heard the distant call of an owl, saw an antlerless mule deer bound off, its white flag flashing from its rigid, flared tail.

He tied up the horses, hobbled them some distance from the downed cedar. He leaned his rifle against the tree where his axe still stood. He picked up the axe and a coil of rope, walked over to the place where he'd topped the tree. He was still tying the rope around the lower branches nearest the ground when McCord walked up, axe in hand.

"You made good progress," he said, picking up the other two coils of rope. "I'm afraid I didn't do as well."

Something clicked in Malcolm's mind when he heard that. He wondered just how far McCord had gotten in trimming the tree he had felled. He tried to remember if McCord had quit before he did the night before. If so, it would tell him something about the time McCord had left before he returned to camp. His suspicions had grown enormously since his search for Two Fires that morning. It made him sad to think that McCord had killed such a fine man, and it made him furious to think that the Scot might get away with it.

He had no proof, of course. Just a dark mammoth of suspicion that was trampling through his mind, smashing all belief that Two Fires had died accidentally.

"Well, maybe I worked harder," Malcolm said, tying the last knot in the rope.

McCord walked over to the tree, threw one of the lines over the middle of the tree. "Think we can work it underneath?" he asked.

"I think so," Malcolm replied, inspecting the underside of the tree. The branches underneath kept the fallen tree an inch or so off the ground. "You poke the rope under with your axe handle. I'll pull it on through."

McCord walked around to the other side, placed the rope under the tree as far as it would go, then pushed it with the axe handle. He worked it past the tangle of branches until Malcolm saw the bitter end within reach.

"Good enough, Randy." Malcolm dropped to his belly and tugged the rope on through. He began looping the rope, tying a half hitch as McCord came around.

"One more midway between that one and the one you tied first ought to do it," he said, looking over at the horses.

"All we need to do is turn it over," Malcolm said. "We can get to the rest of the branches."

"Might as well pull it like that," McCord said. "Most of those branches will rub off on the way back to camp. Be a lot easier that way."

Malcolm saw the sense of it. As long as the log didn't turn over, but it probably would. "We can give it

a try." He didn't want to get into another argument
with McCord just then. Let the bastard think he had
won, that he was not suspected as the murderer of Two
Fires.

The two men hitched up two of the horses to the
lines, holding one horse in reserve.

"We might have to hitch up the other one if these
two can't pull it," Malcolm said.

"Might. I think if we do some pushing to get them
started, they'll do all right. Ready to try it?"

"Whenever you are."

"Do the honors," McCord said.

He seemed to be in a good mood, which further
irritated Flynn. The man was too damned smug and
self-possessed. It was as if he had done nothing. They
might have been two farmers back East pulling a
stump. But Malcolm knew that he was with a man of
treachery, a man who could not be trusted.

Malcolm thought of his rifle leaning against the
tree. How easy it would be to pick it up and put a ball in
McCord's brisket. He looked over at his rifle and saw
McCord's leaning right next to it. He'd have two shots
if he moved fast. For a long moment he was tempted.
As he took a step toward the tree, McCord stepped
between him and the rifles.

"You get 'em started," Randall said. "Then come
back and we'll push on the loose end of the tree."

"All right," Malcolm replied, knowing it was no
use. He couldn't outwit McCord on the best of days,
and this wasn't one of them.

He tugged at the lead horse's halter, urging it on.
The horse took up the slack. Then he slapped the other
one on the rump, and both horses pulled on the ropes.
The tree began to move.

McCord was already pushing on the loose end of
the tree by the time Malcolm ran around to join him.
The tree straightened and began to pull straight.

"Now," McCord grunted, "better get around and lead them to the river. I'll get the axes and rifles."

Malcolm's heart sank like a heavy sashweight two feet inside his chest. McCord thought of everything, damn him!

Malcolm picked up a thin cedar branch and walked behind the two horses, gently slapping their rumps. He could see the ropes biting into their flesh. He heard the crack of breaking branches as the tree moved through the forest, skidding over old pine needles and rotted spruce boughs. The sound made the horses jittery, and they pulled harder to get away from whatever was following them. They peered back gimlet-eyed every so often, and Malcolm whacked them on their rumps so they didn't lag or slack off.

McCord caught up with him a few minutes later, leading the third horse, carrying the rifles, axes, and the last coil of rope.

"They're doing just fine, laddie."

Malcolm said nothing. He reached for his rifle.

"No use you packin' it all," he said lamely.

"Sure, laddie, sure," McCord replied, handing the flintlock to Flynn. "Can't ever tell when we might run into trouble, and we're making a lot of noise."

The log rolled from side to side, but always came back to the underside down. Most of the remaining branches would be stripped away by the time they reached camp, he knew. The heavier underside served as ballast, and the side branches acted as stabilizing outriggers on the log. He hated to give McCord credit, but the man knew what he was doing. McCord didn't rattle as easily as he himself did. He made a mental note to think a lot harder when he was around the man, lest he be caught off guard at the wrong time.

It took them about an hour to lead the horses through the thick woods. As they approached, Malcolm felt his stomach tighten up, wondering if Red Bead was all right. When he saw her waiting for them, the tightness lessened. He was still nervous, and there was still a lot of work to do to make the canoe ready for the river.

Bead had a cook pot on a fire that gave off no smoke. The smell of fish and roots wafted on the bright air. She said nothing to Malcolm, but a look passed between them when McCord was working with the horses to turn the cedar trunk over and expose the underside.

"Do you know where Red Hair cut his tree down?" he asked her in Lakota.

"I can find it."

"When there is a chance for you to slip away, go to that place. I want you to tell me how many branches were left on the tree."

"I will do this," she said softly.

"Do not hurry. Anytime this sun."

"I will do as you ask," Red Bead said, and stirred the pot, turning away from him and McCord.

When they had unhitched the horses, the two men set to with axes to trim the tree. They barked it and began to dig out the hull from the top down.

"Let's get some of that fish in us before we go on," McCord said when the sun stood directly overhead. Both men were naked to the waist, glistening with a sweat that oiled their torsos. They had worked wordlessly from either end of the tree. It was slow, hard work, chipping and knocking out the chunks with the axe blades.

"I'll have to sharpen my axe before we go at it again," Malcolm said.

"Me too, laddie."

After lunch, Red Bead walked into the woods. She carried one of the rifles with her.

"Where's she going?" McCord asked.

"Where women go when they hear nature's call," Malcolm said. "Why?"

"No reason."

"She's not a prisoner, you know."

"Didn't say she was."

"You act like it sometimes."

"That's only a matter of viewpoint, laddie."

McCord was restless after lunch and attacked his axe blade with the file. Malcolm drew the heavy rasp across the dull edge of his own axe, metal screeching in his ears as thin white clouds began to drift over the mountains from the west. The wind picked up, scuffing the waters of the Columbia as it surged upriver, bearing, in its whispery zephyrs, the saline tang of the sea.

Malcolm and McCord worked all afternoon, chopping out the hull from either end. Chips lay around the cedar like odd-sized shingles cut by a wayward froe until the ground looked as if a tribe of beavers with oversized teeth had been at work. Red Bead returned from the woods, then disappeared downstream without a word to either man. McCord watched her walk away out of the corner of his eye, but said nothing. The clouds thickened, and late in the afternoon it began to rain. The men kept on working until the wood got too wet, then covered the gouge with layers of spruce boughs they trimmed from a living tree.

Red Bead returned in the darkness of afternoon, wet from the soaking rain, her moccasins squishing as she walked. Malcolm was trying vainly to light a fire while McCord held a blanket up to protect the spunk from the needling downpour. Every time Malcolm got a spark, the wind blew it out.

"I will make the fire," Red Bead said.

"The wood and tinder are wet."

"I know. I will do it."

"What's she saying?" McCord asked.

"Bead says she will build us a fire."

"Haw!"

"She will too."

"Go find dry logs," she told Malcolm.

Both men went hunting logs for a fire as Red Bead found a dry blanket and disappeared into the forest. McCord and Flynn had a full stack of wood by the time Red Bead returned with the blanket as full as a bundle of laundry. She opened the blanket upside down and squaw wood tumbled out. She had gathered the dry twigs, mountain men called 'squaw wood,' from the pines which grew brittle beneath the boughs and kept them from getting wet. With flint and steel she started the fire, adding the dry rotten logs the men had found. Soon the blaze flickered high, sending orange warmth out in all directions.

When McCord went to gather more wood for the night, Red Bead spoke to Malcolm.

"I found a hawk's feather floating in the river. It was from Two Fires's scalp lock."

"You did? Where?"

"A thousand paces down the river. Tomorrow I will look for the body of Two Fires."

"How?"

"I know a way," she said.

They slept in their tents as the rain pattered all night long. The downpour stopped before dawn, and the sun rose and dried the land before the men started working on the canoe. Red Bead walked away as the men resumed chopping out the hull.

"Now where's she going?" McCord asked.

"I have no idea. But you seem mighty interested in Bead's comings and goings."

"Not at all," Randall replied as he swung his axe downward, slamming the blade hard into the wood.

McCord made the chips fly, and Malcolm matched him stroke for stroke long after their axe blades had gone dull that day. The tension between the two men was so thick and palpable that they seemed like figu-

rines carved out of flesh, moving in contrapuntal
rhythm, as if they were connected by an invisible string.

Red Bead Woman searched along the shore for a
suitable log, roaming in and out of the woods until she
found one that was the size and weight she needed. She
dragged it to the river and stood it on end. Then she
pushed it off the bank with a vigorous shove. It landed
in the water with a loud splash, but she knew no one
had heard it. She no longer heard the clang of the axes,
for the river drowned out all sound as it raced over a
jumble of rocks.

When she walked downriver, she had looked at
both shores for any sign of the body of Two Fires, but
had seen nothing. Now she watched the current take
the log, spin it around, then pull it along. She followed
its course on foot, watching every swirl and eddy in the
river, hoping that it would navigate the white-water
stretches where the boulders studded the banks like
bumps on a buffalo's hide, the same as a drowned man.

She did not care how far the floating log took her
away from camp. She only wanted to know the truth
about Two Fires. She knew that if the Great Spirit was
listening to her murmured chants, he would show her
where the corpse of her friend had landed.

The log became sodden but did not sink to the
bottom. At times she had to run to keep up with it.
Then it would hesitate as part of it caught on something
in the water, and she waited patiently until it broke
loose and flowed once more with the current.

"Ho, Two Fires, let your spirit show me where your
dead body came to rest so that I can read your face in
death. Oh Wakan Tanka, Great Spirit, let the log show
me Two Fires's path in the river."

As she followed the log downstream, she looked
along the sides of the river and among its rocks for any
sign of Two Fires's body. And still the log floated, and

she began to wonder if the Great Spirit had not taken the body of Two Fires all the way to the big water. If so, he must have been very angry and his ears must be closed to her prayers.

The river widened, then narrowed, and suddenly the log disappeared. Her heart beat faster as Red Bead wondered if it had sunk to the bottom. Then she saw it close at hand, snagged in a huge toppled spruce that lay sprawled in the water, its trunk smashed by lightning.

She looked at the log, then crouched next to the downed spruce, searching through its branches for any sign of Two Fires. The water was dark and shaded from the boughs, and she saw nothing until she stood up, dejected, feeling that she had failed in her wish to find Two Fires.

Then she saw the small round object bobbing up and down just beneath a flare of spruce bough. A sodden feather lay against the wood. A hawk's feather, so small it was barely visible.

Her heart caught in her throat as she gave a cry of triumph and despair. For there was the body of Two Fires, all in shadow beneath the lightning-struck spruce, caught in the submerged branches. She saw his legs moving as if he was treading water, just waiting for her to find him. Waiting where the Great Spirit had led him and kept him until she could trace his last journey.

_____ Chapter _____
Twenty-six

---

ared, Gray Cat, and Pettibone gathered all of the canoes left by the Clatsops. Jared even retrieved his own canoe a few hours later, the goods miraculously still lashed to the interior, including his spare rifle, which was stuck between two packets just the way he had left it. They made camp some distance upstream from where the fight with the Clatsops had taken place.

"You got any idea where we're going to set up a post?" Pettibone asked. There was a strong chord of annoyance in his tone.

"I know exactly where," Jared said. "In a few weeks I expect we'll have company, matter of fact."

"You holdin' somethin' back, son?"

Jared smiled sheepishly. From deep in his pack he retrieved an oilskin packet that he had carried all the way across the mountains, all the way from Mackinac. He had not brought it out at any time, but kept it right at the bottom under a pair of spare trousers and some leather for repairing moccasins, pouches, and the like.

Now he opened the packet carefully and spread out a map.

"What is that?" Pettibone asked.

"A crude map of the Columbia River and this whole territory. Sent from the headquarters at New Caledonia, back to Montreal, then to me at Mackinac."

"Well, I'll be double damned," said an astounded Pettibone.

"Couldn't show it to you before. Sorry. I had orders. But here's where we'll go in a few days to set up a headquarters." Jared reached back inside the pack and brought out another bundle, this one larger, also wrapped in oilskin. He unwrapped it, and Pettibone's eyes widened into a pair of boiled quail's eggs.

"British flags."

"We're to contact all the tribes along the Columbia, give them these flags and declare the territory under British rule."

"I'll be triple damned. That ought to stick in old Astor's craw, all this country claimed by North-West."

Jared grinned. He pointed to a spot on the map. Pettibone leaned over, read the words: Spokane R.

"What's that?"

"That was a river we passed, emptying into the Columbia. I determined when we went by it that this would be our first trading post. I had a hunch Astor would already have gotten here by sea, but not overland. But it's for sure, he'll have trappers and traders out here to join up with the Astorians. I couldn't tell Ross that, of course. I'm sure he already knows, but I can't be sure. Our job is to make all the inroads we can before another expedition joins up with McDougal, Ross, and the others. We've got some work to do."

"You say we're going to have company."

Jared folded the map back up and wrapped it in the oilskin. He had not looked at in some time, but had memorized it months ago on Mackinac, when he'd gotten his orders.

"David Thompson should be joining us within the month, I'd say. Early part of July."

"How come nobody told me about all this?" Pettibone seemed to be pouting.

"North-West felt it was best that I keep this information to myself. You know David."

"Yes. He's an astronomer and a partner in North-West."

"As you are likely to be. As I already am. I expect Pierre Lescaux will join us before the snow flies, back with his brigade."

"Well I'm runnin' out of damns. Quadripples."

"Quadruple damned, Fur Face. That's four, and that's quite bloody enough."

"So David Thompson himself is a-comin'. I seen you and him makin' smoke, but I didn't know North-West had planned it all out. Dave himself, eh?"

"With about twenty-five or thirty men."

Pettibone let out a long whistle. Gray Cat sat near the fire, grinning wide.

"What are you grinnin' for, Gray Cat? Don't tell me you knew about all this?"

Jared laughed. "No, he didn't know, but he's enjoying your surprise."

"I'm just right dumbfounded," Pettibone said, and Jared laughed again.

Jared and Pettibone watched the *Tonquin* sail from the harbor on the first of June. The ship beat against the tide and the wind and made little progress. They had left Gray Cat back upriver to guard the canoes and goods while they canoed back down to Astoria to talk to Ross.

The Astorians lined the shore, waving to the ship as it headed for the bar.

Jared waited until Ross turned away and left the clutch of men still waving sadly at the *Tonquin*.

"I've come to say farewell," Jared said.

"You're leaving?" Ross asked.

Pettibone nodded.

"I expect we'll meet again," Jared said. "You look sad. It is because the ship is leaving?"

"Why, yes, that's part of it. Captain Thorn landed but a small part of our cargo, and I feel somewhat destitute. It is his intention to explore the north coast, and upon his return to put the rest on shore. I have a peculiar notion that we've seen the last of the ship. Also, Mr. McKay, as supercargo, has gone aboard with Mr. Lewis, and Mr. John Mumford, the second officer, has been dismissed and left on shore."

"That's bad?" Jared asked.

"On McKay's embarking he called me aside and asked me to watch after his son. I agreed wholeheartedly, and then McKay said something else to me: 'You see how unfortunate we are; the captain in one of his frantic fits has now discharged the only officer on board,' alluding to Mr. Mumford. 'If you ever see us safe back,' said McKay, 'it will be a miracle.' So saying, we parted yesterday, and he slept on board last night. The departure of the ship a few moments ago unfolded to us the danger of our situation."

"I reckon so," Pettibone said, looking around the settlement as the men slowly returned to their work. "You don't seem prepared for any Injun trouble."

"It has been my understanding," Ross said, "that in forming an establishment among savages, the first consideration is safety. Of course we've all been aware that the *Tonquin*'s stay protected our embryo settlement, and that her departure would proclaim to all the hostile tribes around our defenseless state there were no preparations made for the event. Not one."

"None?" Jared asked.

"Not a gun mounted, not a palisade raised. Nor the least precaution to secure either life or property. Such is the character of the man whom Mr. Astor placed at the head of his affairs."

"You've got a garden started, I see," Pettibone said.

"We've planted potatoes, a few other vegetables. I expect we might garner other foodstuffs by learning what the natives eat. If we can ever find some that we trust."

"Well, I wish you good luck," Jared said. "We're heading upriver."

"Be careful, young man," Ross said. "I truly believe that we all face dire straits ahead, Astorians and Northwesters alike."

Jared felt a ripple of chill go up his spine. For just an instant he thought that Alexander Ross's words might be prophetic. They were all interlopers in a strange land, and they had seen both the gentle and violent kinds of Indians in their journey down the Columbia. He wondered if there was some connection between the Indians' behavior and where the whites settled. Perhaps in the mountains the Chinooks and other tribes were more peaceful. The closer they got to the ocean, the more violent the natives seemed. It could be they held the Pacific in reverence and resented any intrusion by sea. It was something to ponder, but not to worry over.

Jared felt amazement whenever he looked at the ocean, realizing he'd seen the Atlantic beginning his journey westward from one coast to another. Now he felt hemmed in and longed for the mountains, where a man knew no boundaries, could not see beyond the nearest range, knew not what lay beyond. He'd come beyond the mountains, and the mystery of what lay beyond had been revealed to him, but he took no comfort in it. He knew the sea had its own mystery, not likely to be plumbed by him or those trying to carve out a small civilization on its shore. The Astorians had blocked themselves off from retreat. The ship that had brought them was heading out to sea, leaving them at the mercy of the savage tribes that prowled the coast.

He shook off the thoughts that crowded his mind. He had things to do and he could not let his feelings prevent him from what he hoped to accomplish.

"Be seeing you, Alexander," he said.

"Luck to you, Jared Flynn," Ross replied. "Pettibone. I hope we meet again."

With that, Jared and Pettibone paddled back up to their camp and loaded their canoes for their trip to the Spokane River. By noon they were well upstream, pulling the captured canoes behind the three they each manned. Jared thought sadly of the little settlement of Astoria. He knew that with the *Tonquin* gone, the Indians would swarm around the settlement and attempt to drive the settlers into the sea. But there was nothing he could do. He had his orders to start a settlement of his own before Thompson's arrival. Still, he felt queasy when he thought about Ross and the others. Despite himself, he hoped they would not all be killed by Indians. Yet he knew that even if they survived, the battle for the territory between the two companies was bound to erupt into hostilities. And wouldn't the native tribes relish that eventuality?

Bead worked the body of Two Fires out from under the spruce branches, then floated him to the bank. She dragged the corpse ashore, using its own weight to advantage by twisting it from side to side while pulling on it until it was free of the water.

She knelt down and examined the dead brave's head for lumps, bruises, cuts. She knew that he could have struck his head on the rocks after he fell in the water, but she also knew the difference between wounds received before and after death. She had treated many a warrior wounded in battle, had bathed many a brave who had given up his spirit.

She looked at the dead man's neck very carefully, touching the blanched and wrinkled flesh with her fingers, feeling the bones of the spine and the throat. She stripped the body and looked at every mark, felt every joint. She traced the bones of his face too, ran her fingers through his wet hair until she had mapped in her mind every inch of Two Fires's corpse. When she was finished, she relaxed and settled into a squat as she gazed at the naked cadaver. She knew that Two Fires had not fallen into the river accidentally. There were marks on his neck from powerful hands, little bones broken in the windpipe, and his voice box had been crushed.

She dragged the body into the woods, out of sight of anyone passing along the river. She lay him in a patch of sunlight, then walked back to where she'd left his clothes. She brought those back with her. They were heavy and sodden with water, and she wrung them out with her small, delicate hands.

She hung the dead brave's buckskins, his medicine pouch, and his hunting pouch, on spruce boughs to dry in the sun while she hunted for two small trees that grew close together and were a certain distance from each other. She would have preferred to have four such trees, but knew that would take too much time.

Bead found three small pines and other saplings growing very close together that would suit her purpose. She quickly went to work with her knife, cutting the tops off the small pines, culling certain limbs so that they made a kind of cradle among them. She bent the other saplings to test their pliability and suppleness. She cut small pieces of wood from other trees, stripping them of bark. These were all of a uniform size and thickness to fit across the cradle's bowl to make a platform.

Red Bead cut shreds of deerskin from her dress and used them as thongs to tie the small sticks to the cradle's sides until she had a sturdy bed. She covered this bed with boughs cut from spruce trees until she had a soft, springy mattress to hold Two Fires's body. By the time she finished, it had stopped raining and the clouds began to disperse.

She made a small travois from two saplings and carried the trees to where she had left Two Fires. His body had grown stiff. His skin had begun to lose its natural color and was darkening. She bathed him carefully and dressed him in his dried buckskins after making them pliant with small amounts of water. She combed his hair with a bone comb she carried in her pouch. She found berries to tie in his scalp lock as ornaments, then placed him on the makeshift travois and carried him to the burial scaffold.

Red Bead stood him up against it and used one of the pines as a fulcrum, placing his head across a limb she had left for that purpose. She lifted his feet up first, swung them over the side. Then she used that end of the scaffold for another fulcrum and pushed his torso up over the top. She laid him straight and even on the fir boughs, flat on his back, looking up at the clearing sky, placed his medicine bag around his neck and his hunting pouch by his side.

Lastly, she folded his arms across his chest.

"I will be back," she whispered. "I will bring your warrior's things for your journey up the star path."

Bead walked through the woods, toward the camp, using dead reckoning as her compass. She waited until dark, then stole up to the camp where Red Hair and Iron Hawk Flynn lay sleeping. She gathered all of Two Fires's possessions, including his rifle, his bow, and quiver full of arrows. She carefully bundled these in his blanket so they did not strike each other. Then she led her horse away from the others and tethered him until her return.

Neither of the men heard her, since she made no sound. She wished she could stop and whisper into her man's ear, but knew she dared not. Before the moon rose she was gone, heading back to the burial scaffold of Two Fires, her heart pounding in her chest. She found her horse, mounted him and rode the rest of the way.

She laid the rifle on one side of Two Fires's body, his bow and quiver on the other. Then she gathered the dry wood for starting fires from under the lowest branches of the tall pines and brought dried deadwood sticks. She made a small fire under the scaffold, and when it was blazing, fed it aromatic spruce boughs. She watched the smoke rise to the Great Spirit and began to chant the ancient prayers to send the warrior on his journey across the great silver band in the sky, the star path that led to the place where the Great Spirit dwells.

She prayed and chanted until just before dawn, then left the scaffold.

Red Bead knew that she could not go back to Iron Heart and tell him what she had found. Instead she must follow the two men down the river, on foot, and hope that her husband would one day kill Red Hair and not be killed himself. She traveled far downriver before dawn, slept, and began hunting for berries and setting snares. She found a place overlooking the river and stayed there, waiting, sending her thoughts back to Iron Hawk Flynn, hoping that he would hear her heart's voice and know she was safe and waiting for him.

"That squaw of yours didn't come back last night," McCord said.

"Yes, she did," said Flynn, who had started the morning cook fire.

"Where is she?"

"I didn't see her, but she was back, all right."

McCord looked around, rubbing the scabs of sleep from his eyes.

He saw that Two Fires's things were missing.

"Came back to steal from us, did she? I see she took the buck's blankets, his rifle and bow."

"Oh, I don't think she was stealing. I think she carried off Two Fires's things to give to him. If you'll look, you'll see she also took her horse."

"You think he's alive, then."

"Randy, you just don't give up, do you? You know as well as I do that Two Fires is dead. You killed him. You either cut his throat or knocked him into the river, choked him or something."

"That's a damned lie."

"Well, Two Fires was a young brave in his prime. He didn't just disappear."

"I wouldn't know about that. You're the savage, not me."

"Am I, McCord?"

"How do you know your Indian friend is dead?"

"I think Bead found his body and put him on a scaffold. Came back to get his things for his journey through the sky."

McCord snorted, threw up his arms. He said no more about Two Fires or Bead from that moment on. Secretly, he was glad the squaw had left. He had meant to kill her before they reached the mouth of the Columbia anyway. She'd saved him a lot of trouble. But he felt sure she'd show up again. She had taken her horse, and that probably meant that she would follow them downriver. He vowed to keep an eye out for her. If he saw her alone and had a clear shot, he would take care of her once and for all.

Two days later the men were on the river in their new cedar canoe. They left the horses to run loose.

As they paddled into the current, Malcolm scanned the surrounding trees and open places, looking for Red Bead.

He knew that somewhere along the way she would be watching for them. And when she decided to return, he would be waiting for her.

McCord, in the front of the canoe, turned and looked back at him.

Malcolm felt his stomach knot up, as if Randall was reading his thoughts.

At that moment he didn't know who he wanted to kill more—McCord or his own brother. He took a deep breath. There was really no decision to make. He would kill them both when the time came.

He hoped it would be soon.

_____ Chapter _____
Twenty-seven

_____

Jared had felt restless all day, an indefinable sense of
anticipation. A stirring in his belly, a tingle in his
brain, as if there was something he was supposed to
do, someone he had to see. Yet he could think of nothing urgent. The feeling persisted as he listened to the
whisper of the wind and looked up at the gathering
clouds for some sign of portentous warning.

He and Pettibone and Gray Cat had worked hard
for over two weeks, cutting pine trees, stripping them,
notching them for logs. First they constructed crude
breastworks behind which they could hide and fire their
rifles should they be attacked. These were three-sided
forts, placed between where they had laid out a design
for the trading post and the river. In addition, they had
built smaller ones to protect their flanks. They used
logs and rocks, spruce bows, and other natural materi-
als to construct these defenses.

They marked out the dimensions of the trading
post where the Spokane River emptied into the Columbia, and set logs for a foundation. Now the post was

rising slowly, log by log. The work was hard since they had to fell the timber and drag each log to the construction site, then strip off the limbs and peel the pine bark in sections.

"You hear anything, Pettibone?"

"Nope. Not a thing."

Pettibone was notching a log for the walls of the fort. Wood chips lay all around him. He was sweating in the cool of morning, as was Jared. Gray Cat ate no salt, so he did not sweat as much. At least Jared had never seen him bathed in perspiration, even in that high humidity along the river.

"I got a funny feeling," Jared said.

"Best keep close to your smokepole, then."

That had been a worry for them. They knew they could be attacked at any moment by hostile bands of coastal Indians. Word had come upriver that there had been trouble at Astoria with Chief Comecomly, but things had calmed down. McDougal had accidentally discharged a blunderbuss, tearing a corner of the chief's robe to shreds. There had been some thieving and a kidnapping of one of the sentinals. Ross and McDougal had put out the brushfire, apparently. They hadn't heard a word from downriver in over two weeks.

But they had been warned to keep a sharp lookout for Comecomly and his pilfering band of Chinooks.

"Mighty quiet," Jared said, realizing, once he said it, that he sounded inane, if not addled.

"Meaning?"

"I don't know. I just feel odd, that's all."

"Maybe you got the second sight."

"What's that?"

"Like you can tell when somethin's goin' to happen."

Jared snorted. "Nonsense."

Pettibone sighed and went back to notching the log. Jared took his rifle with him when he went back

into the woods to cut another tree. The feeling he had
persisted, and he returned a short time later to find
Pettibone and Gray Cat setting another log in place.
The fort was now four logs high. They would cut
shorter ones for doors and windows to be placed on all
four sides of the structure.

"See anything?" Jared asked.

"Yeah, sure did."

"What?" Jared asked, his senses all a-jitter.

"Saw a pair of fish hawks, fifty seagulls, a buzzard,
some swifts, and a big old leaf a-floatin' downriver, just
a-spinnin' like a cartwheel."

Jared's face turned crimson. "That ain't funny,
Pettibone."

"Chile, you're just a scrap heap of nerves. We ain't
seen nothin' but chips fly and clouds bunchin' up west
of us."

"Well, come on. We got logs to skid."

"Be right with you."

Just then Gray Cat signed to them and picked up
his rifle. "Man come," he said.

"Where?" Jared asked.

Gray Cat pointed upriver, along the bank.

An Indian man and two women walked toward
them. One woman was carrying a pack on her back.
The other woman had her hands tied behind her, and
the man held a rope in his hand, leading her like a
horse. They were all dressed in buckskins. The man
wore an eagle feather on his scalp lock. His shirt was
brightly decorated with porcupine quills. He carried a
bow, a quiver of arrows, and a knife and hatchet in his
sash. He stood straight and proud.

"See?" Jared said to Pettibone.

"Looks like you got the second sight all right."

"Stop your joshin', Fur Face. Let's see what this
fellow has to say."

Jared stepped forward, rifle in his left hand. He

held his right hand up, palm out empty-handed in the sign of peace.

The Indian held up his own right hand. In his left he carried his bow, but there was no arrow with it.

"Damned if that ain't a Chippewa coon," Pettibone said. "Looks familiar."

"Damned if he doesn't," Jared said.

"Looks like he's got hisself a prisoner. Comely little wench."

"Lakota woman," Gray Cat said.

"Which one?" Jared asked.

Gray Cat held out both hands, the wrists pressed together to show that he meant the woman who was bound.

"Hello, Fur Face," the Chippewa man said. His woman grinned.

"Who goes yonder?" Pettibone asked.

"Me Night Horse," said the Chippewa. "Me come Thompson man."

"Night Horse," Jared said. "Now I recognize him."

"Who you got there, Horse?" Pettibone asked, making the same sign as Gray Cat had.

"Lakota *wacincila*," Night Horse said. "Red Bead Woman."

"Where'd you get her?"

"River. Back, back."

Pettibone made the introductions. Night Horse's woman was called Little Mouse as near as he could interpret. He spoke to Red Bead in sign and a tongue similar to Lakota. She nodded.

"How come you got her tied up like that?" Pettibone asked.

Night Horse spoke very slowly in French and used his hands in sign.

"When we found this one, she was wandering about like a lost buffalo calf. When I called to her, she ran away to hide like the chipmunk when the owl flies on silent wings. We chased her. When we caught her, she was like a quivering rabbit. She was afraid her man would be killed by the red-haired long knife. She wanted to kill the red-hair. But I told her that many long knives were coming. She would not come with us, so we tied her up. Thompson man might kill her. He might think she is bad-face Indian."

"When is Thompson coming?" Jared asked in French.

"Two or three sleeps. We saw Red Hair and the one she calls Iron Hawk. They come in one sleep. Maybe this sun they come, one crossing of the sun across the sky. They come very fast. Big canoe. Many goods. We had to come fast all night to get away from them. This one says that Red Hair has a bad face. He has killed a Mandan and a Lakota brave."

Jared looked at Red Bead. He started talking to her in sign, asking her who the men were that had the big canoe.

"I speak little English," Red Bead said.

"Where do you come from?" Jared asked as Gray Cat began to make a fire. Pettibone was breaking out the tobacco and pipes for a smoke. Little Mouse set her pack down and squatted next to a skinned log that had not been notched, her brown eyes like little beads as she batted her eyes, looking at the two white men and the Mandan brave. She had not spoken a word, seemed angry at Red Bead for even being alive and in their presence.

"You Jared Flynn?" Red Bead said.

"Yes."

"Me Iron Heart's woman."

"I do not know this Iron Heart."

"Brother. Ma'com. Ma'com Flynn."

Jared's face paled suddenly as the blood raced from its capillaries. Then his cheeks rouged with the rush of blood that suffused the tiny veins.

"My brother? Malcolm?"

"Yes."

Jared closed his eyes for a moment and tried to picture his brother. Married to this Sioux woman. She was comely, petite, with very fine features. She looked tired, worn out.

"I'll untie you," he said, looking at Night Horse for approval.

The Chippewa nodded and laid his bow down, took out his pipe. He sat very straight on the bare ground. Smoke began to curl up from the twigs and faggots as the fire caught. Gray Cat added more wood and sat near Jared. Pettibone joined them. Jared looked at Red Bead's wrists where the leather thongs had cut into them. He rubbed them until the blood filled in the furrows. He threw the thongs and the rope down.

Red Bead did not thank him. She sat on the ground too, as far away from Little Mouse as she could get.

"Do you have hunger?" Jared asked of his guests.

Night Horse rubbed his belly, speaking for himself and the two women.

"We have fish and deer meat," Pettibone said. Little Mouse rose and went to the place where the white man pointed. There, she found bowls and spoons and ladles, food that had been dried and cured in the sun.

Jared turned to Red Bead. "What of Malcolm?"

"Him come soon."

"Why? Is he looking for me?"

"He come to kill brother," she said in her broken English. "Bad white man come too. Red Hair. Mc-Cord."

"Randall McCord? He's with Malcolm?"

Red Bead nodded.

Jared sat back, stunned. The years faded away as he thought of his brother, the last time he'd seen him.

Seen him in a rage, seen him blind mad, unwilling to listen. He thought back to the day when it had all happened, when Malcolm had not been there to see it all with his own eyes.

He could see everything that happened that day as clearly as if it had happened yesterday. He drew in a breath and let the vision spread across his mind, blossom with the vivid memories of that terrible day.

Jared hauled in on the traces when he heard the low scream coming from the barn. The mule lurched to a halt, its long ears twitching to pick up the alien sound. He had agreed to help his father plow the field, since he was feeling poorly.

He was about to cluck to the mule and resume plowing when he heard a much louder scream. This time there was no mistaking it. A woman's voice, or a child's. Jared set the brake and pulled his rifle sling around, took the weapon off his back. He was puzzled. His sister and mother should both have been in the house. Who was in the barn? His pa was laid up with the croup.

Jared set out in a dead run for the barn. He cocked his rifle as he ran. The screams became more insistent, rose shrilly to the highest register of the human voice.

As he drew closer, Jared heard the screams turn to speech.

"Mother, Mother! Help me! Help me, Mother!"

Jared's blood iced as he recognized the terrified voice of his sister, Caitlin. His first thought was that she'd fallen or run into a pitchfork buried in the hay.

He opened the barn door and dashed inside.

Caitlin lay on her back in the middle of the barn, her dress pulled up around her waist, her breasts bare, the top of her frock ripped open, her legs high in the air. Jared saw the naked back of a man straddling her as she lay helpless, fighting him and screaming in terror at the top of her lungs.

Jared made an instant decision. He brought his rifle up to his shoulder and fired point-blank at Caitlin's attacker. He saw the man's right shoulder twitch as the ball struck it, saw the blood spurt from the wound. The man threw both arms straight up in the air, shot to his feet, and turned toward Jared, blood gushing from his chest and spewing from his mouth like a crimson fountain.

The man took a couple of steps before Jared recognized him. He stared in horror at his mortally wounded father.

"Pa . . . Pa . . ."

Then the elder Flynn pitched forward and fell flat on his face. Blood gushed from his chest wound and pooled up beneath him. Jared lowered his rifle, dropped it to the ground.

Caitlin sat up, her hands covering her tearstained face.

She was no longer screaming.

Jared went to her, knelt beside her, took her in his arms.

"What did he do to you, Caitlin?"

Caitlin began sobbing, and the tortured sounds tore at his senses. He rocked her gently in his arms as his mother timidly entered the barn.

"Did you kill him, Jared?" his mother asked, her voice hollow and toneless, devoid of emotion.

"I—I guess so," he said. "He—He was raping Caitlin. I—I didn't know it was him."

"Good," his mother said. "This has gone on long enough."

"You knew about this? He's done this before?"

"Never mind," she said. "It's over. He can't hurt your sister anymore."

"My God," Jared said. "I can't believe this. Caitlin, Caitlin. How long has he been doing this to you?"

"All my life," his sister said, a dullness to her tone that sent shivers up Jared's spine.

"Ever since she was a baby, your pa has been fooling with her," his mother said.

"Why didn't you stop him? Why didn't you tell me or Malcolm?"

"We couldn't," Caitlin said. "He said he'd kill us both."

Jared saw the blood between his sister's legs and pulled her dress down. He felt as if lightning had struck him, shocking his body and brain, robbing him of reason and voice. He sat there in a state of numbness and insensibility, suspended between reality and dream by some unknown force beyond comprehension.

He felt that way now, as the memories flooded through him as if the events had just happened moments before.

Randall McCord. Malcolm had been married to his sister, Lorna McCord. She'd been captured by Shawnees and killed. More sadness in a cursed family. Randall had no reason to hate him. Neither did Malcolm, but he thought he did.

"Why does Iron Hawk want to kill me?" Jared asked.

"He say you kill your father and mother and sister," Red Bead replied.

"I killed my father. My sister killed herself, and my mother died of heartbreak. Do you understand my words?"

Red Bead nodded. "It is a bad thing," she said.

"Well, maybe I can speak with my brother and tell him what happened."

"He does not know?"

Jared shook his head.

The men finished smoking their pipes. The Chippewa and his wife said good-bye and walked back down to the river.

"We will leave the Lakota woman with you," Night Horse said. "Do not trust her."

"Where are you going?"

"We go to Thompson. Bring back."

Jared nodded. He waved good-bye as the two Chippewas paddled up the Columbia. He wondered when Malcolm and Randall would arrive. He stood there for a long time, waiting and looking upriver, but he saw no one. He walked back to the post, anxious to talk to Red Bead Woman again. He had many questions to ask.

That night, after supper, Jared spoke to Red Bead alone.

"You say that McCord killed some men."

"Yes. He wants to kill you. He wants Iron Hawk to kill you. That is why Iron Hawk is coming with Red Hair."

"I have never done anything to McCord."

"He say you Nor'wester."

Jared was surprised that she could say the name of the company so well. "Is that bad to him?"

"He talk about white man name Astor."

"He works for Astor?"

Red Bead nodded.

Jared scratched his head. He wondered what Astor was up to, sending a man like McCord to kill him. And Randall had gotten Malcolm to go along with him. He had known Astor was ambitious, but hadn't realized he would go to such lengths to conquer a new territory.

"I hope I do not have to kill McCord," he told Red Bead.

"I hope you no kill Iron Hawk."

"I would not kill my brother."

"He will kill you I think."

"Not if I can talk to him first."

"Good. You make talk. No kill."

He had many things to puzzle over that night, so he did not question Red Bead further. He needed to think and to sleep on it, so whatever else he had to say could wait until morning.

"We better set watches tonight, Pettibone."

"We set watches ever' night, Jared."

"Particular watches."

"You think McCord might sneak up on us?"

"I don't know what to think. Astor sent him to kill me."

"Don't surprise me none."

"No? Why not?"

"Astor is a ruthless man. So is Randall McCord. He would send a man like that to stop you from setting up this here tradin' post. And Randy, bastard of a Scot that he is, would use your own brother against you. Dogs run together."

"Astor can't stop North-West, even if he kills me."

"Maybe not. But he's a man what won't take second place in any race. He's bound to win at any cost."

"You know all that."

"I know he sent the *Tonquin* out here and he's sending a brigade overland. Like him to buy a little insurance in a man like McCord."

"You may be right. You and Gray Cat take the first watch. I'll take the next."

"You figure they won't get here until tomorry."

"Likely."

"You get in any trouble, son, you just holler."

"I will."

Jared went to bed, but he couldn't sleep for a long time. It seemed he had just fallen into a deep slumber when Gray Cat woke him.

"Huh? What?"

"You take watch. Me sleep."

Jared climbed out of his blankets. He saw Red

Bead sleeping a few yards away. He picked up his rifle
and relieved Pettibone.

"All's quiet, Jared."

"See you in the morning, Pettibone."

"Be careful, son."

Jared walked down to the river and listened to the
soft sigh of the water as it rushed past the banks. He
walked upriver well away from the sound, listening for
any unusual noises. It seemed an eternity until the eastern sky broke open, spilling a creamy light on the horizon.

When he went back to the camp, Pettibone and
Gray Cat were still sleeping.

Red Bead was gone.

Chapter
Twenty-eight

Red Bead appeared on the shore as Randall Mc-Cord and Malcolm Flynn rounded a bend not far from where the Spokane River flowed into the Columbia. She waved to them and the two men turned the craft.

She waited for the canoe to stop. Malcolm stepped out and addressed her in Lakota.

"Winyan Psito Luta," he said. *"Toniktuka hwo?"*

"I am fine, Cetan Mezaska."

"Where did you go?"

"I found the body of Two Fires. I placed him on the scaffold and prayed so that he could walk the star path."

"That is good."

"I have seen your brother."

Malcolm turned to look at McCord.

"What are you two talking about? We don't want to linger here, laddie."

"Just a minute."

He turned back to Red Bead Woman. "Where is my brother?"

"Less than a sleep. Less than a sun away. On the river. He builds a white man's fort."

Malcolm took in a breath to steady himself. He felt a tingling in his veins that he usually only felt when he heard a Lakota flute and the beat of warrior drums. Strange, he thought, that he was finally going to see his brother again after all these years, after trying to erase his memory in the sweat lodge, in the *paha sapa* when the buffalo thundered through those sacred black hills, in those moments when he was alone with the Wakan Tanka, asking the Great Spirit for guidance.

"Did you tell him I was coming?"

"Yes. I told him you come to kill him. And I told him Red Hair has killed Two Fires and the Mandan."

"What did my brother say?"

"He wants to smoke with you. Make talk."

Malcolm's face knotted up in a grimace of anger, darkened as if a shadow had crossed it like a cloud floating over the face of the sun. "I am going to kill him."

"You should kill Red Hair and make talk with your brother."

"How do you know he killed Two Fires?"

"The spirit of Two Fires spoke to me. And I saw the mark of Red Hair's hands on his neck. He squeezed the spirit out of Two Fires with his hands. I saw this in a vision when I prayed beneath the scaffold. I could hear the spirit of Two Fires crying in the night."

"Come, let us go with Red Hair. I will make talk with my brother. Then I will kill him."

"Listen to the Great Spirit. Be still and listen. He will tell you what you must do."

"I will do this, Red Bead Woman."

He knew what a Lakota saw in a vision was very real to her. As real as anything one could see with the eyes. He felt sure that McCord had murdered Two Fires. He knew that Red Bead would not lie, especially about something so important. So, she had found him and put him on a scaffold. That meant she had examined his body carefully, washed it, dressed it. She had taken his personal possessions so he could carry their spirits with him to the star path.

"Where in hell did that squaw chase off to?" McCord snapped as Bead got into the canoe.

Malcolm fixed Randall with a piercing stare. "I told you not to call my wife a squaw, Randy. I'm not going to warn you again."

Malcolm kicked off the shore and moved into the prow of the canoe. He sat down, picked up his paddle.

"I keep forgetting she's your wife," McCord said. "No need to get your dander up. I want to know where she's been."

"She found my brother's camp."

McCord flat-bladed his paddle and spun the stern around, slowing the craft.

"Where? How far?"

"Half a day or less, she says."

"Christ. How in hell did she get this far on foot?"

"I don't know. Maybe she swam."

"See if you can find out where he is exactly. Did she talk to him?"

"No," Malcolm lied.

McCord didn't say anything, but he knew Flynn was lying to him. His squaw wouldn't have recognized Jared unless she heard his name. Something wasn't right. He decided to give Malcolm some rope. Let him hang himself, if that's what he wanted to do. He should have killed Red Bead when he had the chance, he thought. The woman was a nuisance. Worse than that, she couldn't be trusted. Neither of them, for that matter.

"Well, she'd better tell us before we get there. She say how many with him?"

"No," Malcolm said, and that was the truth. He spoke to her now.

"Tell me who was with my brother and how you journeyed there," he said.

"He is with an older white eyes and a Mandan. I was taken there by a Chippewa and his woman, who are with many white eyes who float on the river two sleeps away. The Chippewa and his woman floated on their canoe back up the river last night."

"We did not see them," Malcolm said.

"The Chippewa is a very wise man."

"And you, Red Bead, are a very wise woman."

Red Bead glowed inside with his words and smiled secretly to herself.

Jared stabbed the wiping stick down the barrel of his flintlock to be sure the ball was still seated snug against the powder. He checked the pan to see that it was dry and covered with a patina of fine-grained powder. He worked the lock and the trigger. Then he tested the blade of his knife, and it was sharp. He examined his pistols and tucked them in his sash.

"You fixin' to go huntin', Jared?" Pettibone asked.

"David, I am going upriver to wait for my brother," Jared replied. "I want you and Gray Cat to stay here and wait for me. If I do not come back, you will know that Malcolm killed me."

"That's the first time in many a season you've called me by my Christian name, son."

"I don't want to bring my fight here to this place."

"You know me and the Mandan would back you in any fight."

"I know," Jared said. "But this is what I've decided."

"Worst and bloodiest fights I ever seen was in families."

"I hope I don't have to fight Malcolm."

"Then 'stead of taking all them fire spitters with you, you ought to be packin' a peace pipe."

"Sometimes the best peace is made at the end of a long rifle."

"You got yourself a point."

Jared left shortly after the sun rose, on an empty belly. He knew he'd have a better chance of surviving a stomach wound if he had no food in his stomach. He walked along the river, full of a great and unfathomable sadness, yet his step was light and springy. He watched the smokey wisps of fog rise off the Columbia, saw the circular ripples left by the jumping salmon, heard them splash, saw their arched bodies knifing like sudden metal rainbows as they fed on flying insects just above the slate surface.

He walked for an hour or two, until he was far from the new trading post, until he was in a different wilderness, one he'd never seen before. The sun rose high in the sky, and he thought it ironic how sweet the day was, how precious it had become since the shadow of death began hovering over him like some circling hawk.

The distant mountain peaks rose above the land, shining green in the sunlight, and he felt swallowed up by the vastness of the world before his eyes. He did not think about killing Malcolm, but only of childhood days when they had played together, neither knowing the terror their sister was feeling, the horrible secret she and their father and mother harbored. But that was a distant world, gone forever. This was a new world, where such thoughts should never be born on such a summer day.

He saw the dark speck then, far upriver, and his stomach tugged into a quivering knot. He knew, with-

out seeing, that his brother was close at hand, in that
canoe hanging suspended in space and time for that
single crystal moment. He stopped, in plain view, to
wait, using his rifle like a walking stick, leaning on it to
steady himself.

The speck grew larger, and he made out three figures in the large canoe. Two paddles flashed in the sun,
and the canoe began to move faster in the current. He
knew they had spotted him, and he didn't move.

He saw McCord in the stern, his face a blur, curls
of red hair in coiling spirals over his forehead beneath a
fox cap he remembered from earlier trapping days. His
brother sat at the bow, with Red Bead in the middle.
The canoe struck a course straight for him when it drew
within fifty yards.

"That you, Jared?" Malcolm called.

"Yes. I have been waiting for you."

"You bring that rifle up and you're a dead man,"
McCord yelled, dropping his paddle.

Malcolm turned around as McCord raised his own
rifle and said something that Jared could not hear. But
McCord didn't put the rifle down. Malcolm paddled the
canoe to shore, threw a line around a bush, pulled the
craft to the bank.

"I'm getting out, Jared."

"Yes, come on up, Malcolm. We'll talk."

"I'm bringing my rifle with me."

"Suit yourself."

He heard Malcolm and Red Bead speak in Lakota.
He heard McCord muttering something. And then
Malcolm was stepping from the canoe, his rifle in his
hand, a pistol tucked in his belt, a knife jutting from a
porcupine-quilled scabbard.

Jared waited as Malcolm walked up the shallow
slope above the bank. When he was ten feet away, Malcolm stopped.

"I've come a long way to kill you, Jared."

"Why do want to kill me?"

"You know. Because you murdered our father. Caused the deaths of our mother and sister."

"Before you shoot me, do you want to hear the truth?"

"I know the truth."

"No, you don't. And maybe you don't want to know the truth because you can't change what happened. Even by killing me, you can't change what happened. They're all dead and they're not coming back."

"Dead by your own bloody hand."

Jared saw a movement in the canoe as McCord stood up and put his rifle to his shoulder. His eyes flickered, but Malcolm did not turn around to look. He held his piercing gaze on Jared.

"Kill him now, laddie, or I'll drop the bastard!"

"Stay out of this, Randy," Malcolm shouted back without moving.

"The longer you wait, the harder it's going to be."

"Shut up, Randy!"

There was a long silence between the two brothers standing in the grass of the slope as they stared at each other. Jared stopped leaning against his rifle, stood straight, grasping the barrel with one hand.

"McCord wants you to kill me, Malcolm. Did he talk you into this?"

"McCord doesn't run me."

"Maybe not, but he's tickling that trigger even as we stand here facing each other."

"You have to pay, Jared. An eye for an eye."

"Don't you want to hear what really happened so long ago? Why I shot our father?"

"No. I don't care why. I just know what you did to our family. I hurt every day thinking of Caitlin hanging herself, our mother dying of grief."

"So do I, Malcolm, so do I."

"You bastard," Malcolm said, jerking his rifle to his shoulder.

Jared swung his rifle up and hurled it straight at his brother. It whistled through the air, turning slowly in a spin. Malcolm tried to duck, but the rifle butt struck him in the face. He dropped his rifle and staggered backward. Jared ran toward him, dove at his waist. He knocked Malcolm down, and his brother grabbed his neck with both hands.

Jared shook off the choking grip and they rolled in the grass and down the slope. Malcolm drew his knife. Jared felt his pistols dig into his belly as he rolled over the ground. He reached up, grasped his brother's wrist below the hand holding the knife. He looked up into Malcolm's face.

"Don't, Malcolm. Please don't make me fight you."

"I said I'd kill you. I'm going to. You don't deserve to live after what you've done."

"Listen to me before it's too late."

Malcolm closed his eyes and screamed as he wrestled his hand free of Jared's grip. When he opened them, Jared saw the hatred and the anger flashing like sparks off iron and he knew that it was too late, that Malcolm would never hear what he had to say. His brother was bigger, stronger, and his strength was fueled by his passion to kill.

Malcolm brought the knife down as Jared tried to roll out of the way. He felt it rip through his buckskin shirt and tear his skin. He felt the hot sticky flow of blood gush from the flesh wound. The pain made him wince as he grabbed for his knife.

Malcolm grabbed Jared's arm, jerking it hard. Jared felt the bone bump against the socket as he drew his own knife with the other hand. He felt Malcolm's hot breath on his face, saw the slitted eyes of a madman as his brother's knife flashed in the sun, arcing downward, aiming for his heart.

Jared managed to push Malcolm's knife to the side and brought his knife up hard and fast into his brother's belly. Malcolm stabbed his knife blade into the ground as Jared wriggled out of range. He saw his brother stiffen as he pulled his knife free. The long blade came out crimson with his brother's blood.

"Malcolm, I'm sorry," Jared panted.

Malcolm rolled over on his back. He brought a hand to his waist, sighed deeply. His eyes opened and began to glaze with the pain.

"Well, you killed me too, brother. Sat-Satisfied?"

"Malcolm, listen to me, please. I didn't want to hurt you. Our father raped Caitlin. I didn't know it was him when I shot him. He had been raping her since she was a baby. Mother knew about it. Caitlin was scared. She was hurt bad by what our father did to her. Can you hear me?"

"I—I don't believe you."

"If you had been me, you'd have done the same thing."

"Pa wouldn't do that to little Caitlin."

"He did, Malcolm. You have to believe me. Don't go like this. Believe me. It's true. All true."

Jared looked down at his dying brother and tears filled his eyes. He lifted him up, enclosed him in his arms. Malcolm's eyes fluttered as the blood flowed over his buckskins. Jared knew he was going fast, going beyond hearing, beyond knowing the truth of what had happened so long ago.

"I love you, Malcolm. I love you, my brother. Please don't die now. Don't leave it like this between us."

Malcolm's eyes opened wide, fixing on Jared's face. A shadow seemed to pass over the pupils. Jared felt Malcolm's hand on his arm, felt it squeezing him.

"I would have killed him too, Jared."

"What did you say?"

"If I had caught Pa hurting Caitlin."

"You believe me?"

"I—I . . ." Malcolm shuddered and went into a
final convulsion. Then his eyes closed and he went limp
in Jared's arms. Jared leaned over and put his ear next
to his brother's mouth. He listened, but Malcolm was
no longer breathing.

He lay his brother down and pulled a pistol from
his belt as he stood up.

There was a commotion in the canoe, and Jared
saw McCord hitting Red Bead with the butt of his rifle.

"Leave her alone, McCord."

McCord shoved Red Bead down in the canoe and
stepped over her. "So, did you kill your brother, laddie?"

"McCord, you aren't fit to breathe the same air
Malcolm did."

McCord brought his rifle up. Jared stood steady
and stretched out his arm, cocked his pistol. He took
dead aim and squeezed the trigger. Smoke belched
from the .60 caliber pistol, and he saw dust puff up
from McCord's chest. He drew the other pistol and ran
down the slope as McCord collapsed.

Before he could get there, he saw Red Bead lift a
knife in the air. He saw her bury the blade in McCord's
back, once, twice, a third time, before he reached the
canoe.

She stood up straight, holding the bloody knife in
her hand. "Red Hair dead," she said.

"I have killed your man. My brother."

"You did not kill with a bad heart."

"No. I am very sad."

"Did Iron Heart know the truth?"

"Yes."

"That is good, Jared."

But Jared did not know if his brother really believed him at the end. He wanted to believe it, but he knew that dying men said strange things sometimes and did not always know what was true and what was not.

"Come. We must send Iron Heart to the Great Spirit. You help Bead?"

"I will help," Jared said, his heart empty, his energy drained from him. "I'm sorry, Bead. I did not want to kill my brother."

"I know. Iron Heart walked from the circle. Red Hair took him from the circle."

Jared knew what she meant and that surprised him, for her words were beyond speech, beyond a white man's comprehension. He understood that her words were ancient and holy and true.

"Odd thing," Pettibone said a few days later.

"What's that?"

"You beat Astor by killing McCord, but Astor's going to win in the end."

"I know it."

"You do?"

"Yes, but Astor will find the end of his circle one day."

"Don't know what you mean, Jared."

"The beaver will run out here, same as up in Montreal. Nothing lasts forever. Sioux believe life is a circle. The whole world is a circle. Life is round. Some live shorter circles than others, but each life is complete, finished when it's finished."

"That's a lot in your craw. Where'd you get that?"

"Red Bead explained it to me. But I already knew some of it. There was an old Ojibwa we used to trade with. He spoke some of that to me."

"You talkin' about Little Wolf?"

"Yes. He said a man's life was complete by the end

of twelve summers. So a man should not fear death. He said the circle was holy."

"You believe that?"

"What do you think, Pettibone?

Pettibone did not answer.

Ten days later Jared Flynn shook hands with David Thompson, the Canadian geographer who had been the first white man to cross Horse Pass to the source of the Columbia River in 1807.

"You've made progress," Thompson told Jared as he surveyed the fort that would serve as the North-West Company's first trading post on the Spokane River.

"We've come a ways," Jared said, winking at Pettibone and Gray Cat.

"A hell of a ways," Pettibone said.

ABOUT THE AUTHOR

JORY SHERMAN is the Spur Award–winning author of *The Medicine Horn, Song of the Cheyenne, Horne's Law, Winter of the Wolf,* and *Grass Kingdom,* as well as two previous novels in the Rivers West series, *The Arkansas River* and *The Rio Grande.* Sherman's novel, *Trapper's Moon,* won the Missouri Writer's Guild Award for Best Book of 1994. He is an avid fisherman and hunts with a muzzloder. He currently resides with his wife near Branson, Missouri.

If you enjoyed Jory Sherman's epic tale, *The Columbia River,* be sure to look for the next installment of the RIVERS WEST saga at your local bookstore. Each volume takes you on a voyage of exploration along one of the great rivers of North America with the courageous pioneers who challenged the unknown.

Look for the next exciting book in Bantam's
unique historical series

Rivers West
THE HUMBOLDT RIVER
by
Gary McCarthy

On sale in fall 1996 wherever Bantam Books are sold.

The exciting frontier series continues!

~~~~~~~~ # RIVERS WEST

Native Americans, hunters and trappers, pioneer families—all who braved the emerging American Frontier drew their very lives and fortunes from the great rivers. From the earliest days of the settlement movement to the dawn of the twentieth century, here, in all their awesome splendor, are the RIVERS WEST.